Dead White Female

'It is difficult to remain immune to Sam Jones' anarchic charm. She's a divine dropout who never dropped in, an alley cat with razor wit, the appetites of a scavenger and an extraordinary tolerance for booze . . . enjoy a hedonistic, drunken and irreverently observed prom through London life, high and low, from the grubby squats and Irish pubs to art galleries and vacuous style victims . . . [the novel] zings along, laced with stimulating bitchiness and a fine eye for detail.'

Frances Hegarty, Mail on Sunday

'Sam Jones, heroine by default, prickles with aggressive heat . . . The whole thing radiates with energy and wit. Income support with glamour and attitude.'

Evening Standard

'The tone is delightfully outrageous. A mystery writer is born.'

Time Out

'Debut with bags of promise . . . Gets a high rating on the street cred scale.'

Daily Telegraph

'Promising debut thriller, with an authentic flavour of the youth scene in London.'

Bookseller

'A first novel, bristling with a kind of spiky charm that's hard to come by, harder to resist.'

Literary Review

'An entertaining first novel, written in an edgy, witty style that keeps the story moving fast.'

Times Literary Supplement

About the author

Born in London in 1966, Lauren Henderson originally intended to be an actress, but while reading
English at Cambridge, changed her mind and
decided on journalism instead. Since then, she has
worked for the *New Statesman*, *Marxism Today*,
The Observer and *Lime Lizard*, an indie music
magazine.

Lauren now divides her time between Italy and
London and, when not picking olives, writes full
time. *Dead White Female* is her first novel. *Too
Many Blondes*, her second thriller featuring Sam
Jones, is now available in hardcover from Hodder &
Stoughton.

Dead White Female

Lauren Henderson

NEW ENGLISH LIBRARY
Hodder and Stoughton

Copyright © 1995 Lauren Henderson

The right of Lauren Henderson to be identified as the Author of
the Work has been asserted by her in accordance with the
Copyright, Designs and Patents Act 1988.

First published in Great Britian in 1995 by
Hodder and Stoughton
A division of Hodder Headline PLC

First published in paperback in 1996 by
Hodder & Stoughton
A New English Library Paperback

10 9 8 7 6 5 4 3 2 1

A CIP Catalogue record for this title is available
from the British Library

ISBN 0 340 64915 1

Typeset by Avon Dataset Ltd, Bidford-on-Avon

Printed and bound in Great Britain by
Cox & Wyman Ltd, Reading

Hodder and Stoughton
A division of Hodder Headline PLC
338 Euston Road
London NW1 3BH

To Caroline, without whom . . .

Acknowledgements

Thanks, alphabetically: to Caroline again – she deserves it – Francis, Jenni, Kate, Lisa and Sandy, for all their support and editing skills. And to Bernstein Hounsfield, Giacomo (also, in his case, for thinking it's good even though he hasn't read it yet), Granaiolo, Hartley's, and Pietrafitta. They know why.

1

Alice through the looking-glass learns that if she wants to reach the house she needs to walk away from it, into the garden; only then will she find herself climbing the steps that lead up to its front door. She doesn't have any difficulty following the rule. But then, Alice was a highly sophisticated child. I, on the other hand, can't turn my back on anything, even as a matter of strategy. I have to push and push at what I don't understand, forcing it to give me answers. My way's more direct, but you run the risk that what you're looking for may end up broken in your hands.

By the time it was over, it wasn't only Lee who had died. I started out with her death, and caused two others; I fell in love and got my heart broken. I broke some things myself, for good. Hearts mend. Necks don't.

But I found out how Lee died. Like Alice, I like to finish what I set out to do.

That's not really a fair comparison. Alice never killed anyone, after all.

* * *

Detective Inspector Fincham had a smooth pink face and pale ginger hair. They clashed badly. His eyebrows and eyelashes were so pale that they merged into his skin, giving his features a curious lack of definition, as if he were recovering from severe burns. His tie was secured in a perfect knot precisely above his collar button. Clearly not a natural rebel.

He stared at me and I stared back. We had been working on this routine for some time and by now it was honed down to its essentials. There was nothing else to look at apart from the desk lamp, which had no intrinsic interest. The walls were painted a pale shade of yellow, the yellow of phlegm rather than buttercups. The floor was scuffed linoleum, the desk was grey formica and the chairs grey plastic. Call in Ivana Trump to redecorate, now.

My statement lay on the desk in front of me. Finally, shrugging, I signed it on the dotted line and pushed it over to him.

'I'm still not happy with it,' I said rather sulkily. 'It's all right as far as it goes . . . But Lee was just not the sort of person to wander drunkenly down into a pitch-dark garden at night, fall over and hit her head on a brick. It doesn't make sense.'

'None of the other party guests who have given statements seem to feel that there's anything surprising about it, Miss Jones.'

As a matter of tactics, I decided to let the 'Miss' go. 'No-one else you've talked to really knew her,' I pointed out instead. 'That's why they aren't questioning it.'

'And your acquaintance with her was based on one year at art college, during which she was your tutor. Not that extensive a friendship, would you say? By your own account, you hadn't seen each other for several years.'

'I still knew her well enough. And she wasn't drunk.'

'But she had been drinking?'

'Yes,' I admitted reluctantly.

'She'd had a few drinks, shall we say?' DI Fincham raised his eyebrows at me, wanting my agreement. His pink eyelids, sliding upwards, looked raw, scalpelled, the ginger eyelashes hardly visible. I wondered why he didn't dye them. Pale brown would look plausible. You could buy home dyeing kits nowadays if you were too embarrassed to go to a salon.

'She strolled out into the garden,' he was continuing, 'in search of some fresh air, perhaps wanting a break from the noise. I understand from the neighbours that the party was quite riotous.'

His eyes rested disapprovingly on a rip in my crocheted tights.

'Mrs Jackson wouldn't even need to have been particularly drunk to stumble on a loose brick. The garden was littered with them. And as you yourself mentioned, it was unlit. She tripped, fell over and hit her head on another brick. We found traces of blood on one near where she was lying.'

'So why would she have gone down into the garden in the first place?' I said stubbornly. 'She said herself she was tired and was going home. I told you that already.'

He shrugged. 'That I would certainly be interested to know. Contrary to what you seem to believe, Miss Jones, we do have a policy of treating all deaths as suspicious, at least initially. When we have autopsy results I'll be in a position to see if Mrs Jackson's injury tallies with the theory. Though ultimately it'll be up to the inquest to decide.'

'Then no-one saw her going into the garden?' I asked.

'No. Neither by herself nor accompanied. But quite

3

frankly, Miss Jones,' he said drily, 'from the condition of most of your fellow-guests this morning, I wouldn't be surprised if one of them had spotted her in the company of a large pink elephant. Tap-dancing.'

DI Fincham arranged my statement on top of a neat pile of papers.

'What will you be able to tell from the autopsy?' I persisted.

He looked a little guarded, but he answered the question anyway. I was impressed.

'Whether she did in fact hit her head on the brick found beside her body, and if that's the only cranial injury. Obviously, if there were another, we would have to re-examine everything. Her blood alcohol level, to see if it makes sense that she might have been shaky on her feet. And, of course, whether she was under the influence of anything else.'

He looked at me pointedly. I wriggled slightly in my seat and resisted the impulse to check my nostrils for traces of white powder.

'So I'm the only person who doesn't believe this is as simple as it looks,' I said.

He shrugged. 'So far, from all the statements that have been given, I'd have to say yes. As I say, it depends to a large degree on the autopsy results. But – yes, you're the only one. After all, Miss Jones – ' he looked at me hard – 'it's not as if you have any more evidence to give, is it? There's nothing that you haven't told me?'

I shook my head. 'It's just a feeling. Believe me, if there were something concrete I'd be happy to tell you.'

He must have seen it was the truth, because he relaxed back into his chair.

'Well, in that case—' he began.

'There's nothing more to say.' I finished it for him. I stood up and pulled on my jacket. 'I'm sorry I've been wasting your time.'

He looked as if he were about to say something else, but I was sick of this little room with its talk that was going nowhere and its stuffy air. Turning on my heel, I swept out of the door in as dignified a manner as I could manage, given that I'd only had a few hours of sleep and was still a little high from some self-indulgent behaviour last night at the party. I stalked down a seemingly endless series of smegma-yellow linoleum corridors, too angry to stop and ask anyone for directions, and finally exited into the car park by a sheer fluke. My beat-up little red van, a Ford Escort which I hoped for its sake had seen better days, was half-hidden behind police cars. It looked uncomfortable; it wasn't used to being in such company. I didn't start the motor straight away. I sat in the van and thought for a while about what I was going to do now.

I wasn't surprised that I was the only person who had expressed doubts to the police about the way Lee was supposed to have died. I had already seen the reaction in the house when the news spread that someone was dead in the garden and the police were on their way; the people who had crashed out there overnight had cleared out so fast that I could smell the scorched shoe-rubber in the hall. They didn't care what had happened to whom, they just didn't want to be involved. Ivan, a peaceable hippie who was the house dope dealer, struggled out the front door with his stereo and TV in rapid succession. He was in such a hurry to leave that he dropped his mattress out of his window rather than carry it downstairs.

The group that had gathered in the waiting-room of the police station was thus composed of the comparatively respectable occupants of the house, but it was soon clear to me that none of them wanted any degree of involvement in Lee's death either – despite the fact that she had died in their back garden. I looked slowly at each one in turn.

Tom was suffering such a terrible hangover that he was incapable of speech, hunched over in a ball of misery and blue jumper. Paul and Claire were sitting next to each other, their differences temporarily forgotten in the face of a crisis of this magnitude. My gaze stopped at Paul for a few seconds; I didn't quite believe the calm, relaxed expression on his handsome face. Everyone else was nervous, including myself; why wasn't he? Ajay, the house yuppie, looked as smart as ever, hair brushed, nice sweater, corduroy trousers. Judy, Liz, and Mo, who were the mainstays of the co-operative committee which ran the house and as such were used to dealings with police officers, had managed to achieve a pugnacious slump in the plastic chairs.

It was Claire who put into words what everyone was thinking. She looked nervous and jumpy, but this was her natural state. In the 1920s, they would have said she lived on her nerves, and no-one had yet come up with a better way of putting it.

'Ajay, you'd better tell us – is there anything we shouldn't say when we're questioned?' she asked. There were dark circles under her eyes and she looked half-buried in her heavy sweater and leather jerkin.

'I'm not a criminal lawyer, Claire,' Ajay pointed out with barely concealed impatience. 'Industrial tribunals don't familiarise you with police questioning techniques.'

'Don't be a pompous bastard, you know what I mean,' Claire snapped back.

Ajay sighed. 'Look, there's nothing I can say. Assuming, of course, that no-one's got anything to hide. But to my mind this is a straightforward accidental death. I can't imagine the police getting hot and bothered about it.'

I stared at him, amazed. 'You can't be serious, Ajay!'

He turned to look at me. I noticed, as I always did, how ridiculously long and curly his eyelashes were.

'Come on, Sam,' he said in his most soothing, reasonable tones. Ajay, Mr Conciliator, had never been known to lose his temper, even when people finished his private and clearly labelled tub of margarine. 'In the course of a raucous party, someone who's had a few drinks staggers out to get some air, trips over a brick from that bloody barbecue, and smashes her head in on another brick. It's a miracle something like this hasn't happened before. You know as well as I do how interested the police are going to be in this.'

I changed tack.

'Yes. Fine. I agree with you in principle. But this was *Lee*. Can any of you really see that happening to her?'

'I didn't even know her,' Ajay said rather too quickly.

I looked around the room. No-one seemed eager to meet my gaze.

'Tom?' I said. 'You were talking to her last night.'

He lifted his head for a second. I wished he hadn't. He looked like his own death mask, made from ancient waxy veined marble. This would have suited someone with an impeccable bone structure, but Tom's big chunky Irish face failed to carry it off. His eyes, normally a clear light blue, were small and red and sunken, like those of a pig from hell. He seemed to have splashed on stale beer in lieu of aftershave, without bothering to go through the motions of shaving first. He made a faint moaning sound

like a rabbit that has been hit by a car and is taking a while
to die. I moved hastily on.

'Paul, you and Claire knew her, didn't you?' I asked.

'We'd bumped into each other a few times,' Paul said
carefully, his blue eyes not meeting mine, 'but I wouldn't
say I was a friend of hers. I mean, I knew her, but only to
say hello to. I couldn't really comment on what she'd be
likely to do at a party.'

Claire raised her head. 'Same goes for me,' she said.

I heard someone move restlessly in their chair as if
they wanted to say something. I swivelled my head but
before I could ask who it had been, Liz cut in. She was a
social worker and had attended numerous workshops in
communication skills.

'Sam, I know that this is a friend of yours who's died,'
she began in a tolerant, understanding voice which made
me want to slap her, 'and naturally that's painful. But I
really can't see that any good is going to be done by
stirring up trouble with the police.'

'Someone is dead,' I said, loudly. 'Don't you think we
should at least think about it for a minute, rather than
pretending it hasn't happened?'

There was a pause.

Then Liz said, 'I never spoke to your friend myself,
though I did see her last night. She seemed a nice person.'
(Everyone seemed a nice person to Liz. She would only
have altered that description if she had seen them
laughing merrily while strangling a kitten. Then, in a
serious tone of voice, she would say that they had
problems.)

'But it does seem clear what happened,' she went on.
'And we've got enough trouble with the council as it is.
You don't live there, Sam, it's easy for you to say.'

'They're threatening to raise the rent,' Mo said, eyes flashing in indignation. 'Can you believe it! Absolute bastards! After all we've done to that place! It was a shit-heap when we moved in.'

'As opposed to now,' I thought sarcastically. My skin crawled. I loathed Mo. Liz and Judy were over-serious, knitted their own yoghurt and indulged in psycho-babble from time to time, but neither of them smelt of patchouli oil or jingled with the sound of little bells sewn to their clothing. Mo did both.

'After all, Sam,' Ajay chimed in, 'you don't actually *live* there, you know.'

See no evil, hear no evil, speak no evil – and that goes for you too, Sam – was clearly the consensus reached by the meeting.

'Well, screw you all,' I thought, but didn't say. I would just have to manage on my own. In a way the thought was reassuring.

I had no idea then what it would involve.

2

Alice would have felt at home in the Castle Road house that night. She would have understood its landscape, which, like that of most parties in full swing, was surreal and disjointed enough even for her. It was a rambling old Victorian building covered in ivy; until recently it had been a squat, and now it was run by a co-operative housing association. The spectrum of co-op members ran from no-hoper druggies to rising young professionals who were slumming it for a while to garner street credibility and save up for their eventual mortgage deposits.

I stood outside the house for a while before going in, wondering if I was really up to the challenge of a full-blown party. I had my doubts on this score. People might ask me how my work was going. And back in my studio, squatting on the floor like a malevolent silver toad, was the sculpture I was supposed to have finished months ago, but which I hadn't touched for longer than I cared to think about. I was hooked on it; I couldn't finish it, and I couldn't give it up. It was like being in love with someone who doesn't love you back. I just couldn't say goodbye to it and start anew with another sheet of aluminium.

It was November, cold, crisp, my breath clouding elegantly in the air. The front of the house was matted with a twisted net of twigs, like a shawl thrown loosely

11

over its shoulders. The dead leaves underfoot were sodden with rain, dark and sad, no trace of red left in them. I've never thought autumn was mellow.

I told myself firmly that if I went home I'd only get hopelessly drunk and maudlin. I could do that just as well in company.

Noise spilled out as soon as I opened the front door, as if I had taken the lid off a pressure cooker. The hallway was cluttered with people leaning against the walls, apparently trying to prop up the house; its state of dereliction made this plausible. The corridor was narrow, and full of cigarettes, cans of beer, and plastic cups of warm cheap wine held in unsteady hands. Pushing my way through without collecting an ash and wine slick on my clothes was the twentieth-century version of running the gauntlet.

It was comparatively early yet. No-one looked too wrecked, hair and make-up were still in place. These Castle Road parties always had as weird a mixture of people as the house itself: Ajay's yuppie lawyer friends, the arty lot who knew Tom, Paul and Claire; Mo, Liz and Judy's serious group of social workers and concerned types with their legendary inability to dance; and, of course, a large complement of druggies and layabouts. No-one needed to invite the last contingent; they just turned up. There were always plenty of arguments, seductions, one-night stands, sometimes a punch-up or two, but the atmosphere was essentially good-natured. The really nasty fights would start tomorrow afternoon, about who wasn't helping with the clearing-up.

Tom grabbed me halfway down the hall, with a great deal of enthusiasm. He is tall and wide and I disappeared into his bear-hug for some time.

'Sam! You look gorgeous!' he said happily into the top of my head as I attempted to cough out mouthfuls of his sweater, into which he was squashing me. He released me at last. I pulled off some wool fibres which had stuck to my lipstick.

'Hi, brute,' I said cheerfully. I love Tom to death. 'How's it hanging?'

In reflex, Tom scratched his balls meditatively. 'Oh, nothing much to report. Paul and Claire have been scrapping all day. I wouldn't even notice, but they make so much noise . . .'

'Who's he been paying too much attention to this time?' I wasn't that interested in Paul and Claire; it was an old pattern. She was jealous, he flirted with every semi-attractive woman he met. Ergo plenty of squabbling which both of them must secretly enjoy, otherwise they would have split up years ago.

'Actually, it's Judy,' Tom said. 'Didn't see that one coming, did you?'

'Jesus. No, I didn't.' I was disapproving. Someone who lived in the same house was a no-no. 'He shouldn't shit on his own doorstep.'

'You're so feminine and sensitive, Sam, that's why I love you so much, you need sheltering from this tough macho world—'

I faked a punch at his stomach. It wasn't hard to locate. Tom was one of my best friends, and he had always reminded me of a big, cuddly, sexy teddy bear – slightly over-stuffed, if you were being picky, but endearingly so. Tonight he was as rumpled as ever. I decided not to ask him how the poetry was going. Not to mention his pursuit of his latest blonde love-object, a girl called Julia Seddon. I didn't want to listen to a long moan of frustration, just

13

when I was starting to enjoy myself. Tom has an unfortunate and usually disastrous penchant for blondes, preferably sensitive ones who do appear to need sheltering from this tough macho world. I disapprove, but then I happen to be a brunette who is normally about as sensitive as Conan the Barbarian on cocaine.

I said instead, 'How d'you make a blonde's eyes light up?'

'Uh . . .'

'Shine a torch in her ear.'

'HAHhahahhahahahaha . . .' Tom collapsed against the wall, roaring with laughter. In the right mood, Tom will laugh at almost anything. I envied his happily drunken state.

'I need a drink,' I shouted through his gusts of laughter. 'See you later.'

He was too busy wiping his eyes to notice I had gone.

The kitchen was awash with people and beer cans, the latter mostly full for a change. How nice. I decided firmly that this was not going to be one of those parties where I downed half a bottle of vodka and curled up somewhere to nurse what was left of my personality. In this spirit of maturity I peeled off a beer instead of looking inside the freezer for spirits. There was no food, of course. I wasn't expecting any.

Baby Thompson stuck her head into the kitchen and unfortunately noticed me. She seemed to be imitating those African tribeswomen who deliberately lengthen their earlobes by wearing heavy earrings. In London, however, earlobes which brush gently against one's shoulders are not taken as an indication of fertility. Besides, no self-respecting African tribeswoman's ears would have been seen dead sporting huge pearly chandeliers with plastic people swinging from them. Baby was so thin that I could see every bone in her ribcage through her tight jacket. I braced myself to go through the motions of polite conversation.

'Samantha! It's been ages!' She bent down and pecked both my cheeks. The chandeliers swung dangerously close to my face. I held up my hand in a protective reflex, like Tippi Hedren in *The Birds*.

'Hi, Baby. Incredible earrings,' I said truthfully but disingenuously. Bitch. She knew I hated being called Samantha. Sex dolls are called Samantha. I do actually look like a Samantha, which is why I insist on being called Sam instead. I don't want anyone prodding the small of my back, looking for the valve.

'Thanks. Aren't they wild?' She fingered one, tilting her head to one side. She could carry them off; she was tall and had the necessary sophisticated bony face, fabulously made-up. She did not have an ounce of prettiness or of excess fat and was considered extremely attractive by arty young men. We were in the same year at art school and ever since we met I had been trying unsuccessfully to avoid her. Even at college she had a superb streak of natural pushiness, combined with a total lack of artistic talent. It was inevitable that she would end up working in PR.

'So how are you?' she said, plucked eyebrows lifted. I mumbled something to which she didn't bother to listen; she was looking over my shoulder for other people she knew. I checked out her clothes instead. Baby's public relations firm mainly represented fashion designers and she was always extravagantly dressed. Tonight it was a tight Lycra jacket in psychedelic swirls of orange, yellow and green, with darker green leggings and stacked shoes.

Her eyeshadow was orange and her hair, cut uncompromisingly short, was dyed pale lemon yellow. Weirdly enough the whole effect suited her.

'Have you seen Tom anywhere?' she asked, looking down at me. This was a mistake on her part. I knew that she had always had a thing for Tom.

'He's in the hall,' I said evilly, 'staring wistfully at Julia Seddon. He's had a crush on her for months.'

'That washed-out little thing?' Baby said in a tone that was meant to be dismissive but came out piqued instead.

'That's how he likes them, small, fair and apparently defenceless, like frail woodland creatures.'

Baby snorted.

'She's about as frail as – as—'

'A mechanical digger. Exactly.'

I almost warmed to Baby, for a brief instant. Then she did a big fake pout which made her look like a fag hag and I remembered what a nightmare she was.

'Well,' she said, air-kissing me with tepid enthusiasm, 'it's been lovely talking to you, darling. Stay in touch.'

She went off down the hall, waving her hand at various people (or, as she'd call them, contacts) in an airy, princess-greeting-courtiers manner from the lofty height of her five-feet-ten plus platform shoes. One of the reasons I hate her is that next to her I feel like a midget. Which I'm not. I am in fact the average height of a woman in southern Italy. I threw the rest of the beer down my throat, took a second can and wandered out to look for adventure.

A slow dub was playing in the dance room; too slow for me. But two boys I knew were sitting against the far wall and waved to me, so I wove through the dancers to join them. The room was full of smoke in which the few lamps glowed in a foggy haze. But smoke rises, and there on the floor the air was clearer. I looked up at the dancers through a waist-high mist of cloud. They were making slow, gyrating movements like people on a sea bed, trying to push through the water all around them but moving nowhere, weighed down by cubic tons of liquid. We didn't speak, just sat passing a joint from hand to hand, as if we were playing the hot potato game on tranquillisers. I noticed Ajay, standing by the window, looking preoccupied. I was surprised he wasn't dancing; it was his kind of music. Then I felt someone tapping me on the shoulder.

'Claire!'

She was squatting next to me. 'Come through into the other room,' she said into my ear, 'you can't hear anything here. I want to have a talk.'

She clearly wouldn't take no for an answer. I looked over at Will and Joe for rescue, but by now they had their tongues down each other's throats so far that they were probably blocking off one another's windpipes. I shrugged in resignation. Oh well, at least it would be a gossip. Will's hand was now resting on Joe's thigh, the joint burning away between his fingers. I retrieved it. I would need something to do while Claire talked at me. We went through into the lounge, which was full of people. I couldn't face the thought of one of Claire's keyed-up descriptions of everything that was wrong in her life and so on seeing Paul I headed towards him, ignoring Claire's efforts to turn me back. Hopefully his presence would neutralise the situation. He was sitting on the sofa and shifted up to make room for us.

Claire sat reluctantly next to me, her body as stiff as a board. She was a small, fair girl with very intense eyes, her body thin and wiry, sending off sparks of excess energy. She and Paul were alike as siblings, but Paul channelled his energy into his career, while Claire's seemed to be eating her up. They had both trained as set designers but Paul was doing much better than she was, a state of affairs due more to their respective personalities than their talents. Paul was lubricant-smooth with people who could be of use to him, while Claire didn't know the meaning of the word compromise.

'Hi, Sam! How's it going?' Paul said, his blue eyes bright. I found myself smiling back, seduced by his automatic charm. He knew perfectly well how attractive he was, and he used it shamelessly.

'Forget it,' I said drily. 'Tell me your news instead. It's got to be better.'

That was all the encouragement he needed. He plunged into a description of the new project he was designing, a production of *La Traviata* for an avant-garde opera company; it was to be set in the seventies, in an Australian women's prison, with Violetta serving time for prostitution, Alfredo as a junior guard and his father as the governor. Or something along those lines.

Paul was saying: 'The ball in Act Three is done as a sort of disco for the inmates – mirror ball, revolving lights, great opportunities for pastiche. Then she gets transferred to an upstate prison, drier climate, for her health—'

'To Queensland?' I felt I ought to contribute something.

Paul was interested. 'Is Ayers Rock in Queensland? Because I thought of having it seen from the window, sideways on. Ayers Rock, I mean. And obviously some Aboriginal artworks on the cell walls . . .'

I had had enough of this. 'You didn't say anything about

this when I saw you last,' I said.

Paul waved his hand. 'Oh, it was in the pipeline,' he said airily, 'the grant application was being submitted, but you know how it is, I didn't want to talk about it till it was a certainty.'

'The grant's gone through, then? You've got the funding to put it on?'

'Not officially. But we've heard it's in the bag.'

'Well, congratulations!'

I was impressed. Getting money out of art boards nowadays is harder than mud wrestling a crocodile. Paul must know people on the committee. Paul probably cultivated people in his local church flower-arranging circle, just in case he might need them one of these days.

Across the room I saw Tom, talking animatedly to Julia Seddon, who was staring up at him, eyes wide. From this distance I couldn't tell whether she was fascinated by his conversation or simply glazed with boredom. There was someone else with them; a woman, her back to me, dressed all in white. That was odd enough, in this environment where black was so much the norm that even blue jeans were a variation, to make me take a second look at her. I once knew someone who always wore white . . .

Claire was saying something I only half-heard.

'What?'

'Didn't really think she'd have the nerve to turn up here . . .'

She was leaning forward, and I was too. Vaguely, I wondered why Claire was angry with Julia Seddon, but then I realised who the other woman was.

It was Lee. Lee Jackson. I couldn't believe it.

3

Lee Jackson was not beautiful, but her presence was compelling. In repose she stood as still as if she had been made of alabaster. Her skin, unaided by cosmetics, glowed as if she had a light bulb inside her face. The narrow, delicate tracery of crow's feet round her eyes only made its smoothness more striking. Hardly a line on her forehead, just two near-invisible vertical strokes above her nose, where her brows drew together in thought. Lee was emotion recollected in tranquillity. Her voice was low and calm and her every gesture efficient. Nothing was wasted with Lee.

She was my tutor in my third year at art school. I had spent the first one in wild living and the second in experimenting with a lucky-dip assortment of sculptural techniques. Towards the end of the year I had grown increasingly frenetic, rushing about in a desperate attempt to fix on a style of my own. Nothing seemed to fit, nothing I tried unlocked my imagination; it was as if there were a key to the door which I could not find, and by the time I met Lee I was beating my head against it instead.

In her quiet way Lee revolutionised my efforts. Under her influence I learned to slow down, instead of trying to snatch at something that takes years to discover, and to look inside myself for inspiration. At the time I felt that if she hadn't been my tutor I would have gone mad and though this was an exaggeration it was true that without her I don't think I would ever have found my own way.

Yet I deliberately lost touch with her as soon as I left college. It was wilful of me. But her influence on me had been so strong – despite her dislike of influencing anyone – that I was frightened that if I still saw her, I would find myself working as I imagined she would want me to, rather than in my own style. Lee had showed me how to start thinking for myself, but I was still only in the early stages, and I needed to separate myself from her in order to put this into practice. And the rift had to be abrupt.

I couldn't explain this to her. With every new piece I made, with every exhibition I had, I wanted to send her an invitation, to have her opinion on what I was doing, but something held me back. I must have hurt her. Perhaps she understood; I've never met anyone as wise as Lee.

She must have sensed that I was staring at her, because she turned to look in my direction while Tom was still speaking. I met her gaze directly. Within moments she was crossing the room towards me, her hand held out. I stood up to meet her, heart beating fast. It was the first time that we had met on an equal basis, no longer student and tutor. She was wearing a silky sweater that must have been a hand knit and a beautifully cut pair of trousers, elegantly tapering to a pair of polished brown brogues. Her brown hair was bobbed, and her earrings were small pearls set in silver.

'What are you doing here, Lee?' I blurted out. 'This isn't really your kind of thing, is it?'

'Jesus Christ, Sam,' I thought, 'you haven't seen her for five years and that's all you can say?'

'I'd forgotten how direct you are, Sam!' Lee said, smiling at me.

She closed a hand briefly around my arm in a gesture of welcome. Her eyes were as bright as ever, rich and dark as the mahogany leather of her brogues.

'Julia brought me,' she was saying. 'Julia Seddon. Do you know her? She's another ex-student of mine. We had dinner together.'

'You don't look like you were planning to come to this kind of party.' I grinned at her. 'You look very smart.'

'Well, I've stopped teaching now, you know,' she said. 'I have a part-time job in a gallery instead – it's called Shelley Frank, you might have heard of it – so I have to make an effort. There's a friend who buys things for me, too . . . But it happens with age, you know. You'll find yourself buying classic clothes and taking care of them instead of those PVC miniskirts you used to wear with fishnets—'

'Bleached hair,' I said, 'and black lipstick. All at the same time, talk about overkill!'

We were both laughing now. Lee always knew how to take the edge off a situation.

'It suited you, though. You looked like a beautiful monster. And now you look more – stripped down. No overkill, certainly. Though the skirts are still as short as they used to be.'

'It's not a particularly conscious decision,' I admitted, looking down briefly at my little black Lycra dress. 'I was getting dressed in a miserable temper and I couldn't be bothered with thinking about what I was going to wear.'

'Unlucky in love?' Lee asked.

I shrugged. 'No more than usual.'

Lee smiled briefly, a smile with little amusement

behind it. 'We always assume everyone else is suffering from the same problems as ourselves, don't we?' she said.

The thought of Lee being disappointed romantically was as unlikely to me as an image of her face distorted by uncontrollable emotion. I had assumed that her love life ran on smoothly oiled castors which at worst squeaked quietly from time to time.

'Are things – not working out?' I said, not knowing how to phrase it.

'Well . . .'

She shrugged, a gesture that was very familiar to me. I remembered the many times I had asked her questions she didn't choose to answer, and received only that small, graceful rise and fall of her narrow shoulders. There had been a slight, enigmatic smile which always accompanied the shrug, but it was missing now. Instead her mouth went down at the corners for a moment. 'Unlucky's a self-indulgent way of putting it. Masochistic might be more accurate.'

It was as if a parent were confiding in a grown-up child; I was embarrassed and fascinated in equal measure.

'Do you want to sit down?' I said, indicating an unoccupied couple of chairs. It was a surprise when she drew her brows together for a moment, thinking about it, and then nodded.

* * *

There aren't that many stories in the world, and Lee's was one of the most classic versions; an affair with a married woman. The sex of her lover wasn't a surprise; it was common knowledge at art school that, despite a short-lived marriage many years ago, Lee was gay. Her lover apparently had a high-powered job which meant strict secrecy imposed on their affair. She had told Lee that her marriage was one of convenience only. I didn't point out that this was only what one would have expected her to say.

'Up till the time she met me,' Lee was saying, 'all her energy was going into her career. She works so hard, Sam, I hardly manage to see her at all . . . She hates talking on the phone, so we have to write to each other. Can you believe it? All the rules are hers. I know her position is more difficult but I still find that hard to accept . . . The worst thing is that I feel that she actually resents her feelings for me. Her letters are an extraordinary mixture of passion and the coldest, iciest control. So there's always a tremendous head of steam building up, because part of her doesn't want to, she's always fighting it, so when she lets go, when I make her finally give in to it . . .'

I looked at her sideways, nervous of meeting her eyes. She was still gazing ahead of her, and her features were gathered up into an expression of intense concentration. It was the first time I had been able to see her as a real person, with needs and emotions of her own, not just as my mentor.

Reaching out, I put a hand over Lee's where it lay on the arm of her chair. She did not look at me, but put her other hand over mine briefly, patting it. We sat for a while in silence. There was still some quality of reserve in her that not even the drink in both our bloodstreams could sufficiently dilute. I had been allowed to see one veil lifting, but there were many others which were still firmly pinned in place, and I didn't have the courage to ask her to tell me more than she had already volunteered. Afterwards, I thought that maybe she had wanted me to push her into further confidences, and I cursed my own stupidity in holding back.

She turned to me after a while, her face wiped clean of all but friendliness and interest. This was Lee as I remembered her, and I had to admit that I was more comfortable with her like this. Old habits die hard.

'So what are you working on now?' she said. 'Would I be able to see anything of yours?'

She had pitched her voice just right; she wasn't asking me as a teacher to a student, but as one artist to another, without a hint of patronage. A moment ago I had been dreading this inevitable question, but the magic of Lee's personality meant that as soon as she had asked it, I found myself spilling out my heart to her. The problem of my current sculpture, which I had not talked about to anyone, laid itself bare in a few words.

'It needs something,' I heard myself saying passionately. 'I just don't know what. I can't let go of it and I don't know what it needs. It sits there on the floor of my studio, just waiting for me, when I get up in the morning, when I come home, like some giant *thing* . . . I've been stuck with it for two months now and I don't see any way out.'

I looked at her warily. She did not seem to think there was anything odd in this; she looked concerned and thoughtful. She was studying the silver ring on her index finger with concentration. From experience, I knew this meant that she was about to make a suggestion and wasn't sure how it would be received.

'Perhaps you'll hate the idea,' she said tentatively, still gazing at her ring, 'but I would be very happy to come over and look at it. Just as a friend, obviously. But you might think that, because I was once your tutor, you would feel that I was criticising—'

'No, not at all!' I broke in enthusiastically. 'I can't think of anything I'd like more. You're the only person I would even let comment on it—'

'Really?' Lee looked genuinely flattered, almost shy.

'Yes, I'm very defensive about people seeing work in progress, generally. But you're different.'

'Thank you!'

Lee touched my hand again, smiling at me. For someone so reserved, she made frequent physical contact with those people with whom she felt at ease. I remembered the first time Lee had touched my arm to emphasise a point she was making, after having known me for a term, and how pleased I had been.

'I'm so glad we've met again, Sam,' she said simply. 'I expect it was only a matter of time until we did. But you've been on my mind a lot, you know. I don't like to make contact with my former students; I don't want them to feel any pressure. I usually wait until they get in touch with me. So I would love to see what you're working on now.'

'If you could just give me some suggestions,' I said in a heartfelt voice. 'Just some ideas I can mess around with. Or any criticisms. Anything, as long as I get someone else's point of view – someone I can trust – to give me a new way of looking at it.'

She shrugged, that little eloquent gesture of hers I remembered so vividly.

'Of course. But you know, Sam, you don't need me. You may think you do. But you always sorted out everything for yourself, in the end. I was only the catalyst. All the thinking was always yours.'

I stared at her, not knowing what to say.

'Lee?' said a voice in front of us. We both jumped. I looked up. It was Julia Seddon, and as soon as I saw the yearning expression on her face, I knew that Tom had no chance with her. She had an enormous crush on Lee.

Plenty of girls went through it at art school. For some it was genuine, but for most, probably including Julia, it was on the level of the schoolgirl who gets a crush on a glamorous prefect – perhaps not so much sexual as aspirational, a sort of heroine-worship. I recognised the signs at once, having fallen into the latter category myself for some time.

Still, this information wouldn't exactly cheer Tom up. I wondered if he realised where Julia's affections were really directed. He wouldn't like it much when he found out.

Lee said she was tired and about to go home, so we stood up and kissed goodbye. Waves of dislike were coming off Julia Seddon like a force-field propelling me back from Lee.

'I'll give you a ring,' I said. 'Are you still in the same place?'

'Oh yes. Do call me,' she said. 'I'd love to come round. But remember what I said, Sam – you don't really need me.' She smiled at me, one of her marvellous, light-filled smiles. 'You don't need anyone but yourself.'

* * *

I found Dave in the maelstrom of the dance room, cadged a couple of lines of speed off him and, thus fuelled up, danced solidly for the next few hours. The music was on a roll and wouldn't let go; hip-hop, thrash metal, jazz dance, trash disco, I didn't care, wanting only the sweet oblivion of physical exertion, of pushing my body to its limits. The air was thick with the heady scent of a dance room, a mixture of sweat, perfume, hash and cigarette smoke, brewed in the air; to be sampled only when fresh, because it wouldn't last.

I remember leaning against a wall, drinking more beer, my spirits soaring. The floorboards were rocking beneath our feet, the bass pumping up through them as if we were standing on the house's living heart. Much, much later I found a spare mattress and fell asleep at once, as I had a trick of doing as a child. The mattress was old and yielding; my body curled up into it like a cat settling itself into a warm lap, and then till the morning there was nothing more. No dreams, just oblivion.

* * *

I woke up to the sound of birdsong. The light in the room was clear and pale; it was dawn, or just after it. My head was still buzzing from the speed, and the combination of that and the alcohol had produced a fine blend of raging thirst and pounding head. I would have tried to doze off again but the speed wouldn't let me. And my feet hurt. I wished I had taken my boots off before passing out.

I negotiated the staircase with considerable difficulty. I was trying not to let my head wobble, but it's hard to walk downstairs at a slow, steady pace when great chunks of the treads seem to have been gnawed away by large rodents. On reflection, they probably had been gnawed away by large rodents. The kitchen was exactly what I had been expecting. I managed to locate the sink at last behind the piled-up beer cans, but it was more by luck than judgement.

After drinking about a pint of water I stood leaning against the wall for a little while, allowing the liquid to percolate around my body so that I wouldn't slosh too loudly when I walked. The door to the garden was in front of me, and its glass panel presented a view of green foliage and brick wall that looked very appealing. Back to nature, up with the early bird. I would go outside and commune with the dawn, refresh my inner life . . .

This dream was soon quashed. A barbecue had recently been held in the garden. In an attempt at decorative continuity, the beer can motif from the kitchen had been carried through outdoors, here embellished for added effect with a heavy coating of crumpled pieces of tinfoil and stubbed-out roaches. There was a strong smell of petrol, and a packet of firelighters had spilt its contents underfoot. *Homes and Gardens* were probably ringing right now, begging to send a photographer round. However, it was a big garden, and perhaps if I wandered down to the far wall, the proportion of debris to greenery would be reversed. It would be a nice little excursion for me. I could send postcards back. In the distance I could see a pale heap of person curled up beneath a couple of trees, probably in a pool of their own dried vomit. That would go with the rest of the décor.

The lawn, untended and bare, was covered with fallen leaves. It tailed off into a cluster of huge half-naked trees, their branches sharply etched against the pale sky of an autumn morning, clear and cold. The air circulated briskly through my lungs, and I began to feel properly alive, even with the pounding in my head. Despite everything, it had been a good party. I hadn't taken too many drugs or gone home with anyone I didn't particularly want to. The fresh air was purifying my lungs and my bloodstream. Soon it would be a new year.

In a surge of enthusiasm, I wanted to go straight home, to sit down in front of the sculpture and give myself an ultimatum; either do something to it or tear the whole thing apart and start again. I would ring Lee this afternoon and arrange for her to come round and see it. The thought filled me with excitement. I had a sense, at last, of forward movement in my life.

Leaves crunched underfoot. I shoved my hands into the pockets of my jacket and stood up straight for the first time, hearing the vertebrae click into place up the back of my neck as my spine stretched itself out. I would go over to the person sleeping rough under the trees and check that they were all right, and then I would drive home, stop off for a coffee, open up the studio . . .

I had no idea what I would find. The sleeping figure had its back to me; it was curled up, facing the shelter of the trees. I bent down to shake the nearer shoulder and her whole body tilted, then fell, in an oddly soundless movement, over onto its back.

I knew at once that she was dead. There are some things you cannot mistake.

Lee's eyes stared sightlessly up into the sky, which was as white as her clothes, as white as her skin. Her padded jacket, wrapped round her as snugly as swaddling, would keep her warm no longer. Clear and blue-veined as marble, her skin, and her body stiff with rigor mortis; unyielding, cold, all the things she seemed to be at first sight but was not. But if this was all that was left, her body, her little white ears set, as always, with their little white pearls, then where was she herself any longer?

There was a huge bruise on her temple, dark and heavy, which had leaked a little blood. Her once-pristine clothes were stained with green grass, brown mud, and her hair was damp with dew. She looked like her own ghost.

4

I didn't need to look at the menu. I knew what I wanted already.

'I'll have the breadcrumbed mushrooms with rice and tartare sauce,' I said to the waitress, her opulently middle-aged figure swathed in a white frilled apron and topped with a lacquered, red-tinted pouf of hair. 'And an extra piece of lemon on the side.'

I never believe those people who say that they forget to eat. I don't think it's possible.

I settled back into the peeling green leather booth. The room was warm with steam from the huge old expresso machine. Hot gusts of air surged out from the swing doors to the kitchen, which didn't fit together properly and batted back and forth with a series of dull decreasing thuds. I had come here direct from the police station. It was mid-afternoon now and I hadn't eaten since yesterday evening. Besides, I was struggling with a dangerous temptation and I had decided to eat before making up my mind. Carbohydrates are very calming in times of stress.

On cue my order arrived, an oval white plate piled on one side with deep-fried mushrooms thick and crunchy with breadcrumbs, and on the other with a mound of white fluffy rice. There was a metal cup full of tartare sauce, and my extra piece of lemon. My stomach rumbled in happy anticipation. I squeezed the lemon over the mushrooms, spooned out as much sauce onto the plate as it would hold without slopping over the edges, and set to work.

* * *

An hour later, stomach bulging happily at the seams, I was driving slowly past Warwick Avenue tube station, through the wide streets of Little Venice with their white, square, high-windowed houses. Canal boats, painted in bright primary colours like the plastic ones children play with in the bath, were tied up on either side of the thick green water. Over the canal arched the low pale bridge, a lovely rising stretch of road, and behind it, like a huge dark shadow blocking the sky, hung the network of the Paddington flyover, as grimy and dismal as always.

Pulling up across the street, I checked the number of the flat in my address book, and settled down to wait. It was a large mansion block with plenty of tenants; this part, at least, shouldn't take long. It had better not. Too long a delay and I might start wondering again what on earth I thought I was doing.

After about ten minutes, a young man walked down the street, coming from the direction of a small parade of shops, carrying a green plastic bag stamped with the name of a delicatessen that stayed open all hours and charged its clients double for the privilege. He turned into the entrance to the block of flats, bless him. As he unlocked the door, I was a few paces behind him, and I began to fumble in my bag, clinking my car keys together to make the right kind of looking-for-my-door-key noise. By this time he had opened the door and was casting a swift glance back at me. I smiled ingratiatingly. He held it ajar. What a gentleman.

He was waiting by the lift, so I turned left and started down the corridor, keeping out of sight until I heard the lift start to rise. Then I went back to the hall and up the stairs to the fourth floor.

The corridor was paved with heavy ancient tiles, veined and cracked in places. I was careful to keep to the strip of faded green carpet down the centre, walking softly. The corridor was as silent as a tomb. Or a mausoleum, which it vaguely resembled. The stuffy air didn't seem to have shifted for weeks.

Misspent years of living in squats or paying rent for flats which managed to be even more squalid and derelict than the squats were had taught me a few things about picking locks. In the back of the van, together with various old rusting tools, I had a little gadget which works a treat on Chubb locks; but it has to be plugged in and makes something of a noise. I was very relieved to see that Lee only had a Yale on her door. I gripped the door handle and eased it to the left as far as I could, towards the hinges, creating a little gap between the door and the jamb.

The laminated plastic card I always use for this kind of thing slipped into position easily enough, but the lock itself was as old and tired as the rest of the building and I had as much of a problem getting it to disengage as an arthritic pensioner has with a creaking knee joint.

Finally, the lock yielded. Holding it back, I turned the door handle, which croaked rustily, and opened the door. I was through in a flash, shutting the door behind me as carefully as if it were a precious piece of sculpture which I was levering into position on its plinth. Then I leaned back against it, and took another deep breath, wishing that I had some cigarettes on me. Just now I'd kill for one.

* * *

Lee's flat was just as I remembered it, as pale and bare and shining as it had always been. It was a white box filled with chrome and glass and steel. No plants, no pictures, no photographs. Once I had thought this place an oasis of calm, the equivalent of a cool shower on a humid day. Now I found it strangely unsettling; blanched, like bones in the sun. The sofas were covered in bleached linen, the carpet was a slightly darker shade of neutral. Even the light that poured in through the windows was white, glinting on the metal tubes of the furniture as if on hundreds of knife blades.

No wonder that years ago, when I was tangled up in my own luridly coloured emotions, this place had been so important to me. It was the modern equivalent of a monk's cell, deliberately restrained, as clear of clutter and fuss as Lee herself had been. But now, seeing it through the gap of years, I wondered if perhaps it were too restrained, too stark. For the first time it occurred to me that even Lee – whom I had idolised, as students do when they finally find a teacher who seems to understand them – might have her own flaws, even her own problems.

I had no idea what I was looking for, or even whether there was anything to find. At random I went through into the bedroom and stood there for a moment, feeling a fool, not knowing what I was doing here. Perhaps the voice of reason had been right, the one that had said to dismiss temptation and leave this kind of thing to the professionals. But I was here now, I might as well do something . . . I swung open the cupboard door.

The pockets of Lee's clothes yielded scraps of tissue, receipts, a few loose coins. I checked the two coats hanging on the back of the bedroom door; nothing in their pockets either but a pair of folded tan leather gloves. The floor of the wardrobe was bare of anything but scattered shoes, just as the shelves were bare of anything but clothes.

With a sense of futility, I tried the desk in the living-room. Bills, notepaper, envelopes, nothing at all personal. No packets of photographs, no private letters; no letters at all, come to that. A small accordion file marked 'Accounts', its divisions marked with headings like 'Bank statements', 'Credit card statements', 'Insurance'. I flicked through it briefly, to double-check that all the sections contained what they were supposed to contain. They did. The ball was dropping into zero with predictable regularity.

A clock was ticking in my head, and the sound was getting louder and louder the longer I stayed in the flat. It was an alarm clock, and soon it was going to ring to tell me I should be gone by now.

As soon as I walked into the kitchen I knew something was wrong. The disorder of the shoes in her closet should have told me so already, if I had been thinking. It wouldn't have been obvious to someone who didn't know Lee. But I had, and so I knew how neat she liked to keep her kitchen. The stainless steel and marble-topped counters were as shiny as ever, the white-tiled floor had been swept and polished in the last few days.

On one counter, however, were stacked boxes of cereal and sugar and flour and rice and biscuits, their bright cardboard packets drawing my eye at once. Lee would never have left them out. A memory flashed back to me, of coming here with a group of students for a tutorial, and of Lee making tea for us all. She had taken the packets out of the cupboards, removed teabags and biscuits, closed the packets and put them away again at once. And she had put out more biscuits than our anorexic group would ever have eaten, so she must have known she would have to return the uneaten ones to their boxes later . . . but still, she hadn't wanted to leave the packets out on the counter, even for a couple of hours. So why would she have left these out now?

A few cupboard doors were ajar. I looked inside and saw that the pans and crockery inside were piled higgledy-piggledy, as if someone had taken them all out and then jammed them back in again, wherever they would fit, rather than stacking them up in order of size. It was impossible for me to imagine Lee leaving her cupboards in that state.

All the boxes on the counter were half-empty ones. I checked in the store cupboard and found some sealed packets which were still inside, untouched. An image came to me of someone opening the cupboard, rifling through it, quickly pulling the open packets out onto the counter, pushing their hand down inside each one – flour, rice, muesli – to see if there was anything stored there. It seemed ridiculous. I couldn't take it seriously. And yet no other explanation for what I saw in front of me made sense.

I turned to face the opposite wall. I was looking for Lee's bulletin board, a piece of soft cork, where she had pinned a montage of postcards, invitations and bills, arranged symmetrically around a central photograph of an ice circle. It had been the one splash of colour against the white tiles and surfaces of the kitchen. I remembered the ice circle particularly; for the whole time I had known her, that photograph had occupied the centre of the board.

The board was still there, but now it was just an empty sheet of cork. I had another image, of the same person who had rifled through the packets, moving fast, not having the time to take each card off the wall and read it before pinning it back into place. So they had taken everything – just in case, in their hurry, they missed what they were looking for.

Of course, it was possible that Lee herself had cleared the board of all its bits and pieces. But then she would have put the pins into a drawer, not left them lying in a little pile on the counter top below. So, not Lee. Someone else. And I had no idea who or why.

I went back into the living-room and, now that I was looking for the signs of a search, I could see that someone had been through the bookshelves too. The books were jammed in together; many of them were upside down. But, like the other indications, to a casual glance they seemed tidy enough. I myself had walked straight past the shelves when I came in.

No-one would take me seriously if I cited the cereal packets and missing postcards and upside-down books as proof that the flat had been searched. But I was sure that it had been, and not by the police. They must have been here, but they didn't work like this. If they were really looking for something, they would tear the place apart. And if they were doing a routine check after the owner had died, they wouldn't be searching through opened packets in the kitchen cupboards.

I thought about the amount of space there is in a packet of sugar, or a book. Drugs, in small quantities. I could cross that one out. Lee hadn't been a dealer. I felt safe, too, in discarding the microfilm with the priceless blue-prints for a new smarter bomb, and the Tsarina's missing emeralds.

The alarm clock in my head went off, ringing loudly. Common sense said that the flat had already been searched, and for all I knew the person, or people, who had done it had found what they were looking for. In any case, there was no point in my lingering here to be discovered. I got out fast, and locked the door behind me.

When the lift arrived, I stepped into it quietly and immediately stepped out again. This time, I made a degree of noise walking down the corridor to Lee's front door, where I rang the bell. It made a disappointingly quiet ring. You might not even have heard it from the next-door flat. I knocked on the door, loudly, waited for a short time and then rang the bell again, following up with another nice loud knock. Still nothing. Damn.

I called out: 'Mrs Jackson? Are you there?'

I heard my voice, shockingly loud in the silence, echoing down the long marble reaches of the hallway, past the lines of mahogany front doors. No response. I was just about to give up when suddenly the door of the flat next to Lee's opened, and a head craned out of it. It was a woman's head, and the expression on the face was inquisitive as a monkey's. The body edged out behind it, hunching forward shyly at me, as if it might at any minute scuttle back inside again.

She was small and well-preserved for her age, which was early seventies or so, in a dark green sweater over a long pleated Liberty print skirt. Her fine grey hair was piled neatly on top of her head. There was a silver brooch at the neck of the sweater, set with a large, turquoise stone. Above the brooch, the collar of a lace blouse peeked out demurely. Above the blouse, her eyes were as bright and beady as a snake's.

'I'm sorry to interfere, dear, but I couldn't help hearing you knocking on the door,' she said in a sweet little voice.

I frowned, trying to look perplexed. 'It's just that I was supposed to bring a catalogue round to Mrs Jackson, about this time of day, and I've been ringing the bell, but there doesn't seem to be any answer.'

'Oh dear,' she said, sounding deeply concerned, 'what an awful thing. Are you a friend of hers, may I ask?' Her nose was almost twitching with excitement.

'No, I hardly know her,' I said. 'It's through the gallery where she works. My employer asked me to bring her an exhibition catalogue so she could have a look at it. She didn't want to trust it to the post.'

I patted my rucksack illustratively. It was capacious enough to contain a volume of the *Encyclopaedia Britannica* and instead was full of useless crap which I never found the time to sort through and throw away.

'Well, I'm afraid you've had a wasted journey, dear. The police were round this morning. Apparently she's had an accident. The police didn't exactly say what kind. But she's dead. Awful, isn't it? She didn't come back last night, you see. She was at one of those all-night parties.'

'What a terrible thing!' I exclaimed.

'Oh, I know! Isn't it dreadful? To think of her dying like that, so suddenly, no warning! And an old crock like me still alive, it scarcely seems right, does it?'

She looked me over once more, her little eyes nipping up and down me like a pair of zoom lenses. Through her partially open door streamed a ray of sunlight, which slipped between us and down the faded paper on the far

41

wall. A thousand dust motes tangled themselves inside the sunbeam.

'Would you like to come in for a cup of tea, dear? It seems a shame for you to have come all this way for nothing.'

'No, thank you very much,' I said quickly. 'I'd better be going.'

'Well, I won't keep you.'

I turned as if to walk back to the lift. But after a few steps, I swung tentatively back again, as if I had just thought of something. She was still in the doorway.

'I was just wondering,' I said, casually, 'did anyone else come round today to see Mrs Jackson? My boss said that she might drop in herself, this morning– Oh, but then, of course, if she had come round here, she would have rung to tell me what had happened, so I wouldn't have had the wasted journey.'

Unexpectedly, the wrinkled face creased up, but not with the previous gossipy relish. I had triggered a reaction far beyond what I had been hoping for. Indeed, she looked almost afraid, not of me, but of something she had remembered. She took another step out into the corridor, as if involuntarily, and for the first time her age seemed to render her vulnerable rather than omniscient.

'Nobody's been to see her today, apart from you, dear. But there was something—' She looked at me warily. 'You'll probably think this is just the imagination of an old woman who's hearing things. I didn't tell the police sergeant because I was worried he might tell the social services, you see. I couldn't bear to go to a home. Or even have them coming round checking on me more than they do already.'

'I promise I won't tell them,' I said at once.

She nodded. 'No, you don't exactly look the type to go interfering to the social services . . . Well, it's like this. She was at that party all night, and she died early in the morning, before it was even light, the police sergeant said. I asked him specially. So she didn't come back here at all. But, until he told me she never came back, I'd been sure that I heard her moving around in her flat only this morning. I'm a very light sleeper, you see. The older you get, dear, the less sleep you need, and even when I do finally drop off, I wake up very easily.'

She fiddled with the brooch at her neck.

'Really, I would have sworn that early this morning she was busy in her kitchen. It backs on to my bedroom, you know. And it wasn't light yet, but it wasn't night any more, either. My curtains let a bit of light in, because they're not as heavy as they could be. It wasn't much before dawn. So I distinctly remember thinking what an odd time it was to make yourself a cup of tea. Or even do the cleaning, which is what it sounded like. Of course, I couldn't tell that to the police, could I? They'd think I was batty. But you don't think that, do you?'

Her eyes were imploring. I shook my head and said slowly, 'No. I don't think that at all.'

5

Speculations raced round my mind as I drove home. Whoever had entered Lee's flat early this morning had stripped it bare of everything personal it had once contained. I had not come across a single photograph, a single letter which wasn't connected with her work. That had to be wrong. After all, no-one could avoid accumulating some personal correspondence. I wondered if the police had noticed what was missing.

But they didn't know, as I did, of the existence of some letters which at least should have been in the flat, the love letters of which Lee had spoken so passionately last night. And they were missing too. Unless, of course, Lee had been carrying them in her handbag. But if the thief felt safe enough to rifle through Lee's flat so early in the morning, they probably knew that she was dead; and if they knew she was dead, the first thing they would have done would have been to search her bag for the letters—

A car behind me honked twice. The lights had changed to green and I was still staring into space, hooked by the thought which had just popped into my mind. I put the car in gear and pulled away on automatic pilot. Unconsciously, I had assumed that the object of the search had been the love letters. Well, why not? And if so, had the burglary been successful?

I thought not. People keep their love letters close to hand so they can re-read them often. That means a bedside table, or a desk drawer. But they hadn't turned up in the bedside table, or the desk, because the thief must have tried those first and then gone on looking, unsatisfied, in a variety of increasingly unlikely places. And I didn't believe that they had finally turned up in a cereal packet.

So the letters hadn't been in Lee's bag, or in the flat. But where were they instead? And why was it so important to find them? Had it been Lee's lover in the flat, trying to reclaim her own letters – but then how had she known that Lee was dead? Surely she couldn't have been at the party, running the risk of being seen in public with Lee . . .

The letters might have had nothing to do with the search. They might have been in the bedside table after all, and the thief might simply have scooped them up with everything else that had been taken. But that solved one problem only to raise another: what had the thief been looking for, if not the letters?

I was tired of speculation. I wanted to go home and curl up in bed and finish my supermarket vodka. I had some crème de cassis too and I could mix them together and drink till I was warm and comforted and most of all incapable of asking myself what my name was, let alone whether someone might have deliberately killed Lee.

*　*　*

The street where I live isn't the kind of place that raises your spirits when you turn into it. No-one else lives here but me; all the other buildings are warehouses with filthy cobwebbed windows and peeling paint. Mine was a warehouse too before I moved in and made it into a studio. It still looks as unprepossessing as its neighbours, but I never have trouble finding a parking space at night.

A couple of chipped stone steps lead up to my front door, which is painted the same shit-brown as it was when I first moved in. I didn't want to be accused of yuppifying the area, so I left it untouched. Sprawled across the steps was what looked at first sight like a pile of shapeless blue rags. As I approached, the rags resolved themselves, becoming first recognisably human, and then, when I was closer still, Tom Connelly. My trained eye told me that he was still hungover. Artists are excellent observers.

I stood over him and folded my arms. This made me feel like a dominatrix, especially since I was wearing my leather boots, so I unfolded them again and said: 'Tom, for fuck's sake—'

'A simple hello would suffice.'

He looked up at me. His eyes were now more blue than red, which had to be some sort of improvement on this morning. I knew what was coming; he was going to do his stray dog impression and try to play on my heartstrings. I braced myself to resist it, which wasn't hard. I was not in the mood for calculated charm.

'I just couldn't stay in the house, Sam,' he said pathetically. 'I couldn't. They're all trying to do a collective memory lapse – let's tidy up as if nothing had happened and then we'll go out for a drink and we won't mention it. But Jesus Christ, they just took her body out of there hours ago! I saw it! I knew if I stayed there, tomorrow morning I'd be looking out of my window and seeing her lying there, under the trees, all crumpled up, *dead . . .*'

There was nothing to say. I opened the door without a word; Tom gathered himself up and followed me in. In silence, I walked across to the freezer, removed the vodka, fished two tumblers off the sink, and climbed the high ladder to my sleeping loft; I settled myself down on my futon, filled the glasses to the brim, gave him one, and, in silence, we knocked them back.

I put my glass down and promptly burst into tears. Tom cuddled me into his big sweater. I snuffled like that for a while. I could feel the vodka, syrupy and dense from the freezer, burning its way with icy heat down the back of my neck and into my stomach. It settled there comfortably, and as it did, my tears came to a slow trickling halt.

'She was my tutor at art school,' I said. 'She was so wonderful . . .' I poured myself another glass of vodka and drank most of it down. I remembered that I had forgotten the crème de cassis but it no longer seemed to matter; I was already feeling better – as if someone had punched me in the head, but in a friendly way. 'Didn't you think she was wonderful?' I said.

'I hardly talked to her.'

'But I saw you—'

'Oh, I was telling her about my reading next week,' Tom said, waving an unsteady hand. 'Did I tell you about my reading next week, at the Poetry Club? I'm doing it with Naomi Birtwhistle and that fucking librarian, tax-collector, whatever he does, John poker-up-the-arse Shaw—'

'You didn't see Lee going into the garden with anyone, did you?' I said, ignoring this.

'Bloody hell, Sam, I haven't the faintest idea,' Tom said testily. 'I had a bottle of bourbon in me. I wouldn't have recognised myself in the mirror at that stage.'

'What about Julia? Did she see anything?'

'Leave it, Sam.' Tom refilled my glass and pressed it

into my hand. Common politeness required that I drink it down. I still wanted the answer to the question but I was in no condition to press him on it. Sleep, or at least unconsciousness, was approaching fast.

'I'm going to sleep here, Tom,' I said carefully, patting the futon. 'This is my bed. Where's your bed?'

Tom was quick on the uptake.

'You mean I can't sleep here?'

'Mmmn.'

'But Sam, I can't go home. I can't go back there tonight. I told you.'

'No. Can't sleep here. No.'

'I promise I won't try anything. Really.'

'Bollocks.'

'No, I mean it. I promise.'

'Take the sofa . . .'

'No, please! Not the sofa!'

Tom's face was a picture of misery. People are always rude about my sofa. I don't know why; it's perfectly easy to arrange yourself so that the springs don't dig into you. You just have to shift around a bit. I started to explain this to Tom, but gave up halfway through. I was very tired indeed by now.

'OK.' I started to crawl up the futon towards the headboard. It seemed a very long way. 'Just no funny stuff. Or else you're out. I mean it. Out, out, out . . .'

I pulled the duvet round me. A few tears of self-pity began to trickle down my cheeks. Tom was saying something, but I was too busy snuffling into the pillows to listen. It wasn't what you could call crying myself to sleep. I was unconscious before the pillow was even wet.

6

Shelley Frank Fine Art was located on Devereaux Street, in the little maze of narrow streets between Piccadilly and Bond Street where London's most expensive art galleries are to be found. It belonged to the white and near-empty school of gallery furnishing, rather than the lushly-carpeted brothel madam's boudoir style which features red walls and lots of little gilt chairs. A few paintings were hung on the walls, carefully placed and expertly lit. I paused for a moment outside to survey the effect; very impressive.

I only hoped I hadn't overdone it with the perfume. I had stopped for a moment in Fenwick's to allow a saleswoman as crusted in make-up as a geisha to douse me with Montana and now I could almost see its dark blue aura surrounding me. I couldn't wait; it would take hours to wear off. At least it smelled expensive. Bracing myself, I pushed open the heavy glass door. Inside the gallery, the atmosphere was cool and slightly humid. A heavy pall of quiet hung in the air. It had the same effect on me as school assembly; it made me want to jump up and down and shout obscenities about the headmistress's knickers at the top of my voice.

There were a couple of people strolling from picture to picture, pausing in front of each one to whisper reverent comments to each other. A woman sat at a large glass and steel desk at the far end of the room, head down, making entries in a large book. Like a priest in church, her presence ensured that one talked in hushed monotones and didn't try to enter without decently covering one's shoulders and legs. I walked up to her. She must have heard my patent leather boots clicking on the floor, but she did not lift her head till I was nearly at the desk. Low-pressure selling. I liked it.

'Could I talk to Shelley Frank, please, if she's available?' I said politely.

'Might I ask why?'

She was wearing black-framed glasses for writing, which she now took off to have a thorough look at me. Her eyes were brown and shrewd.

'It's about Lee Jackson, who used to work here. I'm—'

She cut me short, her face tightening up.

'Please. I know exactly why you're here. My God, the grapevine certainly buzzes, doesn't it? You're the third one to come in since it happened.'

So much for my natural air of authority.

'I don't think you understand,' I began. 'I'm—'

'Oh, don't worry, I do. I expect you're a painter?'

'Sculptor, actually—'

'Well, I find it completely distasteful to have people looking for a job so soon after the last employee died. It's only been four days, for God's sake. Go and find someone else's bones to pick.'

'Don't beat around the bush,' I wanted to say: 'tell me what you *really* think of me.' She put her glasses back on and dropped her head to her papers. Interview over.

'I'm not here about the job,' I said smugly.

'*What?*'

'I'm a friend of Lee's. I saw her the night she died. I came to talk to you about her. I assume you're Shelley Frank?'

I based this guess on her air of authority; I couldn't believe that she had a boss. Who would be capable of telling this woman what to do on a regular basis?

She stood up and thrust her hand out at me.

'Shelley Jacobson. My partner's Judith Frank. We split the names.'

I shook her hand. It was that or kiss it.

'Sam Jones.'

'I'm very, very sorry,' she said.

'Sure.'

I smiled. She smiled back. We were practically friends already. The glasses came off again. She looked me up and down once more and made her mind up.

'Look, can I make you a cup of coffee? We'll talk in the back office. I'll get Judith to hold the fort for a while.'

Snap decisions on everything, Shelley Jacobson; not exactly one of your slow reflective types. Not a chess player – squash would be her game. Fast and furious.

She went through a white door at the back of the gallery, indicating for me to follow her. On the other side was a small office. It was like walking through a magic portal which takes you in a flash from one world to another. The gallery had been as cool and clinical as the waiting-room at a very expensive Swiss clinic. The office, on the other hand, was lush and cosy and welcoming. Green carpet, mahogany furniture, a big brass overhead light, a huge abstract oil painting on the back wall in Provençal yellows and blues. There were also a couple of large plants in dull brass bowls, the leaves big and shiny and slightly pointed. Two wide desks, covered in emerald leather, faced each other across the room, with a couple of armchairs between them. The walls were heavily lined with shelves of books and catalogues.

'Jude,' Shelley Jacobson said to the woman sitting at one of the desks, 'this is Sam Jones, a friend of Lee's. Could you take over the front desk while I give her a cup of coffee?'

Judith Frank, a tall, glacially elegant woman with long blonde hair and a long pale nose, raised her eyebrows and murmured a brief hello in my direction. I murmured one back. She pushed her chair back and stood up, revealing a body that went perfectly with the hair and nose; long, pale, and expensively accoutred in a beige dress. She was wearing shiny sheer tights which made her legs look as if they were coated with clear gloss. With a nod to Shelley, she went through into the gallery, shutting the door behind her.

Shelley vanished and returned a few minutes later with a tray, which she put down on the table between the armchairs. We sat down. The tray and the cups were clear Pyrex and the table top and cafetière were glass, so that the coffee seemed to float eerily in mid-air.

'So,' she said, once the coffee was poured. 'You wanted to talk about Lee?'

On looks alone, Shelley Jacobson was nothing to write home about. However, by the time you realised this, it no longer mattered. She had already projected so much confidence at you that she had made herself seem attractive by sheer force of willpower. And she made the best of what she had. She wore a pink Chanel suit trimmed with little gilt chains and plenty of heavy gold jewellery, including a wide wedding band. Her dark brown hair had been tamed into a short, glossy cut which gave her height, as did the three-inch heels she wore. Her brown eyes were outlined with several shades of eyeshadow and her blusher gave her cheekbones. Every detail had been thought about, every defect camouflaged, every asset highlighted.

I gave her a brief outline of the facts as I knew them – the party, my discovery of Lee's body, what the police seemed to consider the likely explanation of her death, and my own doubts on the subject. Shelley Jacobson, who had only heard that Lee had been killed in some sort of tragic accident at a party, widened her eyes incredulously as I described the actual circumstances. Watching her closely, I went on to add that the police had asked me whether I had a key to Lee's flat and, if so, whether I had been to visit it in the early hours of the morning she died.

If this extra information made her nervous, I couldn't tell. She listened in silence, with an almost palpable concentration, but the possibility that I might guess that someone had been into Lee's flat that morning did not seem to trouble her any more than the rest of what I had told her.

When I had finished, she drew a deep breath, and fixed her eyes on me. Their stare had the penetration of road-drills.

'I agree with you,' she said firmly. 'I can't see Lee stumbling drunkenly around outside a party at two in the morning, or whenever. It's totally ridiculous, and I'm surprised that anyone could believe it. But I'm still puzzled,' she added. 'I don't see what you're doing here. After all, you've been to the police, haven't you? You've told them what you've told me, and hopefully they'll at least think about it. So why are you here? What do you want from *me*?'

This was like being thrown straight into the cold plunge pool at the Turkish bath – bracing, as long as you didn't drop dead from the shock. I poured myself another cup of coffee to gain some time.

'This is a little delicate,' I began, watching her carefully. 'I need to be sure you won't talk about it to anyone else.'

'Of course,' she said easily. Too easily.

'Lee told me, the night she died,' I continued, 'that she was having an affair with a married woman. The kind of woman whose career was paramount to her and who couldn't afford to have the truth about her sex life known. I don't know if it has anything to do with her death. Perhaps it's completely irrelevant. But I'd like to find out who this woman was.'

I looked down at my hands. One was holding a half-eaten biscuit. I put it down; it didn't go with the mood I was trying to create.

'I'd like to talk to her,' I said softly. 'Just to talk about our memories of Lee . . . She didn't have any close family that I could go to see. And she meant a great deal to me. It may sound stupid, but I feel that if I could talk to someone who really knew her well, if we could remember her together, that it might help me to get over her death. Mourn her, in a way. Does that sound ridiculous?'

Shelley's eyes were full of sympathy. She reached out and took my hand. I wondered if she thought I had been unrequitedly in love with Lee or something of the sort.

'I understand,' she said. 'Really I do. She meant a lot to you. But I still don't see how I can help.'

'Well, it occurred to me that the way Lee was most likely to meet that kind of woman was through this gallery. I hadn't seen much of her for a few years, since I left college – I used to be a pupil of hers – but her social life, as I remember it, didn't move in those circles. She knew artists, tutors, people like her. They wouldn't want their husband or wife to find out they were having an affair, but they're not the sort of people whose career it would jeopardise. That's the difference.'

I looked her straight in the eye.

'I'm ruling you out, by the way. I saw you were married, of course. But there are a lot of reasons against it.'

It was a calculated risk, talking to her like that, but I wanted to throw her off guard. It had worked. For the first time, she looked genuinely flabbergasted. But I'd read her right; she was too thick-skinned to mind personal remarks. Instead, I had intrigued her.

'Well, let's hear them!' she said. She leant forward, eyes sparkling, as if we were sharing a joke. I held up my hand, fingers and thumb spread wide, and ticked them off one by one.

'Firstly, you wouldn't give a toss if anyone found out you were sleeping with a woman. You'd face it out and tell them to get lost. Secondly, I can't see how it would matter to your career. Why would anyone care? Third, you're not the type of woman Lee described to me, buttoned-up and repressed; her opposite, in fact. Fourth, I can't imagine you in the kind of marriage Lee described. And fifth, if you're gay, I'm a banana split.'

Shelley burst out laughing, throwing herself back in the armchair as easily as a child. It was jolly, robust laughter, in a Henry VIII, thigh-slapping way. It was lucky I hadn't told her the real reason I had crossed her off as a possibility: that I couldn't imagine Lee falling in love with her. Lee's tastes had always been subtle.

'Excellent!' she said. 'So that's me out of the way.'

Still laughing, she went through into the kitchen and

returned with a box of shortbread fingers.

'Very naughty, I know,' she said, ripping the end open. 'But that was such good entertainment. Have one?'

I never cease to marvel at the instantaneous bonding effect that eating rather too many biscuits together has for women. After three shortbread fingers each, we were chattering away like best friends.

'So,' Shelley said, bubbling with energy, 'we want to trace this woman, don't we? If you were thinking I might know, I don't. I didn't even know Lee was seeing anyone. She didn't talk about her personal life at all. I'll have a think about it, though. And as far as her death goes – ' she stared at me thoughtfully – 'you know what I think's most likely? It could have been a kind of accident, though you're right, I don't see Lee going out into the garden by herself at night like that. But suppose she and another person went out to have a private talk which turned into an argument. Perhaps this person gave her a push or something, not meaning actually to do any harm, and she fell over and hit her head.'

'Sure,' I agreed. 'It's the most likely explanation. But if it happened that way, why didn't the person with Lee come straight into the house and say so? All they would have had to do would be to say that Lee had stumbled and fallen in the dark.'

'Maybe they were too scared.'

'Or there was some reason they couldn't come forward, some connection they had with Lee which they didn't want made public. So we're dealing with someone who panics easily, or has something to hide.'

'That doesn't have anything to do with her girlfriend, though, does it? I mean, they're two separate things. Don't you think?'

She looked at me with her clear brown eyes. Shelley Jacobson worried me. She was the kind of person who is hardly ever frightened, not so much because she's brave, but because she's supremely confident. I could easily imagine her seeing a lovely clear stretch of beach and striding straight across it without bothering about the red warning notices. Then, of course, she would be very indignant to find herself knee-deep in quicksand.

Besides, I needed her help to find Lee's girlfriend, and if she thought this would mean involvement in a suspicious death as well I was sure she wouldn't offer it to me. So I nodded in agreement and let the moment pass.

Then she made the proposal to me.

* * *

Claire wasn't at the café when I arrived so I bought a San Miguel and sat down in a corner to watch the clientele. I always meet girlfriends here: what better place to sit alone waiting for someone without being hassled than a gay bar? And there are always plenty of pretty boys to ogle. The fashion students and media trendies are always good value, but the dancers from the Pineapple studio down the road win hands down.

Everything was done in pastel shades of pale blue and orange and the tables, though fortunately not the chairs, were wrought-iron. Next year it would be dark blue walls and wooden furniture, or whatever was the latest thing by that time. Unfortunately for my waistline, I was sitting near the food counter, opposite a carrot cake, and it was calling to me. I was trying to block out its siren song when a voice said, 'Excuse me?'

It was a girl with cropped, bleached blonde hair, red lipstick and a very pretty face. Long legs in faded jeans, and a black, fringed leather jacket over her shoulders. She seemed hesitant. Her hands were pushed deep into her jeans pockets.

'Is this seat taken?' she asked.

'Yes. I'm waiting for someone.'

'Oh.'

She paused. I looked round the room. Only about half of the tables were full; she didn't need my extra chair.

'I expect I can't buy you a drink, then?' she said, very casually.

She really was pretty.

'Sorry, no,' I said, feeling craven. This had never happened to me before – at least not with someone as attractive as she was – and I felt much clumsier than I would have done if she had been a man. I didn't want to be rude. If I hadn't been waiting for Claire I might even have said yes. She obviously wasn't the kind of person to think that a free drink put me under any obligation. But I had other things on my mind. Or that was what I told myself, anyway.

She didn't take it badly. 'OK. See you round.'

She flashed me a lovely smile and was gone. I watched her walk over to the other end of the room, and she knew I was watching her. She rejoined her group of friends; they had a magazine spread out on the table and were laughing over some article. The cropped haircut emphasised the elegant shape of her head, her high cheekbones. It seemed a waste to pass up a rare opportunity; how often did a beautiful blonde ask if she could buy me a drink?

Just then I saw Claire through the window and waved to her, exaggerating slightly so the blonde would see and realise that I hadn't been making it up when I said I was waiting for someone. Claire pushed open the door, looking sulky, as if it should have opened by itself to let her in.

'Do you want a drink?'

She shrugged and sat down. 'Whatever you're having.'

'Beer.'

'No, I'll have tea.'

I went over to the counter and ordered it. A boy with blond dreadlocks and a tartan T-shirt recited a list of ten kinds of herbal tea before I could explain to him that what she wanted was a big pot of English tea, made with two teabags, strong as paint-stripper. I left him rummaging through the back shelves to see if they had a box of it anywhere.

Claire was in her usual clothes: battered jeans, an old high-necked sweater with a suede jerkin over the top, and a deceptively simple pair of brown suede boots. Her short fair hair was pushed back roughly from her face, in a style that suited her strong bone structure. She looked perversely elegant and less like a coiled spring than she usually did.

This comparative calm was explained at once when she said, 'Look what I just bought,' and pulled out a bag from Hobbs in Covent Garden. From carefully wrapped sheets of tissue paper emerged a dark brown leather brogue which, with its twin, must have set her back seventy pounds at least. She had no discernible income and I suspected her of getting handouts from her parents, who were therapists in Hampstead. Her clothes were always much more expensive than they looked.

I made the right appreciative noises about the shoes till the tea was ready, knowing from experience that she would be more approachable when she had a cup of it inside her. Then I said, 'How's life in Castle Road?'

She shrugged.

'Pretty shitty. Ajay's really getting on my nerves. He's always complaining about how much noise we make. He just doesn't appreciate how bloody difficult it is to live with someone else in one room, right, with no money and no work apart from student productions which don't even pay your expenses . . .'

I tried to head her off from this familiar plaint.

'I meant after what happened Saturday night.'

'Oh, that.' Claire looked rather furtive. 'I don't really want to talk about it, you know. Liz wanted to have a house meeting so we could share our feelings and heal together or some hippy shit like that, but I told her to fuck off. I mean, it's not like Lee was a friend or anything.'

'But it must be upsetting, knowing someone actually died in your garden. Besides, you and Paul knew her.'

'Paul knew her much better than I did.'

'Really?'

Claire backed off slightly. 'Oh, you know. Paul gets around. He knows people everywhere to say hello to. Especially women. He's good at getting what he wants out of them. Did you know, I went up to Edinburgh a while ago about a job and stayed for the weekend, right? Didn't get the job, of course. And when I got back I heard there'd been a party in the house and Paul had spent the whole time chatting up some friend of Baby Thompson's. Bloody bastard.'

There was a bitter tone to her voice. I remembered what Tom had told me about Paul's flirtation with Judy, but didn't bring it up. It might distract her.

'It wouldn't have been the same with Lee, though,' I said. 'She wouldn't have been as susceptible to his charm as the rest.'

'What – oh yeah, she was a dyke, wasn't she? I forgot that.'

Her eyes slipped away from mine. She poured herself another cup of tea and said, 'How's things with you? Any news?'

Claire was notorious for the level of her self-absorption. For her to volunteer a question about someone else, rather than bring the conversation round to her own preoccupations, could only mean that she didn't want to continue with the subject under discussion. I felt that there was something she wasn't telling me, but I had no idea what it could be and so I had no way of penetrating the screen she had thrown up around her. I decided to see if I could startle her.

'Yeah, actually. I've got a new job.'

'Oh, right?' Claire seemed more relaxed now the conversation had taken a new turn. 'I thought you were teaching weights classes in that gym in Chalk Farm. Have you given that up?'

'No, I'm still there. But that's not regular work, only when someone's sick or on maternity leave and I have to cover for them.'

'So what's the new job?'

'I'm going to work part-time for an art gallery. Not much money in it, but good commission if I sell anything. And the owner says there should be plenty of opportunity to meet useful people – dealers, collectors. They don't do sculpture themselves but I might find a gallery through them that would take me on.'

'That's great!' Claire said with animation. I regarded her suspiciously; normally she would have been bemoaning my good fortune and comparing it to her own lack of success. 'Which gallery is it?'

'It's called Shelley Frank Fine Art.'

Claire stared at me.

'But isn't that where Lee used to work?' she blurted in surprise.

'That's right,' I said. 'I'm taking over her old job.'

And I wondered how Claire, who had said she hardly knew Lee, was aware not only that Lee worked in a gallery, but even what the gallery was called.

* * *

Shelley wouldn't take no for an answer. She said that she was still feeling guilty that she had been rude to me when we met and offering me the job was the perfect way to atone for it.

'I do actually need someone else right away, despite what I said before,' she explained. 'We're just getting ready to hang a new exhibition, so there's plenty of work. I have another girl who comes in twice a week, called Harriet. I'm sure you two will get on very well.'

That was nice. Maybe Harriet could be my new best friend. Shelley was pacing around the office floor, gesticulating as she spoke, the mass of gold bracelets on each wrist jingling like Christmas chimes in accompaniment. She lowered her voice confidentially.

'You see, although technically Judith and I are equal partners, she hates the day-to-day, business side of it. Doesn't want to be bothered with it. Neither of us are what you might call starving in the streets – ' big shrug here, palms upturned – 'but Judith's never had to worry about making money. She's passionate about art; she has a wonderful eye for new talent. But she's not so keen on the paperwork. And obviously, we need someone on the front desk all the time. Judith only does that when she absolutely has to – she loathes talking to every Tom, Dick or Harry who might come in.'

She looked sad.

'Lee was wonderful about that kind of thing, of course. She was always patient and she never lost her calm. We were so lucky to have her. I can't believe she's gone.'

Shelley caught her breath. 'I'm so sorry, Sam. I hope I didn't upset you.'

I shook my head.

'Well!' she said, brightening up her voice. 'What do you say?'

I pictured myself sitting behind a desk, answering the telephone – 'Shelley Frank Fine Art, good morning' – in my best smart voice. Or presenting plates of posh biscuits to rich morons: 'Another mocca finger, Mr Rich-Moron?' 'Oh yes, I think maybe I will. Thanks awfully.' I thought my talents might stretch to meet the challenge. To say nothing of the investigative opportunities.

'I'd love to,' I said modestly, 'if you're absolutely sure—'

'Oh, I'm so pleased! It's perfect. You're the kind of person I'd have been looking for anyway – I like to employ young artists and you're decorative too, which is always an asset, if I'm honest. It'll be so nice to have a friend of Lee's working here – and you can keep your eye open for the mystery girlfriend at the same time. What fun. But if it's a client, Sam,' she added, her voice all of a sudden preternaturally serious, 'for God's sake be discreet and don't go upsetting anyone. We can't afford to lose clients, you know. I'm sure you appreciate that.'

I nodded with equal seriousness and wondered if Shelley Jacobson could possibly be for real. If she knew more than she was saying, it would be exquisitely daring of her to go so far as to offer me Lee's old job. Yes, she could keep an eye on me here in her own art gallery – but it would still have been much safer to have made all the right, commiserating noises, reminisced about Lee for a while, and regretted her inability to help while walking me to the door.

But maybe Shelley was a gambler. She had enough nerve and more than enough self-confidence. And it was clear that, one way or another, she saw everything as a game.

7

Someone was following me. And making it painfully obvious. The footsteps behind me were matched to mine with unnatural regularity, and there was a prickly feeling between my shoulderblades as if I were being targeted by twin red laser dots: a pair of eyes whose stare was fixed unblinkingly on my back.

It was only a short walk from my studio to the bus stop – I wasn't driving, as I was on my way to meet Tom at a pub in Camden where I fully expected to consume large quantities of fine wines – so the person behind me must be particularly inept to have already made their presence felt. Ducking unexpectedly into a newsagent's, I snatched the briefest of glances over my shoulder. It was a man, surprise surprise, late twenties or so, wearing a tweed jacket; he had frozen in the middle of the pavement, almost palpably twitching with confusion. How gauche.

If I thought that this guy were just the kind of sad creep who got his kicks by following strange women while they did their shopping, I would have whirled round and scared the living daylights out of him. But I was hoping there was more to it than a simple case of perversion. After all, he had been waiting for me outside my studio; there had been no-one on the street when I came out and I had heard the footsteps start up straight away, so he must have been in some alleyway nearby, watching my front door. He hadn't followed me back there in the first place; he was so inept I would have noticed him at once. And he must have been waiting for me in particular, because if you were going to lurk on a street chosen at random, waiting for a front door to open and a girl to emerge whose looks you liked, you certainly wouldn't pick my street; it's the most unpromising stretch of gloomy-fronted ware-houses you ever saw.

I emerged from the newsagents and walked on towards the main road. Seven Sisters is one of London's major arteries, always clogged with exhaust fumes and honking traffic jams. A car ahead of me braked suddenly, squealing as if a small animal had caught its tail in the bonnet. Usually I hated the noise and bustle, but now they were perfect. Various sets of traffic were fretting impatiently behind unbroken white lines at the lights. I strolled up to them as if I were waiting to cross: then, at the last moment, pivoted sharply to my right and turned quickly down the pavement. It was the rush hour, and the street was packed with people; kids hanging out after school, commuters doing their shopping after work, others hurrying to get home.

A few steps away was an amusement arcade, its floor-length windows tinted black. I was through the door and tucked behind one of the game machines before he could even have turned the corner after me. The machine was large enough so that only the upper half of my face was visible over the top. Various large knobs stuck out into me, and the machine beeped insistently into my stomach. I ignored it.

After a few moments, he duly appeared, walking fast. Coming to a halt in the middle of the pavement, he looked up and down the street with quick jerky movements of his head and body, oblivious to the many people who pushed by him impatiently.

He was a very odd-looking person indeed. His face was dead white and shiny, but not with grease; it was as smooth as a china egg, and the features were small and neat, as if painted on with pen and ink. His hair, however, was greasy, if only artificially, slicked back with hair cream from his high brow. It was as black as his face was white and gave him the air of a slightly oriental doll. And it was obvious that he wasn't local. The old tweed jacket, baggy at the elbows, the bright blue sweater with a stripy shirt collar showing at the neck, the corduroy trousers, all said 'Kensington' as clearly as if it were tattooed on his forehead.

The expression on his face confirmed my hopes. He was looking around anxiously, worried, as if he had failed to do something and was going to get in trouble as a result. There was no trace of anything more, no frisson of sexual excitement. Whatever the reason he was following me, it wasn't for a thrill.

He pulled at his shirt collar as if it were too tight for his neck, a short, frustrated gesture, and turned for a last look around him. His gaze swivelled miserably into the arcade, and I ducked at once, heart pounding; how embarrassing to be caught crouching behind a game machine. But the slump of his shoulders said that he had already given up. Disconsolately, he wandered off.

I gave him a little time, and then extricated myself from the clutches of the machine. The arcade was full of skinny, pimply adolescent boys, dressed in the kind of expensive sports gear which, like a ballgown, rustles as you walk. By now it sounded as if every pubescent body in the arcade had swivelled to stare at me in dull fascination. I strolled nonchalantly to the doorway. From there I could see the bus stop, and when the bus arrived there were so many people waiting to board that all I had to do was lose myself among them and be pulled along by forward momentum. As it moved off, I caught a glimpse of Egg-Face on the other side of the street, looking around, still holding up the flow of pedestrian traffic. He looked so miserable I couldn't help feeling sorry for him.

* * *

Tom and I had arranged to meet in a big Southern Irish pub, the Freedom Arms, one of the main rendezvous for London's Irish expatriates. Saturday night revelry spilled out through the doors like falling drunks. The windows, which were decoratively engraved with gold ribbons declaring 'Finest Oysters in London' and 'Superb Porter and Pies', could barely contain the noise. I wedged the door far enough open to squeeze myself through. Inside there was one huge room with the bar in the centre; polished wooden floor, walls hung with photographs and pictures of famous Irishmen, a roaring fire in the iron grate. But tonight the décor was invisible behind the press of bodies. The pub was packed tighter than Sylvester Stallone's trousers.

Tom was in the centre of a large group of people clustered round a table. I heard his voice as soon as I walked in. His accent was, as always in the company of his compatriots, pronouncedly Oirish. You'd never know he left when he was seven and has never been back.

A distracted young man pressed a pint of Guinness into my hand, and I set to work on it before he realised that he had given it to the wrong person. I don't like to look a gift pint in the mouth. A group of people next to me started to sing something about Galway Bay, their heads pressed together. Tom noticed my presence and waved happily at me, already half-seas over.

'Sam, my beauty! How's the girl? Sure, and it's a vision of loveliness you are tonight.'

I assume he knows he's overdoing the accent, but it's annoying just the same.

'God, Tom,' I said, 'if you ever kissed the Blarney Stone, it wasn't with your mouth.'

My words happened to fall into a moment of comparative silence; the song about Galway Bay had broken off because no-one could remember the words past the first few lines. As a result, this comment was hailed as a great witticism. Two men shook my hand and enquired my name with the total sobriety of the very drunk. Someone bought a round of drinks to celebrate. Another song was attempted, with much the same result. I threw the rest of the first pint down the back of my throat and started on the second.

Several hours later someone was crashing away on the piano. I had a chair by this time, and I needed one. People were still trying to sing and by now I was joining in. We were reaching the 'Danny Boy' moment with inexorable momentum. It was well past closing time, but the doors were locked and we were on the right side of them. If a policeman dropped in, he would be told that it was a private party. By now, it wouldn't be a lie. Tom was across the table from me, lost momentarily in a peaceful daze. I had reached a state of clear-headedness myself, a sort of nirvana stage in a night's hard drinking.

Tom's wandering gaze fastened on me. I could see him recognising me, and then remembering something, almost squinting with the effort. He stood up and made a slow, magisterial progression around the table. Standing over the young man next to me, who I think was called Bob, or maybe Doug, Tom asked him politely if he would move, as he had something very important to say to me. Bob, or Doug, not looking up, suggested that Tom perform an anatomical impossibility. Tom stressed again the importance of what he wanted to say. Doug or Bob turned round in his chair, with a suggestion hovering on his lips to which the one before had obviously been only a shy younger sister; then he saw Tom looming over him, large as a rugby player who has been repeatedly capped for Ireland, and said instead that he would be only too happy to move.

Tom sat down, leaning so close to me that his mouth was nearly touching my face. His breath, warm and not unpleasant, smelt of whisky, Guinness and cigarettes.

'I just remembered,' he said unnecessarily. 'It's Judy. She wants to talk to you.'

'Why?' I hardly knew her.

'Wanted to talk to you about Lee.'

'Lee?'

'And Claire.'

'Lee and *Claire*?' I swivelled to face him, my voice rising. 'Are you sure? Do you mean together or separately?'

The close-quarters stare, combined with the interrogative tone, was too much for Tom. His face crumpled and he seemed on the point of tears. I looked at the pub clock; it was two-thirty. If I went round straight away, Judy might be dazzled by my enthusiasm. But then again, she might just think I was drunk. Who could say? Perhaps it would be better to leave it till slightly later on this morning.

On balance, I was satisfied with this decision. I had a swig of beer to celebrate it, then another one. I wondered for a moment if I would be able to get up from my chair unaided, and then dismissed the thought. I don't like dwelling on the negative. Anyway, in extremis, I could always fall off.

* * *

Sunday morning found me waking up in the Castle Road house again with another skull-splitter of a hangover. I had certainly come round full circle that week. Ironically, it was the hangover that saved me from dwelling on this repetition. I was in too much pain to feel maudlin. Judy dosed me with some fruit tea blend. It was a murky shade of orange, with thick particles suspended in the liquid. I couldn't taste it, my tongue being as thick and furry as a toilet seat cover, but it seemed to help.

I had slept, or rather passed out, in Tom's bed, but mercifully had managed to take off my boots and jacket first. This was especially important as far as the jacket was concerned; it was heavily decorated with zips and metal inserts, and I don't enjoy waking up with zip teeth imprinted all down my cheek because I've been resting my head on my arm all night. It makes you look like a skinhead who can't afford a proper tattoo. I was surprised to discover that Tom hadn't tried to feel me up in the night; even my waistcoat was still buttoned. Most unlike him.

'What's the matter,' I said petulantly, 'don't you find me attractive?' But he was fast asleep and didn't hear a word.

Judy, of course, was up and dressed and making tea. Her room smelled faintly of scented joss-sticks and the walls were hung with shawls and bits of material, tacked on with pins. The floor was bare splintery wood, covered in parts with stripy woven rugs in oranges and yellows. Lined up on an old wooden crate was a neat pile of books on meditation and yoga. The main focus of the room was her electric kettle and the various boxes of herbal tea stacked beside it.

I dropped my jacket and boots by the door. This was a mistake. My head was very sensitive and the jingles and clanks of the various buckles and straps made me wince in pain. Judy looked at me with a mixture of pity and disapproval which I was in no state to resent; after all, if I was going to dress up for the evening like an extra in *Mad Max Meets the Amazon Woman*, I should be able to carry it off the next morning as well. Gingerly, I lowered myself to a sitting position. Even through the rugs, the floor was hard and uncomfortable. Floor pillows were probably considered too self-indulgent in the more lofty hippie circles.

Judy handed me a cup of tea in silence. She was sitting cross-legged, leaning over the teapot like the priestess of some obscure sect. Her long thick plait of hair, a beautiful pale blonde, fell over one shoulder. Although her hair was pinned up at the sides, little wisps of it were escaping from the hairpins and all down the length of the plait. They caught the sunlight streaming in from the big window in front of us, making a golden fuzz around her head.

'Thanks very much,' I said with gratitude when I had finished. 'I feel almost human again.'

'I don't know why you do it to yourself,' she observed, not disapproving now so much as bewildered.

'Because it's there?' I suggested. She looked at me blankly. I was in no state for delicate diplomacy, so I decided I would just have to jump in with both feet. 'Look,

Judy, Tom said you wanted to talk to me about Lee and
Claire. Was that right?'

Judy nodded seriously. She did most things seriously:
fun was not a word in her daily vocabulary. But if she
chose to part her hair in the middle and scrape it back into
a plait, to scrub her face bare with soap and, nun-like,
mortify her vanity with horrendous clothes, who was I to
argue with her? Today she was wearing a bobbly brown
sweater and a skirt which looked like a fringed purple
sack tied around her waist with a coloured piece of string.
You can buy better in Oxfam for £3.

'It was about the fight Claire and Lee had,' she said. 'I
thought you'd want to know about it.'

My head cleared instantly.

'What fight?'

'I thought you didn't know,' Judy said importantly.
'Claire asked Lee to recommend her for a job, and then on
Friday she heard she hadn't got it. So Claire started
blaming Lee. She said she – Lee, I mean – hadn't even tried
to help. Lee took her outside to avoid having a big scene
at the party. She was trying to calm her – Claire – down.'

I pounced on the relevant word in this tangled
explanation. 'Outside?'

'They were on the terrace. I was in the kitchen, and
they came past me and went out the kitchen door. I don't
think Claire even saw me. She was already shouting. They
were outside for quite a while, and I don't think they made
it up, because I saw Claire come back in, but she was by
herself, and she still looked really angry.'

'What time of night was this?'

'I don't know. Late, I think.'

That didn't mean anything. Judy thought everything
after nine o'clock was late.

75

'Did you see Lee after that?'

More shakes of the head. One of her hairpins fell out. This was always happening; she picked it up and fixed it back in automatically.

'Probably it isn't important,' she said, looking at her teacup. 'I just thought you might want to know – after what you said at the police station, about Lee not being likely to wander into the garden by herself. I thought you'd want to know what she was doing there.'

There was a little pause. Judy had a long, narrow nose, which flushed a light pink at the tip in moments of stress. It did so now.

'Judy,' I said curiously, 'how do you know all about Claire and the job?'

Judy and Claire had absolutely nothing in common, besides being members of the same co-op. I couldn't see Claire confiding in Judy. And she was too proud to make public the fact that she had failed to get a job despite having asked someone to recommend her for it. I thought I knew the answer already, after what Tom had told me at the party. But I wanted to hear Judy's version.

Judy's nose went slightly redder. 'Paul told me,' she said. 'He often comes in for some tea, and we talk about philosophy and mysticism and, you know, personal things. He says I'm very restful and he can confide in me. He and Claire quarrel a lot, you see. It's mostly her fault, she's so bad-tempered. She even hits him sometimes. I've seen the bruises.'

She wouldn't meet my eyes; she was still staring at the teacup. 'He'd tried to calm Claire down, at the party, but she told him to go away. Well, what she actually said was piss off. I heard her. So he came up here for a cup of tea. He was really worried that Claire would lose her temper completely and there'd be a big scene with Lee. He's very sensitive, you know.'

I didn't, but I let this pass.

'I think he wants to leave her,' Judy said to the teacup. 'But he's frightened of what she might do.'

'Frightened?' I said incredulously.

'She's so temperamental. She could hurt herself, or even him.' Judy's tone of voice indicated what she considered the more important possibility. 'But I'm sure he doesn't really want to stay with her.'

I had my doubts about that. Paul and Claire had been together for years and seemed pretty settled to me. And even if Paul did leave Claire, the last thing I could see him doing was to set up a hippie love nest with Judy.

Still, it wasn't my business to disillusion her. Instead, armed with this information, I went in search of Claire, whom I found in the lounge, nursing a mug of tea so strong you could stand a spoon in it, and making toast. The kitchen had for a long time been so only nominally, unless you chose to use the word 'kitchen' to signify a room filled with beer cans, containing a sink, a fridge and a fluctuating rat population. The lounge, on the other hand, had its own kettle and an extra socket into which a toaster could be conveniently plugged. All the mod cons.

Claire offered me some toast, and I thought it would be churlish to refuse. Besides, if we broke bread together it might bond us in some primal way and make her more ready to confide in me. I try to think of everything.

We sat on the carpet in front of the electric fire, warming ourselves gratefully. The two bars glowed bright orange; the carpet, or to be strictly honest the carpet tiles, were a deep brown, patterned with squares and swirls in orange and yellow. Very seventies. In a few years this lounge would be at the cutting edge of interior decoration – if the carpet tiles could hold out that long.

The hot slices of toast were golden and dripping with margarine and Marmite; I couldn't imagine anything more delicious. We ate for a while in silence. On my part the silence was so that I could give my full attention to the indescribable deliciousness of the toast. I couldn't answer for Claire. After I had thrown four slices down my gullet in rapid succession, I felt much better. Even my tongue seemed to have shrunk to something approaching its normal size. Tea and toast, one of the roaring triumphs of British civilisation. I started to lick margarine off my fingers, wondering how to broach with Claire the subject that was on my mind. But as it happened, she did it for me.

'Do you want any more?' she said.

'No thanks, I'm full. It was just what I needed.'

Claire's face was paler than usual, and there were deep dark shadows under her blue eyes.

'You can have more if you want,' she said indifferently. 'I'm not saving any for Paul, bloody bastard.'

'Oh, have you had a fight?' I said casually.

'*A* fight. God. Where do I start?'

She bit savagely into another piece of toast, clearly imagining that it was Paul's throat.

'Was it about the job you wanted?' I said. 'That you asked Lee to recommend you for?'

She stared at me, her eyes narrowed. 'Did he tell you that?' she said. 'The bastard! He was on at me for ages, telling me I should shut up about it, and then he goes and blabs it out to you. I really hate him sometimes.'

'Was that why you didn't tell me about the job thing on Thursday?' I said provocatively. 'Because Paul said not to talk about it?'

She made a brushing away gesture with her hand. 'I don't do what he tells me. I do what I want to. It's not a big deal anyway.'

'What happened?'

She shrugged and took a big gulp of tea, as if for support. 'It began with this job that came up,' she said. 'A six-month contract at the Playroom. Production designer. I really thought I had it. The second interview went well, you know? Then I bumped into Lee at a do in Covent Garden, and asked her if she'd heard anything about it, because Derek Smithers, the artistic director, is a good friend of hers. And I said that if she could put in a word for me I'd be really grateful. We weren't exactly friends, but she'd seen some of my work and I thought she liked it.'

She shrugged. 'Anyway, it was a mistake. She didn't say anything, but she gave me a pretty odd look. And then last Friday, I got a call from Derek, saying the job had gone to someone else, and he was quite offhand. Which made me think that maybe Lee had rung him up and told him I'd been trying to influence her. I was so angry, I was just waiting for a chance to confront her at the party and have it out with her.'

The memory had worked her up into a fury. Her eyes were blazing and her fists were clenched at her sides; she seemed as volatile as mercury.

'So what happened?'

She shot me a quick look out of the corner of her eye and unclenched her fingers, which had been buried in her palms.

'Oh, it was all a big anti-climax, really.' Her voice was back to normal. 'As soon as we started talking about it I realised I'd been over-reacting. She wouldn't actually have done anything like that. I mean, she was the kind of person who stands back from things, doesn't get involved, right? It was a bit of a storm in a teacup. But I was upset about the job and I got carried away.'

She shot me a suspicious look. 'Why are we going over this? I thought I was talking about Paul.'

'So did I!' I said innocently. 'How does he come into it?'

She lit a cigarette. 'He said I should never have asked Lee in the first place, that it "wasn't appropriate" or some pompous shit like that. So we had a fight. Then I heard I hadn't got the job, and all Paul said was, "Oh well, never mind, these things happen." He expected me to forget about it in five minutes! It's easy enough for him – he's always got some project going on. But it's been ages since I had paid work, not just art – directing some awful student production for the experience and pathetic expenses.'

She looked at me. 'Not only that. Do you know what he's been doing lately? He's been dropping into Judy's room late at night to tell her how awful I am. He's leading her on.' Claire waved her hand dismissively. 'He's not really interested in her, but he needs female attention all the time and if he's not getting it from me he'll find another source. It's not sex he wants, we do enough of that, it's the adoration. She follows him around like a dog. It's beginning to annoy him. But he knows that when we're quarrelling he can slam out of our room and have her make him tea and stare at him with doggy eyes and say how wonderful and deep he is.'

'Can I nick a cigarette, Claire?' I said.

'Sure.' She passed me the packet. 'Didn't know you smoked, Sam.'

'I don't really. I just cadge one occasionally.'

In fact, when she had been gesturing I had noticed some marks on her hand and wanted a closer look at them. As I took the packet from her I saw four red dents on the fleshy part of her palm, which could only have been made by her own fingernails. And around the fresh marks were many other ones, older scabbed bruises of the same shape, faded to purple and green.

Judy had been right. Claire had a very nasty temper indeed.

8

I had nothing to rush home for; Sunday afternoons are miserable without company or occupation. So I hung out at the Castle Road house till the early evening. At two o'clock the lounge filled up for the *EastEnders* omnibus edition and after it had finished we kept the TV on until the *Clothes Show* so that everyone could hurl abuse at what the presenters were wearing. By about six I was ready to go home; the room was thick with smoke from cigarettes and spliffs alike and no-one had much left to say. I had been hoping to talk to Paul but he had gone out early that morning, and Claire didn't know where he had gone or when he would be back. Tom gave me a lift to the tube station. He was meeting Julia to see a film and was twitching with nerves.

I got home to find the red light on my answering machine flashing away, which made me feel wanted. But since two of the callers had hung up without saying anything, they couldn't have wanted me that much. The third message, however, amply compensated for earlier disappointments, despite the fact that the voice was as detached as if it were reading the weather for a recorded announcement.

'Hello, Ms Jones. My name is Laura Archer. I would very much like to talk to you about a private matter.

Would you be able to come to my office on Monday evening at eight? If not, we could arrange another time. For obvious reasons, I would appreciate your not mentioning this matter to anyone.'

I tried the number she had left straight away. Despite it being Sunday night, a receptionist answered at once and informed me that the number belonged to McCott Shaw Associates, a firm of management consultants 'with branches in Europe and America'. Duly impressed, I left a message that I would be happy to meet Mrs Archer – it was Mrs Archer, wasn't it? Thank you – at eight the next evening.

Well, well, well. I filled up the coffeepot and set it on the stove to boil. Brain teeming with possibilities, I leant against the counter and stared meditatively into space. Unfortunately, bang in front of me in the middle of the studio was my current sculpture, the Thing. Four feet tall, it was a huge shiny metal sphere roped loosely around with a thick dulled steel cable. I had frayed the cable in places, pulling out strands, and worked on it with wire wool till parts of it shone like silver. The Thing squatted there like a large malevolent silver toad, tied down by the rope. It didn't look happy; it wanted to be finished and it knew it wasn't yet. I toyed briefly with various ideas. Perhaps it should have a stand, to lift it off the floor a little. Perhaps I should try wrapping some sheets of wire mesh around it, maybe slitting them half-open . . .

With a quick rush of emotion, I found myself missing Lee. She wouldn't have told me what to do but she would have helped me see the Thing with new eyes. I was on my own with it now and suddenly I felt very alone. It was impossible to stay at home that evening. Turning off the light under the coffeepot, I grabbed my coat and walked out the door. Egg-Face didn't seem to be waiting patiently outside but I didn't care if he saw what I was doing this evening. I went to the local Indian restaurant, where I drank three bottles of beer and put away a copious amount of food, drugging myself into somnolence. Back home I threw quantities of blankets on top of the duvet, as if stoking a fire, and burrowed underneath them, stomach consolingly full. And by this time I was glad there was no-one under there with me.

* * *

There was no sign of Egg-Face on Monday – not until the evening. Perhaps he had a day job. He turned up at about six in a navy-blue Golf GTI which stuck out a mile and parked it a few doors down the road. He'd be lucky if it wasn't vandalised with him in it. The smartness of his car confirmed my suspicion about the day job. He couldn't make that sort of money by following people; he wasn't good enough. And just now his timing was terrible. I had a meeting with Mrs Laura Archer and she hadn't invited me to bring a friend along.

I left on the radio and the lights. Then I went up the ladder to my sleeping platform, opened the skylight, and pulled myself up onto the roof, displaying impressive upper body strength. Unfortunately no-one was around to applaud. The roof is leaded, but I was wearing rubber-soled gym shoes. What I proudly call my studio is in fact an undersized, semi-detached warehouse which was originally built as an extension of the one next door. There is a ladder leading up from the roof of mine to the adjoining warehouse, which is still used for its original purpose. Conveniently for me it has its own fire escape. I wasn't afraid of being arrested. Bob, the night-watchman, was very friendly. I took him a bottle of whisky every now and then. And right now he'd be asleep in his nice warm room, with his cat, Fat Shirley, on his lap.

I climbed the ladder and stood for a moment at the top, checking that there was no-one around. The roof was black as pitch, with the occasional smear of pale orange light skewed over it from a streetlamp, eerie and useless, catching on the angles of the skylights set into the roof. No-one was working late; the skylights were as dark as the roof, thick with grime and bird-droppings. It was a starless night. The overcast sky was an indeterminate colour, its clouds thick and heavy with water. I hoped I was back home before the storm.

The top of the fire escape was signalled only by two metal rails at hand height on the far side of the roof. I descended as swiftly as I could without making too much of a racket. My shoes were noiseless, but the ancient rusty iron of the fire escape creaked and moaned loudly enough to set my teeth on edge. I couldn't believe Egg-Face would hear it from inside his car, but all the same I was glad to reach the foot of the stairs and see the van waiting for me, reliable as ever. For a second I forgot that I had driven it there myself earlier in the day, and felt warm and happy, as if it were a good friend who had come to meet me. Perhaps I was spending too much time on my own. I changed my plimsolls for my smart black boots, which I had thoughtfully stored in the boot against this necessity, took off the balaclava, and drove off.

The McCott Shaw building, situated just off Great Portland Street, spoke volumes for the company's corporate image. The towering façade was of pink marble, which on the ground floor was carved into columns like a line of guards standing silently against the front of the building.

The windows were inky glass, and so was the giant door. Framed in a massive Gothic arch of more pink marble, it was a sheer sheet of black. No handles, no buzzer. The whole effect was of a sugar palace designed by Charles Addams on a bad day. I crossed the street and warily approached the door. It split down the middle and swung open. Very impressive.

The reception area was the size of a field, paved in further acres of pink marble. An enormous arc of desk curved halfway into the room, like a huge pink wave which had crashed through the wall and frozen solid. Behind it sat a woman with her hair in a perfect French pleat. She couldn't have seen the hole in my leggings, but she looked down her nose at me as if she knew it was there. She had a shiny coral mouth, a mauve jacket and little rosy pearls in her ears. I wondered if they required her to dress to co-ordinate with the décor.

I introduced myself. She tinkled some computer keys and was visibly disappointed when she found my appointment listed.

'Would you take a seat, please? I will call up to Mrs Archer to tell her you're here,' she said. A professional smile oozed out from between her teeth like toothpaste. Her voice was even more artificially cultured than the pearls in her ears. On a black glass coffee-table was a selection of magazines, meticulously arranged, as pristine as if they had just come hot off the presses. I wandered over to browse, but they all had titles like *Business World* and *Resource Management* – not even any recipes to tear out. *Hello!* and *Woman's Weekly* had probably been nicked already.

'Miss Jones?' said the receptionist. 'Mrs Archer will see you now. Take the lift up to the third floor and she'll meet you there.'

The lift was mirrored on walls and ceiling and carpeted on the floor. I craned my head back to see what I looked like from above. Answer: rather odd, as might have been expected. The light panel flashed '3', a bell pinged politely, the lift settled into place and the doors opened. I was face to face with Mrs Archer.

* * *

She didn't offer me a drink. I found that pretty tacky. But maybe she didn't have a drinks cabinet. The office was so pristine it looked as if she kept it for best and actually worked in another one down the corridor. No pink marble up on the third floor; here it was pale grey walls and black modular furniture. Very restful. The walls were hung with framed Monet prints, doubtless bought in bulk by the decorator, while the desk held only a paperweight, a glass ashtray and a couple of empty filing trays. The ashtray was the only item that seemed to be in use. Laura Archer must be a high-status employee, because she rated a big office with a window and an adjoining one for her secretary. I toyed with the idea of being impressed. Then I dismissed it.

'Won't you sit down?' she said, gesturing in the direction of the window to a pair of armchairs and a black glass coffee-table, a miniature version of the one in the lobby. 'My secretary works next door,' she added, 'but she's left for the day. So we won't be overheard.'

She made a big effect of closing the connecting door between her office and the secretary's; she even bothered to go into the latter's office and shut the outer door which gave onto the corridor. I wondered whether she was indicating to me that our conversation would not be overheard, or whether she was making sure on her own account. The secretary's office was as neat as her boss's; you wouldn't know anyone worked there either. Same prints, same absence of anything personal, same near-empty desk. Laura Archer had hired a secretary as tidy as herself.

She removed the ashtray from the desk, brought it over, and settled herself in the other armchair, pulling down her skirt in a neat automatic gesture. I studied her carefully. She was blonde with hazel eyes and would have been very attractive if she hadn't been wearing such a nondescript suit. It was the kind of thing women wore when they didn't want to be thought of as female in case that meant they didn't get promoted.

'I'm very grateful to you for coming,' she said, making it sound as if she were a Foreign Office diplomat negotiating a peace treaty with a troublesome native. I didn't warm to her, and it wasn't just for lack of a drink; I didn't much like being cast as the troublesome native.

'This is obviously a rather delicate matter,' she said, lighting a cigarette. 'I'd like to ask you something, but before I do I would be very grateful if you would tell me that you will hold it in confidence.'

'Why should I?' I said snappily. The brightly lit room turned everything outside the window into a murky series of shadows. The office was nothing but a grey box with its doors closed. I felt cross and claustrophobic.

She raised her eyebrows. 'A good question. Let me put this another way, then. I want you to do a favour for me. If you accept I can assure you that you will be well rewarded, but on the condition that you employ absolute discretion.'

She spoke like a lawyer. A corporate lawyer trying to buy off a witness who could give inconvenient testimony.

89

I settled back in my chair. 'Well, you'd better tell me what it is, then. I don't buy pigs in pokes.'

She didn't like that, but she didn't have a choice. 'All right,' Laura Archer said, more slowly. 'Basically, I'm trying to obtain some – items connected with a Mrs Jackson, who I understand was a friend of yours.'

That's the way diplomats speak. You can't tell when they pronounce a name whether it belongs to their dead lover or a woman they never met in their life.

'Are we by any chance talking about some letters?' I said.

'Absolutely.' She couldn't keep a trace of eagerness out of her voice. 'Do you have them?'

'Why do you think that I might?'

'If you don't,' she countered, stubbing out her cigarette, 'or if you don't know where they might be, then there's little point continuing this discussion.'

I shook my head.

'Before I tell you whether I have the letters, I'd want some information in return. I want to know how you heard my name and why you thought of asking me for them.'

She lit another cigarette. I wondered whether she always smoked this much or if she were nervous and needed something to do with her hands. She didn't seem nervous; the hazel eyes were clear, the voice calm. But I had already decided that she was a cool customer.

'I'm afraid that for personal reasons I can't do that,' she answered. 'I hope you understand. But if you were able to produce the letters I would see to it that you weren't – out of pocket.'

'And what if I said I'd prefer information to having my expenses paid?' I suggested affably.

The hand carrying the cigarette to her mouth froze for a moment in mid-air, then carried on the movement as if nothing had happened. But she didn't answer straight away. She took an over-long drag on the cigarette and watched the smoke curl away first. Outside the clouds had burst open and the sound of falling rain was loud in the silence of the room.

'All right,' she finally said, 'I can tell you that I am asking you because you are – were – a friend of Mrs Jackson's. It's common knowledge that you were at the party at which she died. She might well have spoken to you about the letters—'

'You'll have to try harder than that.'

She seemed to have come to a decision. 'There are personal reasons why I can't,' she repeated.

'Then no deal.' I stood up. 'You don't get something for nothing.'

She looked up at me, the hazel eyes narrowed with calculation. Her fingers tapped lightly on the arm of her chair.

'If I said that I would tell you when you produced the letters, would you agree to that?'

'I'll think about it,' I said shortly.

I turned to go but she came to her feet, saying swiftly, almost eagerly, 'But you do have them, don't you?'

I smiled at her politely and said again, 'I'll think about it.'

'Please do,' she said. 'I'll be in touch.'

She extended her hand to me as she said goodbye. It was the one without the wedding ring. I still didn't take it.

9

The streets were black and shiny with water. The pointed turrets of the McCott Shaw building turned it into a witch's castle, rain streaking down its black windows and falling onto the Gothic arch of the door. A taxi came around the corner. Its orange 'For Hire' light was switched off but there was no passenger in the back. It pulled up directly outside the pink and black castle. The driver sat there with the engine running. I turned the key in the ignition but didn't switch on the lights yet. Rain pattered in lines on the windscreen.

The black glass doors opened, and Laura Archer came out, wrapped in a camel overcoat which came to her ankles. She got quickly into the taxi and it pulled away. I followed at a discreet distance, the taxi driving too carefully in the rain to notice me on its tail. Laura Archer was sitting up straight on one side of the seat. The rainwashed roads were nearly empty. A few umbrellas, canted at angles to meet the rain, hurried along the pavements, their owners' bodies half-hidden beneath. It was Monday evening, and most people were tucked up snugly in front of their blue flickering televisions with TV dinners on their laps.

Laura Archer lived in a nice peaceful street in Putney, in a medium-sized detached house with a small grass square in front of it; suburbia in the city. She let herself in, but there were already lights on inside the house and a car parked in the drive.

The taxi pulled away. I started up the van and drove past as slowly as I could. The curtains of the front room were drawn, so I couldn't see in. There was only one bell at the door; Mrs, and presumably Mr, Archer were the sole occupants. Mr Archer, of course, would not be told why Mrs Archer was late back from work, Mrs Archer having specified that I ring her at the office only. I wondered exactly how much Mr Archer knew . . .

Egg-Face was still parked outside when I got home. With this probability in mind, I had come back in through the skylight, leaving the van around the corner, but not next to the staircase this time; I didn't want him to come across it there and put two and two together. I was doing some of that myself. He was outside my studio in exactly the same parking space he'd occupied some hours earlier, which meant he had no connection with Laura Archer. If he had, he would have known I was planning to go to McCott Shaw that evening and would have picked me up there later on. But as far as he was concerned, I hadn't left the studio all evening. Which meant that there was someone else besides Laura Archer who was interested in my whereabouts – and that probably also meant the whereabouts of the letters.

I had an idea about the letters myself. I looked up the number of someone called Stephen Baldring who lived in Highgate. Since he was the reclusive sort, I was worried he might be ex-directory, but I found his number at once. He was in. I explained what I wanted and we arranged a time for me to see him tomorrow. I went to bed with the hummus pitta sandwich – extra chillies – and bottle of beer which I had picked up from the kebab shop on my way home. I was feeling smug and organised.

It didn't last long.

* * *

'We've called it "Flora and Fauna", rather tongue-in-cheek.' Shelley had the phone cradled against her ear and was caressing it lovingly with the special voice she kept for art journalists. 'Three up-and-coming young British painters, a complete re-interpretation of the concepts of landscape and still-life painting . . . mmn hmmn . . . mmn hmmn . . . absolutely . . . drinks and canapés from six-thirty . . . mmn hmmn . . .'

The gallery was in the messy birth throes of preparing for the exhibition, which had its private view on Friday evening. It was Tuesday and half the paintings were still to be hung. The huge canvases by Susan Durrit were the star of the show; Victoria Davenant's featured beheaded flowers in vases, while Mark Martin seemed mainly interested in electricity pylons, which he reproduced in loving detail down to the last rivet. Occasionally he introduced a bird or two, sitting on a wire, by way of variety. I hoped I wouldn't be called upon to compliment him. What could you say about pylons?

Shelley laughed sweetly into the phone, said 'So we'll see you on Friday! Wonderful!' and replaced the receiver, sighing loudly.

'What do I do with this one?' I said, indicating the next painting to be hung, imaginatively titled *Irises #3*.

Looking harassed, Shelley shouted: 'Judith! What about the next one of Victoria's?'

From the doorway to the office Judith said with an apparent lack of interest, 'On the far wall, don't you think?

Next to the other one?' then drifted back through the door as if blown on a light gust of wind. It was only Judith's manner that was vague. And I had noticed that although Shelley seemed to be the one in control, she almost always deferred to Judith's judgement.

I picked up my spirit level and started marking out the wall. Shelley went back to dialling the number of another newspaper. A small buzzer went off briefly, indicating that someone had come into the gallery. Out of the corner of my eye I saw a man wandering slowly round the paintings which were already hung. They were mostly Susan Durrit's; huge surfaces, thickly encrusted with paint in great clusters and trails, seeming to tumble in slow motion down the canvas. They needed to be viewed from a distance; if you stood too close to them, your eyes went out of focus, unable to put the whorls and swirls of the picture together into a whole. The man stepped further and further back, nearly bumping into me.

'Sorry,' he said unapologetically. 'Am I in your way?'

I was concentrating on the spirit level, which I had just lined up, so I didn't answer. I ruled a neat line over the top and took it away. He wasn't deterred by my lack of response.

'Are you new here?' he said.

He looked in his late twenties, tall and verging on thin. His clothes hung off his bones as if from a wire hanger; dark faded jeans, a pale pink shirt and an ancient blue zip-up jacket under an equally faded jeans jacket. It looked as if he had picked them all off the floor that morning at random. I like my men on the scruffy side but this one was well beyond scruffy and into scuffed, like a worn-out trainer.

I put the spirit level down on the top of *Irises #3*, which was leaning against the wall at waist-height. For some reason the way he was looking at me made me feel off-balance.

'Why do you ask?' I said. To my surprise, it came out almost hostile. It was as if we were taking each other's measure.

'I come in here sometimes,' he said, shrugging. 'I haven't seen you before.'

His face was narrow and bony, the cheekbones high and sharply etched beneath skin so pale that it might never have seen the sun. His short brown hair was ragged, as if he cut it himself. But it was his eyes that caught the attention, with their distant gleam of buried wickedness; long, slightly slanted eyes, under straight brows, of an indeterminate colour that could have been green or grey, but was light against the pallor of his skin. I couldn't read his expression. There was something buried below his eyes I wanted to excavate. I felt myself returning his stare with the same kind of detachment.

'You might have come in on my days off,' I said casually.

There was a momentary pause, and then he broke the tension by laughing, completely naturally, a laugh which creased up the whole of his face like india-rubber. His mouth was very wide and mobile.

'You're trouble, aren't you?' he said cheerfully. 'Why are you so stroppy? What have I ever done to you?'

I could think of a few things he might start with.

'OK, I just started here a few days ago,' I said, smiling too.

'When's it open, then, this exhibition?' he said. He had a north London accent, and he treated words like 'exhibition' with deliberate, over-precise deference, as if he found them pretentious.

'Have an invitation,' I said, giving him a card. He hardly glanced at it, but folded it in two and shoved it into his back pocket. I made a bet with myself that he would tear it up for roaches. He smiled at me and loped over to the door.

'Maybe I'll be back when it opens, then.'

'Maybe,' I said, picking up the spirit level again, glad to see that my hand was steady.

'What did that man want?' Shelley called over, her hand covering the mouthpiece of the phone.

'Just looking.'

'Fine, fine.' She took her hand off the mouthpiece. 'Hello? Yes. I was holding for Brian Fisher on the arts desk. Well, is anyone else available?'

My instinct said that I would see him again. There had been a sexual attraction, or better, a kind of sexual tension, crackling between us which our casual conversation had somehow acknowledged. I let my mind drift off into speculation for a moment. In the long run he would probably be bad for me; the ease with which we had both fallen into verbal sparring suggested that we could fight like cat and dog without much excuse. But the short term – that could be a lot of fun.

* * *

I left early, having told Shelley that I had a doctor's appointment, and stopped off at a nearby phone to ring a friend of mine who had a motorbike shop in Balham and the right connections to check out the Egg's licence-plate for me. He took down the numbers and said he'd ring me back that evening. I kept an eye out for the navy-blue GTI, or any other car for that matter, which might be following me, even doubling round a couple of times to make sure. Everything looked fine. Half an hour later I was in Highgate, ringing a rusty old bell outside an even rustier set of iron gates set into a high encircling ivy-covered wall. If Lee's letters were in here, they were well-protected.

Stephen Baldring was expecting me. We knew each other by sight, since I had once been to visit Lee here, and he greeted me with old-fashioned politeness, taking me down the driveway which led to the building that Lee had used as a studio. It had originally been a double garage, but many years before a couple of large skylights had been knocked into the roof, and windows had been set into the front and back walls. Stephen's house stood in about half an acre of land, straggled over with weeds. Here at its back the air was still and quiet. Occasionally a particularly noisy lorry would roar down Highgate Hill, wheels clattering, or an underground train would rumble faintly in the distance like buried thunder.

The silence was not a tranquil one. The atmosphere was stagnant, brooding, as if the house, unhealthily sealed off from the world, had infected the air around it. Things that are not used rot away, and can take their immediate surroundings with them. I shivered. If something lived at the bottom of this garden, I wouldn't like to meet it, even by daylight.

It didn't look as if Stephen had been in the habit of visiting Lee's studio; it took him ten minutes to locate the right key on an enormous bunch of hardware. Lee's sudden death had thrown him into confusion – he was transcendentally vague at the best of times – and I got the impression that he would be happy to leave the studio locked up for ever rather than have to think about what to do with her possessions.

'Were there only two sets of keys to the studio, yours and Lee's?' I asked.

'Absolutely!' Stephen froze with the key in one hand and the padlock in the other. 'I wouldn't have liked anyone else having a key . . . It was rather pleasant to have Lee coming back and forth. She was so quiet, you see. One knew she was there but one wasn't made unpleasantly aware of it. But Lee was very much a special case.'

He unlocked the padlock and I helped him pull open one half of the big garage doors. Inside it was airy and full of light from the big skylights and the high windows, with all the space one could wish for. Stephen hovered on the threshold, unwilling to come in.

'What was it you said you were looking for, Miss Jones?' he said.

'Sam, please . . . Some sketches of mine that I gave her to have a look at, a couple of weeks ago.'

'I'm afraid I wouldn't even know where to start,' he said helplessly.

'Oh, don't worry. I shall just have to go through everything.'

He was staring beyond me, across the room, at a couple of pillars, each about five feet high, made from rolled sheets of metal etched with various shapes. Into the top of each was incised a mouth.

'That would be her current work,' he said thoughtfully. 'She often came up to the house for a sherry, you know, after having finished for the day, and would tell me how it had gone. She was rather excited about those . . .'

His voice trailed off as he realised that they would now never be finished.

'Well, I'll leave you to your task,' he said rapidly. 'Drop

the keys back to me, won't you, when you've found your sketches?'

He was already retreating down the path, his back as bony and awkward as that of a giant, underfed, flightless bird. I closed the door behind him and went to work.

Two hours later, I had found absolutely nothing, even having looked inside the cistern in desperation. I stood in the middle of the studio, and turned slowly round 360 degrees, hoping that my eye would fall on something I might have missed. It didn't. I couldn't believe it; I had been convinced that the letters would be here.

I stared at the two metal pillars which Lee had been working on before she died. Each had a figure posed on its domed top. I traced my finger over one of them. It was of an archer, bow held taut by her strong arms, an arrow nocked against the string. Her hair was cut short and slicked back over her scalp, and though the lines of her body were slender and muscled there was something about her poise, the calm expression on her face, which suggested that she was not a young girl but a woman. She stood on the domed top of the pillar, and at her feet was what looked like a sign of the zodiac. I assumed it must be Sagittarius.

The figure on the other pillar was a woman with the body of a lion, or perhaps a lioness with a woman's head. The head was very beautiful, its bones sharp and clear, the hair pushed back behind the delicate ears; it fitted with disconcerting naturalness on top of the lioness's body, which stretched out along the dome as elegantly as if she were reposing on a chaise-longue. Her tail, falling down the far side of the dome, was so lifelike that I half-expected it to twitch itself from time to time. In one paw, the lioness held a mask. It was the face that properly matched her body. The mane of hair curled wildly around the snub-nosed face with its pretty whiskers; the smooth paw held it casually but securely, as if at any moment the lioness might put it on, uncurl herself, and jump down from the pillar, lithe and agile.

Two zodiac signs, Sagittarius and Leo. Ten more to go. And with the care which Lee had taken over these two, the rest would have been a long time in the making. It was not only the figures which were beautifully executed; over the whole surface of the pillars themselves were etched patterns, trellises over which climbed strange animals, serpents, flowers.

Lee's work was usually more angular, less lush, than this; the figures on the pillars almost seemed alive. There was a romanticism, not only in the figures but in the decoration of the pillars, which made me believe that they had been made with love. I ran my finger around the edge of the mouth shape on the lioness's pillar. It was smooth and cold.

In a sudden impulse, I put my hands around the dome and tried to lift it up. It wouldn't move. Nor would the figure herself, who was firmly welded to her perch. I tilted back the whole pillar; nothing underneath. A search of the Sagittarius pillar had the same result. I squatted down and looked into the little mouth hole, so narrow the range of vision it provided was minimal. There was nothing to be seen, anyway; just dark empty space.

The faces of the archer and the lion-woman seemed to be mocking me. I swore at myself. I had failed. And no-one had been ahead of me this time. The padlock had not been tampered with, and there was no sign of forced entry on either window. Besides, the only way to reach the studio was to pass by the main house, through the creaky old iron gates. Even if the person who had searched Lee's flat also had the keys to her studio, Stephen would have heard anyone opening those gates. Depressed, I returned the keys to him and went home.

10

'More wine?'

Smile, refill all glasses in the immediate vicinity, move on to the next group, say 'More wine?', repeat ad infinitum. The private view had been going strong for over an hour and I was already exhausted. I had never realised entertaining people was such hard work. I wouldn't cut it in PR.

Shelley Frank Fine Art was packed with people: smartly dressed, carefully made-up people wearing their best public faces and shouting at each other with big public smiles. A handful of skilled operators were working the room, talking to everyone important and waving at people who might be important one day. The other guests were wondering wistfully why everyone else seemed to know more people than they did.

I caught sight of Shelley through a momentary gap in the crowd. She was holding a glass of red wine; her face was flushed and her voice was happily raised, relaxing into the certain success of the exhibition. A few of the gallery's most steady clients had been invited to "preview the show" yesterday and today, and as a result there were already red dots next to three Durrits and two Davenants. Shelley would be able to afford some more gold ropes from Chanel if this kept up.

My face was strained with smiling. I can only manage to be friendly in fits and spurts and smiling at strangers doesn't come naturally to me. I headed back to the drinks table for a respite. Harriet, my co-worker, was already there, filling more glasses with white wine. Tall and slim, she was a pretty girl, or she would have been if her face hadn't been drawn back too tightly over its bones. She was wearing her usual outfit; hair smoothed back into a ponytail, silver hoop earrings, Lycra body and jeans. We'd met already but hadn't exchanged more than a few words. I couldn't decide if she was unfriendly or just withdrawn.

'Doing anything tonight?' I said in an attempt to make conversation.

'Oh, my boyfriend's coming in and we're having dinner with some of his friends,' she said, sounding un-enthusiastic. 'At some expensive place I can't afford, as usual.'

'Why don't you suggest going somewhere cheaper?'

'Oh, I couldn't. I mean, they all decide.' She opened another bottle. 'And Johnny'll check to make sure I haven't ordered anything too fattening and everyone will throw bread rolls at each other and make jokes about the girls' tits.'

'It sounds like hell,' I said frankly.

She shrugged gloomily. 'I love him,' she said.

I fought the nausea down. Fortunately, at that moment Johnny arrived and I was saved having to answer. Harriet introduced him to me and he shook my hand, making some asinine comment about what a jolly nice job it must be to stand around and open bottles all day. He was tall, fair, and looked as if he had played rugby for both his school and his agricultural college. He had blue eyes in a face that was already pink from alcohol, wide shoulders and an air of absolute authority conferred on him by inherited wealth.

His friends were much the same. They wore stripy shirts and pressed blue jeans; their faces were pink and their voices were loud and confident, rising to a bray when they laughed. The women wore velvet Alice bands to hold back their hair and pearl studs in their ears. Harriet did not fit in with these people. Johnny seemed somehow to dwarf her, to make her lose her colour. She was prettier than any of the other girls but their complete self-confidence cancelled out even this advantage.

'Had a hard day being arty, Hatty?' Johnny said, chucking her on the nose. 'Isn't she lovely! Let's have a kiss, then!'

'Wouldn't mind some of that myself!' chortled another young man.

'Now, hands off, Simon,' Johnny said over his shoulder. 'Find your own bird. Ask Sophie, she's always game for a laugh.'

He gestured at a girl who was wearing the ubiquitous velvet headband, an oversized yellow cardigan, a blue-striped shirt and jeans. The collar of her shirt was turned up and held by a pearl necklace. Her lips were frosted a paler shade of pink than her face. It was her one effort at colour co-ordination.

She retorted heartily, 'You must be joking, Johnny? Don't you remember that skiing trip last year?' She turned to a girl next to her. 'When Simsy got it out to show the chalet girl and we all fell about laughing? Seen bigger ones on the Labradors!'

They all chuckled nostalgically. Simon seemed no whit abashed; he was ho-hoing along with the rest.

He said, 'She was jolly pretty though, that girl. What was her name?'

'Belinda Something-Something,' said a Sophie-clone. 'Johnny had her, didn't you, Johnno?' She looked at Harriet's face. 'Ooops!' she said and started giggling. 'Dropped one there!'

Though they had a certain appalling fascination, I dragged myself away from this noxious little group, finding a vantage point from which I could look round the room. The crowd seemed to be thinning out slightly, and I hadn't yet seen the man in tatty clothes; I had been sure he would show up, but by now I was beginning to worry that he wouldn't. Someone tapped me on the shoulder and I jumped, thinking it was him. It turned out to be Judith.

'Sam? Come here a minute. There are some clients I'd like you to meet.'

Judith had a large gin-and-tonic in her hand, which I knew wasn't her first; but unlike Shelley, who was positively merry by this time, she seemed as composed as ever. She was standing near an alcove at the top of the stairs with a man and a woman, slightly out of the way of the through traffic. She introduced the couple as Clifford and Catherine Hammond. We all shook hands. Even when we were touching, Clifford Hammond didn't meet my eyes, and as soon as the contact was over he returned to his conversation with Judith, ignoring me completely. Doubtless a mere employee was beneath his notice.

Catherine Hammond, however, made polite conversation with me. She was extraordinarily beautiful; tall and slim, verging on thin, with very pale olive skin and startling light grey almond-shaped eyes. Her cheekbones were high and underneath them were hollows deep as wells. Her short light brown hair was pushed loosely off her face. She was groomed with maximum simplicity: little make-up, unpolished nails, her only jewellery a small pair of gold stud earrings. She wore a superb navy-blue crepe trouser suit with dull navy satin trim by Yves Saint Laurent, which I had recently seen in *Vogue*. The minimalism didn't stop there, as she did not seem to be wearing anything at all under the jacket. She was thin enough for this to look elegant rather than vulgar.

'Mr and Mrs Hammond have just bought one of Susan Durrit's paintings, *Grass Slide*,' Judith said to me.

Clifford Hammond was almost as good-looking as his wife, but in a much more conventional style, that of the successful businessman. He had glossy silvering hair and a face which would look excellent at the top of a company report.

'We wanted *Cloud Formation* too,' Clifford Hammond was saying. He sounded peeved. 'But Andrew Forme beat us to it.'

'But I didn't want you to take two of Susan's so soon, Clifford,' Judith said, putting her hand on his arm. 'I want to spread Susan round a bit. She won't be known so well, not in the beginning, if greedy people like you with too much taste buy her up so fast.'

The tension was diffused. Clifford Hammond said self-importantly: 'You may have a point, Judith. But with the next batch, the prices will have gone up, won't they?'

Judith mimed horror at him. 'Clifford, darling. Please don't use the word "batch", particularly in front of our artists. They're sensitive souls, you know.'

'I talked for a little while to the boy who did those paintings of pylons,' Catherine Hammond said drily. 'Sensitive is not the first adjective that would spring to mind. Or perhaps you wouldn't call him an artist?'

'Perhaps Mark isn't to all tastes, Catherine,' Judith returned, not at all fazed. 'But he's very high concept. Now, I think you two should have a little talk with Susan herself – she's rather retiring, the opposite to her canvases, but I'm sure she'd love to meet you. Sam, do you think you could fish her out of whatever corner she's in?'

I found her standing next to Victoria Davenant while the latter dealt with a keen young journalist. The two artists presented an odd contrast: Susan Durrit was a thin little thing with mousy hair and dull skin, while Victoria was positively Junoesque. I conveyed Judith's message to Susan, who looked petrified at the idea of meeting buyers of her work.

'Go on, Susie,' Victoria bellowed. 'They won't bite your head off!' She laughed, showing a set of teeth which could easily have done so. 'And they can't be as bloody boring as Dennis here!'

'Daniel,' corrected the keen young man, who was looking increasingly frayed at the edges.

'Dennis, Daniel, what's the difference? I wouldn't mind if you got my name wrong, it's only a poxy little rag you write for anyway. Any more in that bottle, Sam?'

I filled her glass to the brim. She downed it in one and turned back to the unfortunate Daniel, who was fiddling nervously with his glasses.

'More wine?' I said to him sympathetically.

'No, no, thank you,' he said hurriedly.

'Wants to keep his wits about him,' Victoria added. 'Such as they are!'

She threw her head back and burst into laughter. The teeth flashed, even in the tastefully muted lighting. Daniel and the lioness. No prizes for guessing who would survive.

110

I took Susan upstairs myself and pushed her gently in the direction of the Hammonds and Judith. If I hadn't, she would have run away. Judith immediately put on her most soothing voice for the trembling Susan's benefit, as if she were calming a frightened puppy. I moved away, looking for a glass. I had earned a drink of my own.

'Your bottle's empty,' said a voice behind me. 'I don't call that very good service, do you?'

11

He had materialised apparently out of nowhere, but without the traditional accompanying puff of brimstone. I turned round slowly. He looked, if anything, more scruffy than before.

'I see you made an effort to dress up,' I said ironically.

'I think you did that for both of us,' he said, looking me up and down appreciatively. I was wearing a close-fitting chocolate-coloured wool dress with a deep scooped neckline, over fishnet tights and my newly polished black leather boots. I had a black velvet choker around my neck, my hair was piled up in curls on top of my head and my lipstick was a warm dark crimson, nearly blood colour. Vampira with bovver boots. I was pleased with the effect myself. Though I had wanted to throw him off-balance as he had done to me, it didn't actually matter what he was wearing; he was sexy as hell anyway.

'I might do something about the state of this bottle,' I said as coolly as I could. 'Do you want a glass?'

He shrugged, keeping his eyes on mine.

'Might as well.'

There were only a few bottles of rotgut left at the drinks table. Harriet was sorting out trays of dirty glasses. She looked up at us with interest.

'This is Harriet,' I said, 'who works here too.'

'Hello, Harriet,' he said. 'I'm Nathan. Nat for short. And you're Sam,' he said, taking a glass of wine. 'Cheers.'

'How did you know my name?'

'Curiosity killed the cat.'

He grinned wolfishly at me and drank some wine. Johnny detached himself from his group of friends, who were standing nearby, and put his hand proprietorially on Harriet's bottom.

'Time to go, Hats,' he said.

'Oh, but I can't, Johnny!' Harriet said. 'I have to help with the clearing-up.'

'We have a table booked, darling. I did say.'

Johnny's jaw was set tight, and so was his grip on Harriet's behind.

'But I can't just leave, Johnny. It's my job. I'm supposed to stay till everyone's gone—'

'Oh, they'll understand. Come on, there's a good girl.'

The young man called Simon, now even pinker than he had been before, appeared at Johnny's elbow. 'Are we making a move then, Johnno?' he said.

'I certainly hope so,' Johnny said bluffly. 'We seem to be waiting for Hatty here.'

'She doesn't have to go if she doesn't want to,' Nat said, mildly. His eyes were gleaming.

'And who the hell are you?' Johnny said, noticing him for the first time.

'He's a friend of Sam's,' Harriet said quickly.

Johnny's head was thrust forward, bull-like, the eyes tight and small. The thick meaty face and neck were flushed with wine and irritation; he looked like a pig in a temper. Nat, by contrast, was lounging against the edge of the table, seemingly relaxed. Sensitive as I was to him, I felt the coiled tension in his body, but his legs were still casually crossed at the ankles, his hands shoved in his pockets. Johnny took his hand off Harriet's bottom and stepped a pace towards Nat. They stared into each other's eyes as if they were locking horns.

'No-one tells me what to do with my girlfriend. Is that understood?' Johnny said angrily.

'Haven't you read *Cosmopolitan* recently?' Nat said. 'I'd say your attitude was past its sell-by date.'

Johnny stared at him, uncomprehending. Harriet grabbed hold of his arm.

'Look, Johnny,' she said swiftly, 'you all go along to the restaurant and I'll join you in ten minutes. You order me something nice to eat, whatever you think I'd like.'

'Come on, Johnno,' Simon added just as fast. 'Harriet's right, we'll let her catch us up.'

Johnny shook his head like a big animal shaking off a fly. 'Right,' he said. 'OK. We'll be off.'

Harriet and Simon sagged visibly with relief.

'I'll see you there in ten minutes, Harriet, or I'll know the reason why,' Johnny said to her. 'And you – ' he looked at Nat, stabbing a finger towards him for emphasis – 'I never forget a face.'

'Save you having to look in the mirror every morning,' Nat said. 'Must be a welcome relief for you.'

Fortunately, at the same time that Nat was speaking, Simon had said something fatuous to Johnny about ill-mannered oiks and was already ushering him to the door. Harriet looked at Nat. Her expression indicated that she hadn't found the joke particularly amusing.

'You shouldn't have annoyed him,' she said nervously. 'He'll take it out on me now. Because I saw it.'

'Don't go then,' Nat said, shrugging. 'Dump him.'

'It's not that simple.'

'It should be.'

Harriet looked at me for support, but I agreed with Nat. Still, he wasn't exactly being sympathetic. I'd only known him for a few minutes, but he was clearly no Sir Galahad; Johnny's manhandling of Harriet had just served as the excuse for Nat to enjoy a little aggro. Perhaps he was trying to impress me with his high testosterone level.

'I've got to help Harriet clear up,' I said to him. He nodded as if he didn't care what I did.

'I'll have a wander round, then.'

I noticed that sometimes he half-dropped his 'h's, and sometimes they were firmly in place; talking to Johnny his accent had been more upmarket than it was with me. He sauntered off, and I took a deep breath. Harriet and I stacked the dirty glasses into their boxes. They would be returned to the caterer's tomorrow morning, to be washed there. The wine had finally run out. Not before time, judging by the state of some of the people in here. Across the gallery, I saw someone who looked eerily familiar. Harriet, damn her, was waving in the same direction.

'Hello, Baby!' she called. Heads turned. It was a ridiculously incongruous nickname. Probably that was why she had picked it, for the gap between the signifier – the name 'Baby', denoting something small, round and cute – and what it signified – Baby Thompson, PR personality, fashion victim and stick insect extra-ordinaire. She swayed over and enthusiastically kissed the air in front of both of our faces, bending over on her platform shoes and leaving the heavy reek of Obsession in her wake. I coughed pointedly. I hadn't seen her since the party and I hadn't missed her much.

'Hello, darlings! Being busy?' she said, not even listening for a response, but staring over our shoulders for famous people, as was her usual practice. Harriet had perked up. She probably thought Baby was fabulously cool and that she, Harriet, must be nearly as cool, for knowing her. How sad.

Tonight, Baby was modelling a look which was a nineties version of beatnik, crossed with a soupçon of trash queen: beret, beaded choker, tiny hoop earrings. I noticed that the tight stripy top outlined what could only be described as a bosom. It had to be a Wonderbra. Unaided by upholstery, Baby had tits like midge bites. Two young men had trailed after Baby and now stood one on each side of her like ineffectual bodyguards.

'Some of us are going on to Altered States afterwards,' Baby said. 'Do either of you want to come?'

Generally I prefer to eat my own congealed vomit than to be seen in Baby's company. I didn't say this. Harriet's face fell.

'I can't,' she said regretfully. 'I'm going out to dinner with Johnny and some friends of his.'

'What about you, Sam?' Baby said.

'I think I'm busy,' I said firmly. I was expecting Nat to return shortly and ask me out for a drink.

'Oh, OK. Well, we have to meet some people here, and they haven't turned up yet, so we'll be around if you change your mind.'

Harriet looked at her watch and gasped in dismay.

'Oh no, I'm late already!' She dragged her bag out from under the desk. Spraying on some perfume at random, she checked her make-up frantically in the small mirror, then dashed out the door, calling goodbye in her wake.

Shelley said behind me, in a grim voice, 'Was that Harriet going out the door?'

I explained the situation as best I could. The

expression on Shelley's face boded ill for Harriet's job security.

'It won't do,' she said. 'Especially when we have so much on. I can't afford unreliable staff. I want to do a stocktaking as soon as the exhibition's over.'

I felt that I was expected to say something.

'Really?'

She nodded. 'We usually do them in August, when it's quieter. But we've been so busy, I want to be up-to-date with what we have in stock. I told Harriet the same thing just now, and she looked like she understood . . . and as soon as I turn my back she's running out the door. It just won't do.'

She broke off. 'I came over to ask you something else. Judith's just told me that Mrs Hammond's secretary hasn't turned up yet to collect the Hammonds – he's the chauffeur as well, apparently. Could you just see if he's hanging round outside?'

'Sure,' I said. 'They're an impressive couple, the Hammonds.'

'My God, yes. Do you know who they are?'

'Should I? She does look familiar, but I couldn't place her.'

'Clifford Hammond is the managing director of the Wallenstein Trust,' she said, naming a famous merchant bank. 'And Catherine works for the Economic Research Foundation. I think she's the deputy chairman.'

I whistled. Now I remembered that I had seen Catherine Hammond's picture in the papers a couple of times. And I had heard of the right-wing think-tank for which she worked. The Hammonds were clearly to be treated with chamois gloves. I set off at once to find their missing chauffeur and was nearly at the door when I felt a hand on my shoulder. I swivelled to see who it was. To my surprise, it was Catherine Hammond herself.

'Sam? It is Sam, isn't it?' she said quickly.

'That's right—'

'I wanted to ask you if you knew if the gallery has any prints by Philip Guthrie. Judith said you could look it up for me.'

She ran her fingers through her hair, which parted in their wake and then fell back, perfectly in place. I had seen her do this while we were talking earlier. It had struck me as a nervous gesture then.

I said, 'Shelley's just asked me to see if your chauffeur's arrived.'

'Oh, thank you, but he's here already. I've just seen the car outside.'

'Fine,' I said, shrugging. 'I'll look up the prints for you instead.'

'Thank you so much.' She favoured me with an unexpected smile and turned away.

I went through into the back office to look through the artists' index cards. These were kept in blue boxes, with separate headings for each artist; within this each work of art had its own card with details of its subject, size, medium, artist's dates and so on. The system was due to be computerised but its simplicity worked very well. It only took me a minute to flick through the 'G's to Guthrie and see that although we had had two prints by Philip Guthrie in stock, each card carried a note in Harriet's neat little writing, informing me that each print had recently been sold. I emerged from the office and looked around for Catherine Hammond.

She was with her husband and the Franks, all of whom were donning their coats. Catherine Hammond's was the same navy as her crepe suit, a long expensive swathe of cashmere. She was tying the belt around her narrow waist when I told her that we didn't have any Philip Guthries in stock. She thanked me politely for my trouble, as one might have done a chambermaid for making up the bed, and went back to drawing on her gloves. I was dismissed.

Baby was at my elbow. Behind her stood the bodyguards and an unidentified couple; I thought it was composed of a male and a female but I wasn't sure.

'Now, Sam, are you coming to the club with us?' she said persistently. 'It's going to be fab. Jacques has flown the DJ over from New York for the evening . . .'

The Hammonds and the Franks were making a royal exit, as if down an invisible red carpet in the middle of the room. They were a striking group; the women elegant, the men handsome, an aura of money and power floating around them. Catherine Hammond had turned up the navy fur collar of her coat to cover her throat, holding it with one suede-gloved hand. Judith Frank smiled a goodbye at me. The Hammonds did not favour me with anything.

Their departure seemed to mark the end of the evening; the rest of the guests started shuffling into the back room, looking for their coats. Across the room, Shelley waved at me, indicating I could go. Baby was still hovering to see if I was coming to this club of hers. I scanned the room, looking for Nat. He was leaning against the jamb of the half-open door, watching me, waiting for me to find him there. I was expecting him to shrug his shoulders at me in a way that meant: 'Well, are you coming or what?' or jerk his head at the door, eyebrows raised, to mean the same thing . . .

A moment of acknowledgement passed between us. And then he raised a hand to me in farewell and walked through the door and away down the street without looking back.

I felt as if I had been kicked in the stomach. But I wouldn't let it show. And I certainly wasn't going straight home. Turning to Baby with a bright smile, I said, 'Sure! Sounds like fun,' and tried to make myself believe it.

12

By the time we reached the club a queue of fashion
victims had already formed outside the door. Baby swept
up to the head as haughtily as if she were Evita Peron and
they a line of peons waiting for the soup kitchen to open,
and did an exaggerated wave, with much Commedia
dell'Arte pantomiming of her face, at a man I assumed to
be Jacques. He was slumped morosely on a red velvet
stool just inside the door. Behind him was a desk staffed
by two girls with their hair in curlers. A couple of
bouncers stood in front of him, blocking the doorway like
a pair of stone lions.

'Jacques, darling!' Baby carolled. 'It's me!'

Jacques, a preternaturally thin man with a bum-fluff
goatee and a woolly hat, made some gesture at the lions,
who moved apart with much reluctance. Baby kissed him
and they engaged in a lively debate about how many
people she was allowed to bring in with her. Taking the
opportunity of Jacques' temporary distraction, I strolled
unobtrusively through the door and down the grey-
carpeted stairs. The essential part of this manoeuvre is to
keep walking straight ahead as if it would be unthinkable
for anyone to challenge your right to do so. I noticed that
I had been joined by one of Baby's bodyguards. A curlered
girl called something after us, but I waved my hand

dismissively, saying 'Jacques said to go ahead,' and kept moving. We were not pursued.

At the bottom of the stairs, I exchanged a smug smile with my companion and bought us both beers to celebrate the success of our lig. We leant on the bar and watched the club slowly fill up. This was a plush little place, like the inside of a jewellery box; even the ceilings looked carpeted. It was early yet and the dance floor was nearly empty.

'Nice work,' the bodyguard said cheerfully. 'I'm Tim.'

'I'm Sam.'

'How do you know Baby, Sam?'

'Art school. And various parties since then. She keeps turning up.'

'Like thrush,' I added to myself. Once contracted, never shaken off. I looked at this Tim person again. To my surprise, he was actually quite nice-looking; tall and thin, with a pleasant bony face and a quiet air of self-possession.

'So how do you know Baby?' I asked curiously.

'I'm her cousin.'

That fitted. He seemed too sensible to be interested in Baby. He offered me a cigarette. I was in dire need of oral reassurance and took one gratefully. I was still baffled by Nat's disappearance. Years of experience had taught me not to search for rational explanations of male behaviour, but occasionally the temptation was hard to resist.

'So do you work full-time at that gallery?' Tim was saying.

'No,' I said, dragging my thoughts firmly away from Nat. 'I sculpt. I take odd jobs when I run out of money, which I do frequently. And sometimes I stand in for a woman I know who teaches weights classes. It doesn't pay much, but I get to use the gym for free.'

Just then we were rudely interrupted by Baby, who descended on us like a hurricane in a beret.

'Where did you go off to?' she demanded.

'We just walked in,' Tim said. 'It seemed easiest.'

'Did you pay?'

'Nope.'

'Oh. Well, I expect it helped, because Jacques would only let me bring in four people free. So you've met my clever cousin, have you, Sam?' Baby continued, draping herself around Tim's shoulders as if she were showing him off to me. 'Tim's the brains of the family, you know. He's a journalist, isn't that impressive? I'm sure he looks down on us humble PRs.'

'Do you want a drink, Baby?' Tim asked in a shut-up-now tone of voice.

'Oh, Phil said he'd get me one,' Baby said absently, as usual looking around her for people she knew. She was completely impervious to hints, tones of voice, or anything short of a bazooka assault. 'Oh look,' she suddenly exclaimed, waving semaphorically so that everyone in the club turned round to stare at her. 'There's Gabby! Gabby darling! Over here!'

She disappeared as fast as the platform shoes would take her.

'Who do you work for?' I said to Tim.

'Baby has a mouth as big as a white shark's,' Tim said, resigned. 'The *Herald*. If you must know. I'm mainly on the newsdesk, but I do the odd feature.'

'Why didn't you want me to know you work on the *Herald*?'

'It's not that,' he said, looking me in the eye. 'It's my moron cousin boasting about me to an attractive girl – as if I couldn't do my own trumpet blowing.'

'Oh.'

'Can I ask you something?' he said.

'OK,' I said, rather uncomfortable. I had been enjoying the conversation and now it looked as if he were going to chat me up, which I couldn't deal with at the moment. I did have someone else on my mind, after all.

He read my thoughts.

'That guy at the gallery – the tall one with the hungry eyes – are you with him?'

That was quite perceptive of him.

'No, not at all,' I said. 'I'm off that sort of thing at the moment – I'm too busy with my work and it's a distraction.'

This of course is never true. If someone says it to you, it means that they know you find them attractive and are trying tactfully to discourage you. I hoped Tim was au fait with this convention.

'I think Baby knows him. That guy, I mean,' he said, taking me by surprise.

'Really?' It seemed unlikely. 'I don't get the impression they move in the same circles.'

'I'm probably wrong,' he said quickly, perhaps thinking he had put his foot in his mouth. 'I think she said hello to him earlier, that's all.'

Just then the opening of 'Jamaican Funk' started up on the dancefloor.

'Sorry,' I said, simultaneously finishing my beer and stubbing out my cigarette in a small miracle of coordination. 'I have to go and dance to this.'

'I'll be here,' he said. He raised his beer to me.

For the next couple of hours I danced practically non-stop in a haze of pleasure. It would have been bliss, if only the man waiting for me at the bar had been Nat instead of

Tim. Damn, damn, damn. Don't think about it now, just keep moving. The majority of the clientele had come to show off their latest Gaultier and wouldn't dream of getting it sweaty, so the dancefloor, though small, was not overcrowded. I only had to jab a couple of people with my elbow. A few prats tried to dance in front of me seductively but I ignored them. And the music was excellent. I made a couple of pit-stops at the bar but I didn't want to talk to anyone, just dance till I was pleasantly exhausted and my head was spinning and I couldn't think about Nat at all.

Closing time came fast. Like a police raid, large people in uniform shone blinding spotlights at us and chivvied us out in orderly file. Mayfair at two-thirty in the morning was as peaceful as a cemetery and the silence was like a blow to the face, my ears already buzzing as if to compensate. We had lost the couple who came with us but Tim, fresh as a daisy, was guiding a sleepy Phil and a wasted Baby. The fresh air was wonderful. Rain was falling, a light, refreshing drizzle. I didn't need to worry about it; I was damp through with sweat already.

We set off back to the gallery, where we had left our cars. Baby had been abusing substances in the toilet with Gabby all night and was distinctly the worse for wear. She couldn't stop talking, but her mouth had lost connection with her brain. Also she kept falling over on her platform shoes.

We reached my van first.

'Good night,' I said to Tim. 'It's been fun.'

He kissed me on the cheek.

'Can we go out for a drink some time?' he said.

'Sure,' I said. 'I'd like that.'

'Good. I'll call you at the gallery. I hate fumbling around writing phone numbers on cigarette packets at three in the morning. Have a safe drive back.'

I started up the van and drove past them, waving out the window. Baby had stalled again, and Phil and Tim were holding her up between them. The beret was skewed madly over one ear; she looked like a psychedelic bag lady.

I headed home, wondering if I should stop at the all-night bagel place and then deciding that I couldn't be bothered. For some reason I found myself making a list of all the things that are bad for you but you still want, like vodka and coke and cigarettes and chocolate and speed and cherry cheesecake and unreliable men with hungry eyes . . .

I had a strange sense of déjà vu when I pulled up outside the studio door. There was another heap of rags sprawled over my doorstep. What was it about my front door that attracted the dregs of humanity to it, as if it were a magnet? But my heart was pounding as I got out of the van and propped myself against its side. I needed to lean on something. In a single movement, the rag pile uncurled itself and stood upright, like a piece of film wound backwards where the debris of an explosion magically reassembles before your eyes.

'Hi,' he said, both hands shoved into his jacket pockets, tilting back on his heels, as nonchalant as if we were still at the private view. 'You took your time coming home, didn't you?'

I've never liked being taken for granted. My tone was as sharp as a surgeon's knife.

'You were lucky I came home at all,' I said icily, as if he were a specimen I was about to dissect with my voice. He grinned, unabashed. His teeth were yellow and chipped like bits of old bone.

'Are you going to let me in, then?'

'You're a bossy bastard, aren't you?'

'Are we going to stand out here and ask questions all night?'

I gave in. I would say with reluctance, but that would be disingenuous. I unlocked the door. He stood behind me, so close I could feel his warm breath on my hair. I shivered, but not with cold.

'You don't know me from Adam,' he said. 'Very reckless.'

I shrugged. 'You don't know me from Eve.'

The last bolt slipped back. I pushed open the door.

'Bloody hell,' he said, coming in behind me, 'it's no warmer in here than it is out there!'

'Feel free to leave at any time.'

My tone was still acerbic. I walked away from the door, leaving him to decide whether to go or stay. I heard the heavy door swing shut, and for a nasty moment thought that he was on the wrong side of it. Then his footsteps were quick on the concrete floor, and he was in front of me, his face serious.

'Look, I'm sorry,' he said. 'I didn't mean to piss you off.'

'How did you know where I lived?' I wasn't giving an inch.

'Your address book was on the desk in the gallery. I just opened up the cover.'

I didn't need to ask how he'd known it was mine. My address book is a tattered old notebook I've had for years, spattered with paint, SAM written in huge letters on the cover in marker pen. It's hard to miss.

'I know it was a bit of a liberty,' he went on, head tilted to one side. 'But if you'd told me to go just now I'd have gone, and no hard feelings.'

'Mmmn. So why did you doss down on my doorstep all night?'

'All night? It's only three o'clock.'

'You didn't answer the question.'

'You're a hard woman to hounds, Sam Jones. If you must know, I didn't like the look of those people you were with. I thought I'd come over here and catch you on your own when you didn't have Madame Fifi with the false tits hanging about.'

'How did you know they were false?' I found myself asking.

'She kept fiddling with them, couldn't you see? Hauling up the straps. And they were a funny shape to start with.'

His mention of Baby reminded me of what Tim had said.

'How *do* you know Baby?' I said curiously.

He stared at me. 'Who?'

'Madame Fifi.'

'Oh, her,' he said dismissively. 'She came up to me and said very drunkenly that I was the only person in the room tall enough to appreciate her earrings properly, or something like that. I got away as soon as I could.' He looked me up and down. 'She didn't do anything for me. I don't like girls who look like clothes hangers.'

'Oh? How do you like them, then?'

'Dark and gorgeous with plenty of curves,' he said at once. 'Call me old-fashioned.'

I felt myself smiling. A silence fell, charged with electricity. I could almost see the blue sparks darting between our bodies. I heard his breath and mine, and heard, too, the relentless pounding of my heart inside my ribcage. The nervousness which can never be avoided, no matter how old and experienced you feel yourself to be at this, made me as shy as a schoolgirl; we were a man and woman alone in a room and attracted to each other, and it seemed blazoned across our heads in neon letters ten feet high. I needed a drink.

I extracted a vodka bottle from the freezer, filled a couple of glasses and handed him one. He was looking around the studio, unashamedly curious. He took the glass, wandered over to the sculpture and stood in front of it as if he were staring it out.

'What's this, then?'

'I don't know. I don't think it knows, either. That's the problem.'

'It needs something.'

'I know,' I said rather snappily. We surveyed the Thing in silence.

'It looks like it just fell out of the sky,' he observed.

'What, you mean it looks squashed?'

'No, not exactly . . . It looks like a meteor fragment or something.'

'Hmmn.'

I saw what he meant. But I was completely sick of the Thing; even discussion on the subject depressed me. I said as much, shortly, and headed up the ladder to the sleeping platform, taking the bottle with me. By the time his head popped up the top of the ladder, I had already downed another glass and was feeling much better.

'This is a brilliant place,' he said admiringly. 'Bloody cold, though.'

He bent over the futon and rifled through the heaps of blankets and quilts thrown over it.

'Bet you need all of these in the winter.'

'And more,' I said, meaning only that no matter how many duvets I had, they never seemed enough; but as soon as the words were out of my mouth I felt self-conscious. He looked at me, sitting on the edge of the futon, and smiled, long and slow. When he smiled his whole face creased up around it in a rictus. He bent close to me. My heart raced, and I concentrated on holding my glass steady.

He said, 'I like your mole.'

'It's a beauty spot,' I said firmly. I have had to make this clear to others before him.

He took the glass out of my hand and put it down on the floor, then knelt down in front of me and kissed me, almost in the same movement. It was practically the first time we had touched, and we both jumped on contact with each other's bodies. Then our lips moved together; tentatively at first, but not for long. It happened so quickly, the change from light exploration to deep wrenching desire, that when I pulled away we were both gasping.

'Jesus,' he said. He poured us both some more vodka. I was incapable of speech.

He was grinning again. It was a grin without a trace of humour, full of recognition. He sprawled lithely across my futon like a big dangerous cat.

'Well, well, well,' he said, softly, never taking his eyes off me.

My body felt as if someone had outlined my sexual parts with a red felt-tip pen and then, to be doubly sure, had added large arrows pointing them out. I surveyed him over the rim of my glass.

'If you're going to lounge around on my bed,' I said, hearing that my voice had sunk at least half an octave, 'you can at least take your shoes off.'

He didn't say anything, but looked at me, his eyes unreadable. Slowly, he sat up and bent over, unlacing his shoes. I watched him, noticing afresh how big men are in comparison with women, how long their legs and arms are, how wide their shoulders. I thought of the blonde in the bar and how pretty she had been. But how could I give all this up?

The nape of his neck as he bent away from me was milky white under the tangle of brown hair. I wanted to sink my fingers into it and pull him over to me right now, this minute. I told my body firmly that it was always better if you waited, but my flesh was weak and wouldn't listen. I had never before thought that the sight of a man taking his shoes off was particularly sexy. You live and learn.

'All right?' he said, his eyes bright, his mouth a straight line. I looked him up and down.

'And the jacket,' I said. 'It looks filthy.'

'OK.' He took both his jackets off together and flung them deftly at the screen. They hit the top and hung there. He lay back on the bed, his arms behind his head, now in his black T-shirt and jeans, which were held up by a tattered old leather belt. His arms were as white as his neck and unexpectedly muscular, considering his thinness. His eyes were still sparkling.

'I think you should take off your boots, as well,' he said, thoughtfully.

'You have a point.'

I started to unlace my boots. They came high up my calves, and it took a while. He sat up behind me and started to undo the back of my dress.

'And this,' he said. 'This should come off. Or it'll get creased.'

He unzipped it slowly, kissing my back all the way down to the base of the zip. I managed, finally, to drag my boots off, the leather creaking protestingly. They fell unnoticed to the floor.

His hands were underneath my dress now, around my waist. Slowly they moved up the front of my body. The feeling of him on my bare skin was almost unbearable. My head fell back and he took one of my earlobes between his teeth, nipping it lightly, caressing my ear. Any minute now I was going to explode. There would be nothing left of me but my earrings.

His hands moved up my body, the fingers long and confident, reaching my throat, circling it. He ran one slow finger underneath the black velvet choker. Then he bent his head and traced its outlines with his tongue.

'You can keep this on,' he said.

* * *

I woke up all at once, my head pounding. For a moment, disoriented, I thought I had a hangover. Then I remembered what, or rather who, had happened to me, earlier on that day. Nat was moving around at the foot of the bed. Light was streaming in from the window above, clear white unwelcome morning light.

Oh dear, I thought, what have I done? I couldn't face the prospect of conversation. Perhaps I did have a hangover, a sex hangover. I pulled the pillow out from under my head and tried to go back to sleep. If I couldn't see him, then he couldn't see me.

An unceremonious hand plucked the pillow from my face. I scrabbled around, trying to get it back.

'Open your eyes,' Nat said.

'Mmmuh,' I said, shaking my head.

He kneeled over me, a hand on either side of my head, shaking it to and fro.

'Open your eyes. Come on.'

Finally, reluctantly, I did. His face was above me, his hair hanging down over it. He was wearing his jeans, the belt threaded through the loops but not yet buckled. I could see all the bones of his ribcage under the white skin. I blinked, accustoming my eyes to the light.

'Are you awake?'

'Mmmuh.'

'Sam! Bloody wake up when I'm talking to you!'

'What?' I finally mumbled. I reached up to put a hand over my eyes, to shield them from the light, but he misunderstood, thinking I was trying to block out the sight of him, and gripped my wrist tightly, holding it above my head.

'Look at me! Do you even know who I am?'

'Nat,' I said. That part had been easy. Maybe he would let me go back to sleep now.

'Yeah.' His voice softened slightly. He shifted back a little on his knees.

'Sam? I have to go now. I'm late already.'

'Well, go then!' I said reasonably. 'I'll go back to sleep . . .'

I started to turn over and cuddle back into the pillows, but he grabbed my other hand and held it above my head too, both of my wrists secured firmly in his right hand. With his left, he tilted my chin towards him.

'Do you mean that?'

'Oh, for God's sake—' I shook my head away from his hand crossly.

He bent over me and kissed me hard, taking my whole mouth in his, drinking it in, his teeth sharp on my lips. Then he pulled back, looking satisfied, and bent again to kiss my neck. I arched towards him. One of his ears was close to my mouth; I ran my tongue around it, breathing out warm air in a sigh at the same time. Then I took his lobe between my teeth and bit down. A shudder ran the whole length of his body. I felt him jolt hard against me. He raised his head and looked into my face, breathing as hard as if he'd just run a race.

'Jesus,' he said. With his free hand he pulled the duvet off me completely, tossing it to the other side of the bed. I gasped at the cold. He laid himself on top of me, his jeans scraping down the length of my legs.

'Let go of my hands,' I whispered against his mouth.

He untwisted his fingers from my wrists. As soon as he did I sank my fingers into his hair and rolled him over in a sudden spurt of energy until I was on top of him, holding him fast between my legs. I lowered myself onto him slowly. The belt buckle was icy against my skin. I started to undo his jeans. His eyelids fluttered shut, his lips parted. I stopped just as I had prised free the final button. His head was moving from side to side on the pillow in anticipation.

'Nat?' I said. His eyes opened.

'What?' he said in frustration.

'Don't you have to be somewhere now?'

'Jesus H. Christ—'

He surged up till he was sitting level with me, dragged my head towards his, his fingers tangled in my hair, and kissed me till I thought he had worn my lips away. Then he pulled away and stared at me, his eyes burning. I lay back on the bed and watched him dragging off his jeans, swearing vigorously because they weren't coming off quickly enough. He was a marvel to watch, so thin that his bone and muscle were clearly limned beneath the skin, as full of nervous energy as a hungry cat, and as graceful.

The jeans slithered off like a discarded snake skin, the belt buckle striking the floorboards with a noisy clink. I felt my mouth curving into a smug little smile. He saw it, and his eyes narrowed. He pounced over me, grasped my wrists and pulled them over my head again. I let him.

'You're a right bitch,' he said, whispering it against my ear like a caress.

It was not the first time I had been told this, and it wouldn't be the last.

13

After Nat left I curled my arms around a pillow and fell asleep again at once, drifting in and out of hazy dreams about skeletons and giant cats and moving through a crowd of dancers, looking for someone whose face I would not recognise. It was the phone which finally woke me; it rang and rang but the answering machine didn't pick up. I must have forgotten to set it. I rolled over slowly and looked at the bedside clock. It was two in the afternoon. If I didn't get up now I wouldn't sleep this evening.

To my surprise, once out of bed I discovered that I was brimming with energy. After the various excesses of last night I had assumed I would be thoroughly wrecked today, but apparently something had invigorated me. I decided to drop in unexpectedly at the co-op. I wanted to see what they knew about the investigation into Lee's death. And I also wanted to talk to Claire again. I didn't quite believe her version of what had happened that night. It was too sanitised to ring true.

The Castle Road house looked unkempt and crumbling. I parked my car on a thick rotting carpet of leaves and stood for a moment in front of the house, remembering how I had seen it only a few weeks ago, music and light and chatter spilling out from the windows, old and rickety but still very much alive. Now it looked like a target for squatters. The community spirit was splitting at the seams.

There was a yellow plastic crate of beer bottles outside the door. The cat was sitting on it, mewing pathetically. I bent down to stroke him. Communal living had taught him to be undiscriminatingly friendly and he promptly started licking all the parts of me he could reach and winding himself through my legs as if I were his long-lost mother. The cheap prostitute. He'd give himself to anyone for half a tin of Whiskas.

The interior of the house was equally slum-like. Change and decay in everything I see. Cobwebs in doorways, dirt trodden deep into the carpets, and the smell of stale smoke and old beer hanging like a pall in the air. Even I, who have a battle-hardened stomach for this kind of thing, was taken aback. I tripped over something in the hall and looked down to see a silver foil takeaway container, scraps of dried curry even the cat had rejected clinging like yellow worms to the sides.

Just then Tom came down the stairs. He too looked tired and uncared-for. It must be the prevailing malaise.

'Sam! Were you looking for me?'

'I was really after Claire,' I admitted.

'Oh well,' Tom said sourly, 'catch her while you can.'

'What do you mean?'

'Haven't you heard? She's got a job in Manchester. She's moving out tomorrow or the day after.'

I stared blankly at the stains on Tom's jumper.

'And what about Paul?' I said.

'He's going with her, I think. This opera he was doing fell through. They didn't get their grant renewed. Apparently the arts committee wasn't too happy about the down-and-out *Tosca* with the symbolic fire-eaters, and the Australian women's prison idea for *Traviata* was the final straw.'

'That's a shame,' I said, momentarily distracted. 'I thought the fire-eaters worked very well. And the bit at the end when she throws herself off the rubbish dump was great.'

'I don't know. I thought having Cavaradossi being tortured onstage with the live rats was a bit over the top. They usually don't show the torture part, do they?'

'No, I think you just hear his screams.'

'Well, then. I didn't really believe in the rats, either.'

'No, they were too sweet,' I agreed. 'I felt quite affectionate towards them by the end. You could see they weren't really biting his balls.'

'Brave of him, though, that singer,' Tom said, shuddering. 'Catch me dropping my trousers onstage and smearing rat food over my bollocks for Mickey and Minnie to lick off.'

I dragged the conversation back to pertinence with an effort.

'But when I saw Paul at the party he talked as if it were definite,' I objected. 'The opera, I mean.'

Tom shrugged. 'That's Paul for you. He'd say anything rather than tell you his next engagement is down the Job Centre next Wednesday for a Restart interview. No, it's kaput, finito, dead as that tenor's balls after Minnie and Mickey had been chewing them for a fourteen-night run. No money for degenerates like you in these hard-pressed times, sonny, we're funding the Mozart Greatest Hits String Quartet instead.'

With my usual perceptiveness, I detected a note of bitterness in Tom's voice.

'How did your reading go?' I said, trying to cheer him up. He glared at me.

'It was shit,' he said curtly. 'I didn't sell a single copy and Julia never turned up, the bitch.'

'I'm sorry, Tom—'

'Don't be,' he cut me short. 'It's your friend that screwed it all up for me.'

'I don't understand.'

'That Jackson woman. Julia can't stop talking about her even now she's dead. I never even got a look-in.'

Without thinking, I said: 'I didn't think you'd noticed—'

'Oh great!' That just inflamed Tom's ire. 'Brilliant! Everybody bloody knows what's going on but me! I make a fool of myself over some woman and when I finally realise she's got a major crush on another one it turns out everyone else knew all the time!'

'Tom—'

It was too late. He had already slammed out of the front door, shoving it so hard it almost bounced out of its frame.

Touchy, touchy. He was probably premenstrual. I headed upstairs to Claire and Paul's room and found them in the throes of packing. Streams of pale autumn light fell through the high windows across piles of cardboard boxes, some already taped up with a note of their contents scrawled across the top. Claire looked better than I had seen her for months; imminent employment had obviously done wonders for her morale. She was sorting things out energetically, while Paul, smoking a cigarette on the bed, seemed like just one more item which she would have to remember to pack up and take with her. He was idly watching her unscrew and fold up the drawing board, and occupying himself by tossing out suggestions for its dismemberment; she, in return, was disregarding his advice and snapping back at him about how useless he was being.

I congratulated Claire on her new job and at once she lit up like a hundred-watt bulb, launching into a flood of descriptions of the theatre, the designer, the fantastic opportunity offered by the assistant designer's pulling out at the last minute to take up a film offer instead and the designer's remembering Claire's work from a couple of years ago and giving her a ring on the off-chance that she might be available . . .

When she finally wound down, I said innocently to Paul, 'But what happened about your Opera London project? The Australian *Traviata*? It sounded so interesting.'

'We never got the funding,' Paul said shortly.

'But I thought it was all settled!'

'Yeah, well, join the club: so did we. But the London Arts Committee dumped us.'

'That bloody Lee Jackson,' Claire said vehemently. 'I'm glad she's dead.'

'Shut up, Claire.'

'I will not!' Claire glared at him. 'It's true, isn't it? You'd think she had it in for both of us.'

'Claire's exaggerating,' Paul said reluctantly. 'It's just that Lee was on the LAC this year, that's all.'

'I know she didn't like the *Tosca*,' Claire said. 'She hated the rats. And after what she did to me—'

'She didn't do anything to you!' Paul said. 'When will you admit they didn't rate you enough to give you the job and just leave it at that instead of blaming other people?'

'God, you *bastard*—'

'Sorry,' I said, trying to lower the temperature, 'but I don't understand. That Saturday night you still thought the funding was OK, but that was the night Lee died.'

'The meeting was the day before,' Paul said. 'We just didn't hear the result till Monday.'

'Bitch,' Claire said. 'Having the nerve to come to a party here after knifing us like that—'

'Shut up, Claire,' Paul said, leaning forward.

'I will not!' Claire yelled back. 'You're always trying to tell me what to do! Look at you now, lounging round as usual not doing anything and expecting me to sort things out for you—'

I was hoping the argument would come round to the night Lee died; Claire was quite capable of letting something slip in anger. But a few minutes more made it obvious that the subject under discussion was simply what was wrong with each of the participants in turn. Paul raised his voice. Claire started screaming. I made a discreet exit, disappointed.

As I left their room I nearly bumped into Ajay going into his, which was next door. The sounds of Claire yodelling with rage were clearly audible even with the door shut. We exchanged speaking glances. He was carrying a glass jar on which was stuck a white label reading: 'Ajay's. Please ask before using.'

'I'm glad to see you, Sam,' he said, surprising me. 'I was just going to make myself a coffee. Would you like one?'

I nodded, my curiosity triggered.

I had never been into Ajay's room before. In contrast to the rest of the house it was fastidiously clean and tidy. The desk and bed were a matching set, the kind you buy in plastic packets and assemble yourself. The duvet and pillow covers also matched, a pattern of diagonal lines in burgundy, black and grey. Very masculine. Even the stacks of paper on the desk were neatly aligned and held down with thick books which I presumed were legal text books. Or case studies. Or something. The bedside table held more books, an alarm clock and toiletries: aftershave, deodorant spray and shaving foam, all the same brand. Ajay wisely didn't want to trust these to the communal bathrooms.

The only discordant note in the room was the noise of Claire and Paul's domestic tiff. This was mostly confined to upraised voices, though occasionally there was a dull thud against the connecting wall, as if small items of furniture were being hurled and dodged. Ajay's eyebrows were raised in disapproval.

'I can't be sorry they're leaving,' he said, stirring three sugars into his coffee. 'At least we'll get some sleep at night. Do you know she once gave him a black eye?'

'Judy told me.'

Ajay shook his head in disbelief. 'I would never dream of raising my hand to a woman, but I wouldn't be very happy if Vicky tried to hit me, I can tell you! And then she'd work herself up into a state of hysteria and come in here for us to calm her down, no matter what time it was.'

He sipped some coffee delicately. 'The night of the party was terrible. I was about to give them an ultimatum when it turned out they were leaving anyway. And not a moment too soon as far as I'm concerned.'

'Yes, I heard Claire got very upset.'

'The worst she's ever been. She simply staggered into the room without even knocking. Vicky was furious. We had to give her half a bottle of Valium and sit next to her for nearly an hour before she went to sleep. Of course I looked for Paul, but as usual he was nowhere to be seen. And just as we'd got Claire off to sleep, he emerged from Judy's room and said they'd been having a conversation about meditation and he hadn't heard me shouting his name all over the damn house. I think he was just lying low until we'd dealt with her. As it turned out, of course, it was very lucky for her. But it wasn't so much fun for us.'

I put my mug down. 'What do you mean, lucky?'

'Oh, because of the row she had with Lee Jackson,' Ajay said. 'Judy told me about it. She was ready to go to the police, if I hadn't nipped it in the bud. Judy hasn't got much time for Claire, you know.'

He looked at my uncomprehending face and explained patiently: 'Don't you see? The police would have been very interested in the fact that Claire had a fight with Mrs Jackson that night, you see. As far as I can tell they're treating it as an accident – which I'm sure it was,' he added quickly. 'But Judy was bursting to tell them what had happened, and if she had it would have complicated things tremendously. Fortunately I cleared that up before they heard about it.'

'But—'

'Sorry, I haven't been clear. We put Claire to bed dosed with Valium, as I said. She passed out completely. She always does after these hysterical scenes.' As if by way of punctuation, something in the next room hit the connecting wall and shattered loudly. We both looked at the wall as if expecting to see shards come hurtling through. Ajay continued, wincing.

'And then we went back down to the party. I saw Mrs Jackson and went over to apologise for Claire's behaviour. I felt rather responsible, considering it had happened in this house. I am the co-op chair this year, you know.'

I tried to look respectful.

'But she was charming about it. Very understanding, considering some of the things Claire had been shouting

146

at her. So you see, Claire couldn't have had anything to do with her death. Lee was alive after the row with Claire and certainly Claire wouldn't have been able to get out of bed with those tranquillisers in her.'

He looked at me, his huge brown eyes wide, the lashes long and curly as a cow's.

'Claire would certainly have been capable of it,' he said frankly. 'But she didn't do it.'

I looked at him, not yet understanding his motives.

'Why have you bothered to tell me this, Ajay?'

'Because of what you said at the police station. You were suspicious and I thought you were talking about Claire. I'm glad I've had the opportunity to clear this up. As you can see, I'm scarcely prejudiced towards her, but I didn't want you to go haring off on the wrong track and stir things up unnecessarily.'

'Is that the only reason?'

I was only fishing now, and when he answered I couldn't help believing that he meant what he said.

'What else could there be? I know Lee Jackson was a friend of yours, but don't you see, her death must have been an accident. After all, how else could it have happened?'

14

I had assumed Laura Archer would leave for work early in the morning, and I had been right. It had been seven-thirty when she had emerged from her neat little house, climbed into the waiting minicab and been driven away to the pink marble castle where she worked. She liked her cabs, Laura Archer. Fortunately I had previously stopped to buy myself a cheese croissant and a takeaway expresso, so I was well fortified for sitting outside the castle waiting for her to come out again. I planned to stay here till I started getting bedsores, if necessary.

I didn't know what else to do. Until I had the letters I couldn't exert pressure on her to tell me what I wanted to know; and since I was still letterless, I could only hope to pick up some information by following her. Maybe if that didn't yield anything, I could try to bluff her instead. But I had a feeling that she was too smart to be easily bluffed.

There was a constant stream of people going in and out of the McCott Shaw building, so I didn't notice Laura Archer's second minicab of the day till she came out of the black glass portals, looked around for a moment and then stepped into it. Before I knew it the car was pulling away in the wrong direction for me. I had to execute a snappy U-turn, annoying two cyclists and seriously offending a Ford Sierra. Fortunately the driver was too polite to honk;

she just flashed her lights in a disgusted manner, which meant that Laura Archer's attention didn't seem to be called to my wilful obstruction of a busy thoroughfare. She didn't swivel round to look, in any case.

It was a nightmare to follow the car. This morning had been straight-forward by comparison; after all, I had had a pretty good idea of where she was going. But now she was heading deeper and deeper into the heart of London, through streets clogged with seventeen kinds of traffic, the kind where bike messengers slip along on either side of you, slapping their hands on your bonnet for balance, and people who are apparently under the impression that the West End is a pedestrian-only shopping mall step unexpectedly into the road, eyes fixed on the façade of Marks and Spencer's, turning their heads with expressions of surprise as your vehicle skids to a halt inches away from them.

By the time we reached Laura Archer's destination my palms were slippery with sweat. I had nearly lost the cab several times and though I hadn't killed anyone on the way, it had been a near thing a couple of times. We were in the heart of the City, where fabulous new post-modern monsters rubbed shoulders with ancient grey stone buildings. The cab was dawdling down a street off Old Jewry in the way they do when they're looking for a place to stop. Taking a risk, I pulled into a parking space which had just come free and earned some curses from a man who had been waiting to back into it. Down the street I could see Laura Archer's camel coat and briefcase swinging into an impressive-looking building. I waited until the swearing driver had run out of insults and pulled away; then I locked the car and strolled along to investigate Laura Archer's next port of call.

This was faced, or fortified, with grey granite and looked like a privately run high-security prison. Its entrance was a heavy, brass-studded steel portal about as welcoming as a tombstone. Maybe the design was supposed to reassure clients of the bank that their money was safe inside. Getting it back out through that giant door might be another matter. I knew it was a bank, because there was a legend carved over the frame of the portal in big square letters spelling out the name of the company.

That was interesting. It was the Wallenstein Trust building. Of which, if I remembered correctly, my genial acquaintance Clifford Hammond was the big white boss.

The door was about a foot thick and looked as if it were made from solid steel. I hoped it was propped open with something equally heavy; I didn't fancy being mashed to a pulp behind it. At least it would be easy to clean me off the wall. The designer prison effect was not confined to the façade of the building. Shiny grey granite floor and walls stretched across to a series of lift doors in ribbed steel. The ceiling was so high I couldn't even see it.

Laura Archer had disappeared. I looked around. The reception desk was staffed by two warders in grey frogged uniforms and peaked caps which shadowed the upper halves of their faces. The lower halves wore expressions slightly less welcoming than those of British immigration control officials. One of the warders was engaged in conversation with a very fat man in a very large suit who was smoking a cigar which in his hand looked like a toothpick. I approached the other guard. His skin was pockmarked with old acne scars, his mouth fixed into a straight line as if glued shut with mastic.

'Oh, hello,' I said in my poshest voice. 'I wonder if you could help me.'

'Certainly, miss,' he said, the lips parting only a fraction, the mouth still remaining as straight as a ruler. However, his tone was more civil than I was expecting. He gave me a swift glance to check me out for respectability points and seemed to approve. It was lucky I'd been feeling smart this morning.

'I'm so sorry to bother you,' I went on, trying to sound rich and stupid, 'but I think I just saw an old schoolfriend of my sister's come in here. Her married name's Archer, Laura Archer. Do you know her?'

'Mrs Archer? Yes, miss. You only missed her by a minute or so.'

'Oh, super. Do you know if she'll be long? Is she here for a meeting?' I asked ingenuously.

'A meeting?' He looked confused. 'Well, miss, I really wouldn't know. I could ring up to her office—'

'Her office? What do you mean?'

'Well, of course, she has an office, miss,' he said blankly. 'She works here.'

I stared at him, feeling my mouth fall open. Sounding stupid was getting easier by the minute. 'But I thought that she worked at some management consultancy firm in the West End. Are we talking about the same woman?'

'Oh yes, miss. I know Mrs Archer. I've only been here for six months or so but she was here when I came.'

He was beginning to look unsure of himself. He glanced over at his fellow warder, who was obviously his senior; his cap fitted his head so precisely that it might have been grafted there. The fat man was waving his cigar, sending plumes of thick smoke into the air, and saying something in a deep fruity voice at which the warder was chuckling in an ingratiating sort of way.

'Reg might be able to explain, miss,' he went on. 'But

he's just having a word with one of our partners. Is there some kind of problem?'

'No, no, not at all,' I said brightly. 'I know she and Veronica have been out of touch for a while, so Laura's probably changed her job since they talked last. So she's always here, then? Mrs Archer, I mean?'

'Oh yes, miss. Or if not you can leave a message with her secretary.'

The fat man was now lumbering in the direction of the lifts. Luckily no-one else was waiting there too; he'd need one to himself. Reg, the other warder, whipped the servile smile from his face and replaced it with the expression of a constipated bulldog. I assumed this was him *au naturel*. He was strolling magisterially over to us, hands clasped behind his back. Fortunately, the desk was huge and Reg was too important to hurry for anyone. I thanked the junior warder and left promptly. Reg would probably ask me to leave my name and I felt that a false one would only confuse Laura Archer unnecessarily. She must have plenty of work to do already, considering that she seemed to be holding down two jobs at the same time.

There were a couple of messages on my answering machine. One was from my friend Dave from the bike shop in Balham; his contact at the DVLC had looked up the name that went with Egg-Face's licence number. The Egg was called Walter Quincy, of 14c Randolph Terrace, Fulham, an address that went with the Golf GTI. The other was from Tim, asking if I still wanted to go out for a drink with him and leaving his home and work numbers. He must have got my number from Baby. I only half-listened to it. I was searching for my address book, where I had written Laura Archer's work number and address. At least I'd remembered to collect it from the gallery yesterday. Finally I found it on the kitchen table, dialled the number of McCott Shaw and asked for Laura Archer.

'I'm sorry,' the receptionist cooed regretfully, 'but I'm afraid that Mrs Archer is out of the office at present.'

'Could I talk to her secretary, please?'

'I'd be happy to take a message for Mrs Archer myself,' she suggested in the same dulcet tones.

'I'd rather speak to her secretary, thank you.'

The sugary charm vanished. 'If you'll hold on,' she said shortly, 'I'll put you through to someone who can help you.'

In a couple of seconds, a woman's voice said confidently, 'Hello, how can I help?'

'I was calling for Laura Archer,' I said. 'Is she available?'

'No, I'm afraid she's out of the office at the moment. Could I take a message?'

'Do you know when she's expected back?'

'I really couldn't say. I'm sorry.'

'But aren't you her secretary?' I said politely.

'No, I'm the assistant of one of our senior partners.' There was a little pause. 'Mrs Archer doesn't actually have a secretary at the moment,' she said finally. 'But I would be very happy to take a message—'

'Oh, don't worry,' I said airily. 'I'll ring her at home. Thank you so much.'

I put down the phone and stared blankly at the wall. At our meeting, Laura Archer had gone out of her way to tell me she had a secretary who worked in the next room. I remembered the office, empty of anything but the most basic furnishings, and the similarly empty one of the non-existent secretary. She had obviously been trying to hide her connection with Clifford Hammond by pretending she worked somewhere else. But why would McCott Shaw cover up for her, to the extent of taking her phone calls and letting her use their offices?

I had no idea myself, but I knew someone I could ask. I played back the last message and wrote down his number.

'Sam!' said Tim happily. 'I was beginning to think that you'd turned into an answering machine! How are you?'

'I'm fine,' I said. 'And I'm sorry I didn't ring you earlier, but I've got something of a crisis on my hands and I can't think about much else till it's sorted out. Do you mind my picking your brains?'

'Not at all. Fire away.'

'OK, I wanted to ask you about someone called Clifford Hammond. He runs—'

'The Wallenstein Trust,' he said at once. 'Why on earth do you want to know about him?'

'Well, firstly, there's a woman who works for him who seems also to work for a firm of management consultants. I wanted to ask about that.'

'Hmmn,' Tim said, thoughtfully. 'If that's the kind of thing you want to know, you'd be better off talking to someone on the City desk. Hold on.'

He was back in a couple of minutes.

'Sam? I'm going to put you through to Anne-Marie, our City editor. She'll be able to help you.'

'Thanks very much,' I said gratefully.

'But in return, I want a couple of concessions. First—'

'Let me guess,' I said. 'First, you ask me what's going on, and I promise that I'll tell you as soon as I can. And secondly, you say do I want to meet for a drink some time, and I say yes. But not for a little while – not till I've sorted this thing out.'

'Fine, I understand.' Tim didn't sound like he understood – in fact he sounded disappointed. But he took it well. 'Call me when you can. I'll put you through to Anne-Marie. Don't worry if she talks through you, she does that to everyone.'

Anne-Marie sounded as crisp as freshly washed iceberg lettuce.

'I don't have much time,' she said right after she'd told me her name. Clearly, she wasn't into conversational niceties. 'Tim tells me you're not a journalist. Is that right?'

'Yes—'

'And that you want to know something about Clifford Hammond?'

'Yes—'

'OK. What do you want to know?'

'A bit of background on him, I expect,' I said hopefully. 'But the main thing is this woman who works for him, called Laura Archer.'

I gave a brief summary of the mystery of where precisely Laura Archer worked. True to form, Anne-Marie interrupted me halfway through.

'I take it you don't know much about management consultants?' she said.

'No—'

'OK. Well, what they do is to go into companies and advise them how they could run better – cutting out over-staffing, speeding up production, targeting markets more clearly, that kind of thing. McCott Shaw is one of the best-known management consultancies. However, most companies don't like it to be known that they've called in outside observers to tell them how to run their business better. So the connection between the consultants and the clients is kept very quiet indeed. And occasionally a consultant will stay on at the client company for years. It's called going native. In the end the consultant isn't much more use to the client firm than a member of its own staff would have been, because they lose the fresh perspective for which they were hired. That's what's happened here. As far as I know Laura Archer has been on secondment to Wallenstein's for about a year now.'

'But McCott Shaw still say she's working there—'

'Effectively she is,' Anne-Marie pointed out. 'She's paid by them, not Wallenstein's. Think of her as being an incredibly well-salaried temp.'

'Why do they bother with the pretence?'

'Company policy,' Anne-Marie said at once. 'They all have rigid rules about secrecy.'

'So there's nothing particularly strange about it?' I was disappointed.

'Well . . .' Anne-Marie's tone loosened up slightly. 'She seems to be Hammond's right-hand woman by now. There's a lot of resentment about it at Wallenstein's. Obviously, she's seen as an outsider, and she and Hammond seem thick as thieves. That's a very ambitious woman. She's quite dependent on him, though, because technically she's still on secondment from McCott Shaw. The rumours have it she's angling for a top job at the bank.'

'Will she get it?'

'That,' said Anne-Marie drily, 'depends completely on her influence with Clifford Hammond.'

'And what do you know about his wife? Catherine Hammond?'

'God. Talk about ambitious women!' Anne-Marie now sounded positively gossipy. 'I really admire what she's achieved. She's the deputy chairman – that's what they call it still, I'm afraid – of the Economic Research Foundation, but in practice she heads it up. Sir Neil Fisher, her boss, is a senile old drunk who's contributed so much money to the Tories that he got the job as a prestige booster on the understanding that he wouldn't actually try to do any work there. And when he finally drops dead of DTs Catherine Hammond will step into his shoes, no question about it. Apart from her ability, everyone's desperate at the moment for high-profile women.'

'What's their marriage like?' I said.

There was a small pause. 'That's an unknown quantity. They're always out together in the right places, in a way they make the perfect couple. But as to their private life . . . There have been rumours about him and Laura Archer, you know. Nothing substantial. And Catherine Hammond has an assistant who follows her everywhere, like a devoted slave. The Hammonds seem to go very much their own ways out of the spotlight, if you know what I mean.'

'You don't happen to know the name of Catherine Hammond's assistant, do you?' I could always try the Economic Research Foundation. But I didn't have to. Anne-Marie wasn't City editor for nothing.

'God. Let me think – something a bit Dickensian – Quincy, that's it. Maybe William, the first name—'

'Not quite. It's Walter,' I said.

I could even tell her his home address if she were interested. I thanked her and hung up thoughtfully. Things were rather falling into place.

15

This part of Fulham was a yuppie enclave. Pine shops and wine merchants and boutiques run by girls called Virginia who sold stripy shirts and floaty silk skirts and big straw hats to be worn at garden parties. The kind of people who lived here didn't hang net curtains over their windows to protect their privacy; they drew them to the sides with little tie-backs so that passers-by could see what a nice chintz they had chosen for their Habitat sofa and how well it went with the fresh flowers on the pine table.

Randolph Terrace was a street of tall white houses which had long since been divided into flats. In the evening the cars must be parked bumper to bumper. I managed to park just down from number fourteen, on the other side of the road. Since Egg-Face – or Walter Quincy, as I must now learn to call him – already knew what my car looked like, this wouldn't have done me much good if I wanted to follow him. But I didn't. I wanted to talk to him and I didn't much care if he saw me coming.

Walter Quincy seemed to be the weakest link in the chain. If I got nothing out of him I'd try Laura Archer, but Walter's nerviness and incompetence at anything remotely cloak-and-dagger suggested that I might well be able to catch him off guard.

His car wasn't parked nearby. I tried the doorbell but he wasn't in so I went back to the car to wait. I had a tuna sandwich and a bag of plums for sustenance. Nothing to drink. I didn't think Walter's neighbours would let me in to use their toilet, even if I explained the circumstances.

A very long time passed. I spent most of it running down my battery listening to Radio 4 and cursing the bastard schedulers who shifted *Woman's Hour* to a morning slot. It got dark. By eleven I was onto Kiss FM and Walter still wasn't home. He must be driving the Hammonds back from a dinner rendezvous. I was dog-tired and in no fit condition to question anyone, so I gave it up for the night and headed home sulkily. I should have gone to the gym instead; at least I would have felt I had done something meaningful today.

There were three messages on the answering machine. I was starving, and all I could find to eat was half a tub of vanilla fudge ice cream which was set hard as rock. I pressed the Play button and started to chip off pieces of ice cream with a spoon, which soon started to bend ominously.

'Hello, Sammy. It's Tom, the lovable slob from Tipperary. Sorry I was so stroppy the other day, you caught me in a filthy mood. There's a party on tonight somewhere, do you want to go? I might drop round on my way. Bye for now.'

Beep, click, whirr, beep. Someone hanging up without leaving a message.

'This is Laura Archer. Could you please ring me as soon as possible to let me know your progress on the matter we discussed? I look forward to hearing from you.'

Oh no you don't, I thought cheerfully. I had just chipped off a big chunk of ice cream when the doorbell rang. It would be Tom, dropping round as promised. My heart sank. I wasn't in the mood for company. I went over to the door but didn't start to unbolt the locks.

'Tom?' I said.

'No. It's me.'

'Oh.' I hovered, my hand on the top bolt. I told myself that, though I didn't really want company, he had come all the way here and it would be rude not to let him in. He would probably just kick the door down anyway if I didn't. I could tell him he could only stay a little while, pleading fatigue. Who was I kidding? I was already undoing the bolts.

If I had been expecting a huge bunch of roses and a tender kiss on the lips, I would have been disappointed. Fortunately, though I hadn't known Nat for long, I already knew him better than that. He marched in pugnaciously, as if he owned the place and I were merely the housekeeper, and went straight over to the kitchen area on the opposite side of the room. He slapped down two packets wrapped in newspaper and a six-pack of beer on the table and swung round to face me.

'Who's Tom?' he said.

I shrugged.

'A friend.'

'Why did you think it was him, not me?'

'Will you please stop making a scene about this!' I snapped. 'If you must know, he rang earlier to ask me to a party and said he might drop by. And that's more of an explanation than you deserve.'

I went over to the kitchen table and pulled a can of beer off the pack, then opened one of the packets of newspaper.

'Fish and chips! Excellent!'

I sat down on the table and started stuffing my face. Nat was sprawled on the sofa, looking sulky.

'Comfortable?' I said.

'No, there's a bloody great spring sticking into my arse.'

'You have to sort of bend yourself around it.'

'I'd need to saw my legs off at the knee.'

'Don't exaggerate. D'you want a beer?'

He didn't answer. The green-eyed monster was gnawing at his gut still. There was nothing I could do about it; if I let him think he had any right to cross-examine me, he would never stop. I ate some more chips. Then I shook up a can of beer and threw it at his head. He caught it with one hand, and I saw that he was grinning again.

'You could have done me a nasty injury with that,' he observed.

'You could have ducked.'

'When a girl throws something at me, I usually stay right where I am. That way it never hits me.'

'I was the champion fast bowler in my year at school.'

'You played cricket at school?' he said incredulously.

'No, rounders.'

He snorted with laughter.

'I'm not opening this,' he said, still holding the beer. 'It'll go everywhere.'

'Spoilsport. Well, you'll have to come over here and get another one, won't you?'

He walked over, throwing the beer can high up into the air and catching it behind his back with one hand, without looking. That was probably supposed to put me and my ability to throw straight in our respective places. I slid the pack of cans along the table, out of his sightline.

'Where's the beer, then?' he said.

'Behind me.'

He leant past me to reach for one. I wrapped my legs tightly around his waist. He slid his hands up my thighs. 'I like this velvety stuff,' he said, stroking my leggings, 'very sexy . . .'

I was busy pulling his T-shirt out from his jeans. His bare skin was cool under my palms. I moved my fingers slowly up the front of his body and he drew in his breath sharply. He threaded one hand through my hair, his fingers stretched tight over my scalp. I pushed back against them as a cat butts itself into a stroking hand.

'This friend of yours, Tom,' he said. 'Do you fancy him?'

'Give it a rest—'

'Do you sleep with him?'

'Same answer.'

His mouth tightened. But then something seemed to uncoil and his face relaxed. 'All right,' he said at last. 'I give in.'

He looked down at me, his eyes glinting, and pushed the table back and forth to see how steady it was. It rocked slightly.

He said, 'Do you think it'll hold?'

He lifted me slightly so he could slide down my leggings. I shivered at the touch of his hands on me, cold at first, skilled as a surgeon's but infinitely more gentle. They stroked my thighs, parting them, moving me where he wanted me, as if I were a doll. He didn't bother to take off his own clothes. He knelt in front of me, as he was, jacket, boots and all, sinking his mouth into me, hard and soft, lips and teeth and tongue. I heard my own voice cry out as if it were a stranger's. He held me tight around my hips all the time, as if I would try to escape if he didn't. And I sank my fingers into his hair and kept him where I wanted him till I thought I would die of it.

The table held up. Barely. I was impressed; I hadn't known that it could take that kind of punishment. And the fish and chips tasted wonderful when I reheated them in the oven. We also discovered our first taste rift; I liked vinegar on my chips. He preferred ketchup.

16

Nat left early the next morning. He had somewhere to go – he didn't tell me where and I didn't ask. I wasn't due at the gallery again till the next day so, like a responsible investigator, I slept in. At noon I hauled my carcass out of bed, washed it, dressed it and gave it some lunch. Two Sainsbury's Garlic and Cheese Veggieburgers. I'd found them lurking at the back of the freezer when I was putting back the ice cream.

Walter would be at work now. I had decided to revisit Randolph Terrace this evening and hopefully catch him at home. That still left the problem of what to do with the afternoon. Nat had said he might drop back later but that wouldn't be till tonight.

I paced around the studio, which brought me from time to time in contact with the Thing. I didn't glare at it though, and it seemed less malevolent than usual. Not friendly, but almost communicative, as if it were trying to tell me something. But I didn't have time to listen to it now; I had too much else on my mind. Any excuse not to do some work . . .

A thought struck me. I could ring the police station and ask DI Fincham about the autopsy results on Lee. I didn't even know if they had held the inquest yet – how did you find out about things like that? He might not tell me anything, but it was still worth a try.

Three police officers, all sounding stressed and preoccupied, put me on hold before I got through to Fincham himself. He too sounded stressed and preoccupied and his tone didn't soften noticeably when he realised who I was.

'What can I do for you now, Miss Jones?'

I decided again not to correct the 'Miss'. I didn't think he'd take it well.

'I was wondering if you'd had the autopsy report yet.'

'That would be on Mrs, um—'

'Jackson. Lee Jackson.'

I could hear him rifling through papers. He came back on the line and said, 'Didn't you go to the inquest?'

'I didn't know when it was.'

He made a humphing noise.

'One of the people from that house gave evidence. The young Asian man. He seemed the most sensible of the lot. It was all quite straight-forward. The verdict was accidental death.'

'What did the autopsy say?'

He sighed. 'I don't have the exact results to hand. The paperwork's been filed away now after the verdict. But I can assure you that the injury to Mrs Jackson tallied completely with the theory we'd formed. She had been struck once only and the angle of the blow was consistent with her having fallen and knocked herself out on the brick.' He paused for a moment and said more sympathetically, 'She would have died at once, Miss Jones. I doubt she even realised what had happened.'

'And you mentioned the blood alcohol level before—'

'That also was consistent. Enough to assume she was moderately intoxicated, but not so much that she would have been unconscious. That would have been strange, you see – it wouldn't have been possible for her to be walking around outside. We would have had to think again. But as I say, it all checked out.'

'I see.'

None of this really surprised me. What did take me aback was when Fincham said in an almost friendly tone of voice, 'The case is closed now, Miss Jones. But if you have some information you want to give me, you can still do so. I'm happy to listen.'

I wanted to burst out laughing. Where would I start?

'Thanks for the offer,' I said. 'But – no thanks.'

He didn't press me on it.

* * *

After I'd hung up I still had several hours to spare. It was a toss-up between pigging out on the remnants of last night's fish and chips or going to the gym, and I took the virtuous option. But as I was assembling the collection of ragged T-shirts and leggings which I wear while exercising, I realised that my current favourite tape, an indie-grunge compilation I had painstakingly put together a few weeks ago and still played constantly, was at present in my Walkman, and that my Walkman was in one of the drawers of the front desk at Shelley Frank Fine Art. Well, hell, I was killing time anyway, and I wanted to put the tape on while I was working out. I might as well make a detour by way of Devereaux Street.

When I got there, the Walkman wasn't in the drawer. Shelley had moved it for safety to the back office and only produced it once she had given me a motherly lecture about looking after my possessions. I listened with docility and made my escape, noticing that Harriet looked terrible – her face was pinched and showing strain. Shelley must have given her a hard time about skiving off the opening.

I had just left the gallery when I saw a familiar face coming down the street towards me. It was Paul.

'What are you doing round here?' I said by way of greeting. It wasn't very polite, but then I was surprised to see him in this neck of the woods.

His smile was as charming as ever and as usual it betrayed no trace of what was going on behind it.

'Looking for you, of course!' he said. 'Claire told me you were working here now.'

'Actually, it's my day off.'

'Yes, I know. Do you want to come for a drink?'

'OK,' I said, curious now, 'but nothing alcoholic. I'm on my way to the gym.'

There was a sandwich bar on the corner of the street that had a few tables inside, none occupied; it was a quiet time of day. Paul had one of those enormous chocolatey things stuffed with nuts and pieces of biscuit, and enviously I watched him eat it as I toyed with a glass of mineral water.

'What did you want to say to me?' I asked.

Paul fixed me with his bright blue eyes. He was wearing a big sweater with a suede jerkin over the top, the way Claire did, but in his case the bulky clothes suited him. He looked like a fashionable Frenchman's idea of an Englishman dressed for the countryside.

'It's like this, Sam,' he began. 'When you came round on Sunday and dropped in to see us, Claire was pretty worked up, and when she's like that she tends to say a lot of things she doesn't really mean.'

I stared at him.

'You mean like what she said about Lee?' I asked.

'Exactly.'

'But Ajay's already explained that to me.'

'*Ajay* has?' He looked completely bewildered.

'He told me that he and Vicky dosed Claire to the eyeballs with Valium to calm her down that night, and that once they'd got her to bed, he himself had a conversation with Lee downstairs. So there was no way that Claire could have been involved with what happened to Lee, because by the time Lee died Claire was happily up in the stratosphere on Planet Valium.'

'Oh, right,' Paul said rather blankly. 'Well, good. So that's all cleared up, then. Excellent!'

He turned his head towards the man behind the counter and asked for the bill.

I said, '*Claire's* off the hook, yes. But that wasn't what you wanted to talk to me about, was it?'

Paul's head snapped back towards me. Reflexively he said, 'How did you know?'

I had caught him off-balance again and he had lost his usual composure. The conversation was clearly not going the way he had planned. I was enjoying this.

'Because you were so surprised when I mentioned that Vicky and Ajay had looked after Claire. It was obviously the last thing on your mind. I think you were really talking about what Claire said about you on Sunday. That Lee had been on the committee which had turned down the grant application for the opera you were going to design.'

Leaning back in his chair, Paul directed the full beam of his smile towards me.

'You sound awfully suspicious, Sam! You don't really think I had a quarrel with Lee about that, do you? There are seven people on the committee, you know. One person's vote doesn't make that much difference – and I don't even know the way she voted.'

I thought back. Nothing Claire had said indicated that she knew for sure whether Lee had been for or against the application.

'Anyway,' Paul was continuing, 'you should know that I'm not the kind of person to take setbacks personally. I simply get on with the next idea. I wouldn't even have mentioned it to Lee when I saw her again; it might have created bad feeling. I would just have let it slide. Claire's the one who gets herself worked up and can't accept failure – and since Ajay's given her what's effectively an alibi, she's out of the picture too.'

Reluctantly I had to agree with him. I couldn't imagine Paul complaining to Lee about the committee's decision; as he'd pointed out himself, that would be the quickest way to give himself a bad name. You were supposed to take this kind of thing in your stride. Paul was easy-come, easy-go; I doubted that he would have nursed a grudge against Lee even if he knew she had voted against his project. Still, I had one more arrow left.

'So why did you bother to come to find me at work?' I asked.

Paul smiled again, smugly this time. The advantage had shifted back to him and he knew it.

'Because I knew how upset you were about Lee's death. I understand that – she was a friend of yours. I know you're very sensible, but it just occurred to me that it would be a good idea to have a word with you when Claire wasn't around, to clear up what she'd said in case you'd taken it the wrong way. I've had to do this kind of thing before, you know – when Claire's angry she opens her mouth and doesn't much care what comes out.'

'I see.' I had to admit that it all made perfect sense. I felt rather deflated.

Paul was putting some money on the table.

'I don't want to keep you,' he said. 'But it was very nice to see you, even if we had to talk about something unpleasant. I hope next time we bump into each other this is all over and done with.'

We walked outside.

'Aren't you going off to Manchester soon?' I said.

'In a few days. Claire has had to rush off because the theatre wanted her straight away, but I've still got some loose ends to tie up in London. I'll see how it goes. If it doesn't work out for me career-wise in Manchester, I'll come back.'

He kissed me goodbye and held my hand for a moment.

'I'll give you a ring, Sam, if I'm back in London,' he said, his blue eyes looking into mine. 'We can go for a drink or see a film. You're looking really good, you know.'

I couldn't help being flattered, even though I knew that with Paul it was simply a reflex to chat up every half-pretty girl he met. He was a slut, that boy. I bet Claire wouldn't be happy at the idea of him alone and on the prowl in London.

I hadn't been to the gym in a couple of weeks, as Lou's disapproving glance reminded me when I checked in. She informed me tartly that I didn't have any classes to take for at least another fortnight and suggested I use the intervening period to bring my fitness level back up to appropriate teacher standard. I atoned by working out for an hour and then dropping into Rachel's aerobics class, already nice and sweaty. Despite all the stretches I'd done, tomorrow I would feel as if gnomes had been pounding my body with small hard mallets all night.

Then I headed off for Randolph Terrace. Having showered first, naturally. I have some manners.

It was dark when I left the gym, cold and lonely after the warm changing room with its peeling yellow paint, filled with half-naked women all talking at once. I was in velvet leggings, a big chenille sweater and my fake-fur coat and I needed every bit of warmth. I fished in my bag and pulled out my furry hat with the ear flaps. I had just washed my hair and I didn't want to catch cold.

It was the wrong look for Randolph Terrace; much too bohemian. As I had thought, it took some time to find a parking space, now that the yuppies were back from work for the evening. I had to park streets away. But the navy-blue Golf was right opposite Walter's house. What bliss, no car sores on my bottom today. I jumped lithely up the steps of number fourteen and pressed the bell marked 'Quincy'. The speaker panel buzzed with static and a faint voice said through the atmospherics, 'Who's that?'

'It's Sam Jones, Walter. I'd like to talk to you.'

Even the buzzing went dead.

'Walter?' I said louder. Still nothing.

I went down the steps and looked back up at the house. A white blur of face darted back from one of the third-floor windows, like a nervous ghost. This was not polite. I had come all the way to Fulham to see him and the least he could do was let me in. I returned to the doorbell and leaned on it for a couple of minutes. The ring it made was hardly audible to me, but I hoped that it was causing a din chez 14c.

It must have had some effect. After a while, his voice said imploringly down the speaker, more a question than a command, 'Go away.'

I didn't answer. After a moment he said helplessly, his

voice tinny with the distortion, 'Please, go away! Why are you here?'

'Why were you outside my house?'

No answer. My right index finger was getting sore. I switched over to the left one.

I stared down at the square of grass at the front of number fourteen. It was completely bare apart from the rhododendron bush in the centre. Too neat. What it needed was a whacking great asymmetrical metal sculpture in place of the rhododendron. After terrorising Walter Quincy I could pop downstairs and flog a sculpture to the people in the basement. Shame I didn't have any photos on me.

'If you don't talk to me, Egg – Walter,' I said, 'I'll go and talk to Catherine Hammond instead. I'm sure she'd be interested in what I have to say.'

'No! No, you can't!' Walter squawked in his metallic little speakerphone voice.

'Then talk to me.'

There was a long pause. I thought he was still holding out. Then I heard another kind of buzzer. It was the front door unlocking. I pushed it open quickly before he could change his mind.

Walter's flat was the top one, and he was waiting at the door, holding it half-open, obviously wanting to shut it in my face but unable to summon up the nerve. He was smaller than I had remembered, and his face was even whiter and smoother than it looked from a distance; it was perfectly still, apart from the way his eyes were flickering nervously in their sockets like a pair of black balls in a pinball machine.

He took me into the living-room and I sat down in the only armchair. Walter sat primly on the sofa, knees together and his hands on them. The sofa and armchair were covered in navy Dralon, the bookshelves and coffee-table made from heavy brown teak. The shelves were overflowing with books, mostly, as far as I could read, ones on economic theory; the coffee-table sported the current issues of the *Spectator* and the *Economist*. The sofa and armchair had antimacassars on the back. I hadn't seen those in a long time. The room smelt of mustiness and stale takeaway food, like a graduate's study at university.

'You know why I'm here, don't you, Walter?' I said.

Walter had a wide forehead and a small round chin. His black hair was plastered back as smoothly as ever. The resemblance to an egg was just as strong under close scrutiny as it had been from across the street. He sat on the sofa as still as a china statue.

'You've been following me,' I prompted, in case he had forgotten who I was but was trying to be polite. 'I know who you are and who you work for. And that you don't want me to get in contact with her.'

'No!' Walter said, coming to life at once, his hands clamping tightly around his kneecaps. 'Please, you mustn't! Catherine – you mustn't tell her that you've talked to me.'

'Unless you tell me straight away what you know, Walter,' I said deliberately, 'I'll go immediately to Catherine Hammond and tell her that you've told me everything.'

Walter's face was incapable of going whiter. Instead it took on an extra sheen, a glossy film of sweat.

'No, no . . .' he stuttered.

I shrugged, and made to stand up. Walter started in horror and said quickly, 'No! Please!' His knuckles were white around his knees. His head was bent. I waited, half out of the chair. I was uncomfortable but I wasn't going to break the tension by making a movement. At last he reached a decision.

'All right,' he said, his head still bent, his voice issuing from the floor. 'I'll tell you.'

'Good,' I said, sitting back in the chair.

'But please,' he said, 'please promise me you won't go to see her.'

'No, I can't do that. But I will promise you that I won't tell her that we had this conversation.'

He could see that was the best he was going to get. His hands had loosened their throttling grip on his kneecaps.

'All right,' he said, almost inaudibly. 'But *please* don't go to see her if you can help it.'

I didn't answer. Instead I deliberately changed tack. 'Do you have anything to drink in the place, Walter?'

'Over there.'

He indicated the shelves behind the armchair in which I was sitting. In a shiny teak alcove stood a small collection of bottles and glasses. I squinted at them. Cheap blended whisky, gin, and some tolerable brandy, the lesser of the three evils.

'I'll have some brandy,' I said. 'And get yourself a drink too.'

He seemed to be used to taking orders. I told him to bring the bottles over as well, to save us getting up later, and he obeyed immediately.

Walter knocked back a large tot of whisky at once. He pulled out a handkerchief from the pocket of his cardigan and wiped his face matt-smooth again. Then he looked at me expectantly. This tendency of his to wait for me to do all the conversational work was beginning to annoy me. I didn't want to keep having to ask him questions; that would only reveal the gaps in my knowledge.

'OK,' I said, sipping lightly at the brandy. I only wanted one of us to be intoxicated. 'Start from the beginning.'

Fine lines of confusion cracked the even glaze of Walter's forehead.

'Well, then, what would you call the beginning?' I said sharply.

Walter said simply, 'I suppose it would have been when Catherine met Lee Jackson.'

There was a long silence during which I did some quick thinking. I wasn't really surprised. Catherine Hammond was the kind of woman to lose your head about, to seduce even someone as calm as Lee. Various knots unravelled themselves before my eyes. But now where was Laura Archer? Off the board?

I took a slug of brandy against the shock.

'OK,' I said, shrugging. 'That'll do. Start from there.'

Walter's voice was quiet. He didn't look at me, which was useful as I was having a hard time trying to look as if I knew what he was telling me already. It was as if he were pretending to himself that he were telling his story to the whisky glass.

'It was different right from the start,' he said. 'She was different. It was as if she'd been hypnotised. I don't think anyone else noticed the change in her besides me and Clifford – I mean Mr Hammond. She was working just as hard as she always had, but I could see that all she was really thinking about was that woman. Whenever I walked into her office she'd push what she'd been writing under some papers, and I'd know it was a letter to her—'

'Yes, why was that?' I broke in, curious. 'Why didn't they just phone each other?'

'Catherine didn't trust the phone,' Walter said enigmatically. 'She never knew when there might be someone listening in.'

'Do you mean she was worried her husband would find out? But I thought he knew about the affair.' I only half-remembered what Lee had told me. 'I heard it was sort of a marriage of convenience.'

Walter winced. 'This was different,' he repeated petulantly. 'She said she was in love with Mrs Jackson.' He placed 'in love' between inverted commas, as if he were handling the words with sterilised gloves.

'And how did her husband react?'

'He didn't talk to me,' Walter answered obliquely. 'He doesn't trust me, he thinks I only do what she wants. And he's right.' His eyes flashed suddenly. His face came alive. 'I was the one she trusted to drive her to that woman's flat in Little Venice, where they used to meet. She trusted me with everything. Oh, he knew she was seeing someone. He even asked me, but I didn't say a word, not a word.'

He snuffled to himself. It took me a while to realise that he was laughing.

'It was Mrs Frank who told him in the end. He was nearly going mad. He knew something was happening with Catherine but he didn't know what it was. He was very worried.' He sounded positively gleeful at Clifford Hammond's humiliation. 'Mr Hammond was in and out of the gallery, dealing with that Jackson woman, for about a month before he realised who she was.'

More snuffles of laughter. Walter Quincy didn't like Clifford Hammond one little bit.

'You mean before Judith Frank told him that Catherine and Lee Jackson were having an affair,' I said slowly.

'That's right. He came to me and asked me if it were

true. His face was a picture. Because, you see, the funniest thing of all was that he liked her – Lee Jackson – before he found out. Once I even heard him say to Catherine that he thought Mrs Jackson was a real asset to the gallery. I didn't confirm it, when he asked me. But I didn't deny it either. And he trusts Mrs Frank, you see. He's got money invested in the gallery, and she's a friend of his – if you could say he has friends. She's not the gossiping type, Mrs Frank, not like that other woman there. Oh yes, he believed it.'

I had finished my brandy. Walter's glass was empty too. I promptly refilled it with whisky and handed it to him like medicine. He took it and started to drink from it at once.

'So what happened then, Walter?'

He looked up at me, puzzled.

'I thought you knew all of this,' he said. 'From her. Lee Jackson.'

'Oh I do, don't worry,' I said smoothly. 'I want to see exactly how much you know. And if you're trying to exaggerate or make things up I'll know at once.'

This put him on his mettle. He was happy to boast about how much Catherine Hammond confided in him.

'They had a terrible fight, she and Mr Hammond,' he said, his voice louder now with the whisky. 'He told her she was endangering everything, her career and his too. If it came out there would be a huge scandal. She told him not to be ridiculous, but he insisted. He's always been terrified that anyone will find out about them.'

'That their marriage isn't a real one, you mean?'

'People know about that already, or guess,' Walter said dismissively. 'They can see she doesn't care anything about him. But he wouldn't want people to find out about her, and not just because it would make him look a fool.'

Walter took a breath. His eyes were shining now. 'But that's not the main reason. Oh no. He's petrified because he thinks that if people know that she's had an affair with a woman, they might get curious about *him* too. What *he* does.'

'What he does,' I echoed neutrally. The atmosphere was very still, and behind the stillness something unpleasant was hovering. For the first time, Walter was controlling the conversation.

'Everybody does *some*thing,' Walter said in a malicious, evil little voice. 'I know what he does.'

He looked sharply at me, his currant eyes alert.

'You don't know *that*, do you? You don't know as much as you think you do. You don't know about his boys. His young boys.' He sniggered, and reached for the whisky bottle, emboldened enough by his own revelations to be able to pour himself a drink on his own. 'He likes them just right.' More snuffling laughter. He was beginning to remind me of a psychotic mole. 'They have to look just right or he's not interested.'

'Why?'

But Walter seized up. That was as far as he was prepared to go on the subject. Reluctantly, I shifted tack.

'You were talking about the argument they had,' I said. 'Catherine and Clifford.'

'Oh yes.' Walter seemed relieved to be back on safer ground. 'He told her that she had to stop the affair, and she said it would be dangerous to make her choose. Dangerous, that's what she said. It scared him.'

There was something Walter wasn't telling me. I could feel him picking his words with suspicious care. I probed the wound.

'And you didn't like it either, did you? This affair.'

I had touched a nerve. His voice sank so low that I had to crane to hear him.

'She always used to talk to me,' he said rather pitifully. 'About what was going on. Make a joke of it for me. She said I was her right hand. I did so much for her, you know. I still do. I was working as a researcher in the Foundation library, it was my first proper job after I left college, and she picked me out, promoted me, made me her assistant. I'm closer to her than her secretary, than anyone else. I knew everything she was doing, I drafted all her reports—'

'And then Lee Jackson came between you.'

It was the right choice of words.

'Catherine wasn't mine any more, she was that woman's. I'd always had her – she'd always been – I'd always been the closest to her, and now I wasn't any more. It made me so angry. When I drove her around she would just sit there, in a dream. It was as if I'd lost her.'

'So what did you do about it? You must have done something.'

He looked on the verge of tears. 'I – I told Clifford,' he mumbled into his lap.

This took me completely by surprise.

'But he knew already!' I said, bemused. 'Judith Frank had told him!'

'*No*. Not *that*.' His tone dismissed my ignorance with contempt. 'About the *letters*. I told him about all the letters Catherine had been writing to her.'

A lot of pieces clicked into place at once.

'And he was terrified of scandal,' I said slowly, almost to myself.

'He nearly had a heart attack,' Walter said gleefully. 'He thought Mrs Jackson would go straight to the newspapers.

I could have told him it wouldn't happen. Nobody would be interested. They were just love letters. It's not like she's Princess Di, after all. He thinks he's so clever but he can be stupid, more stupid than you'd believe. He was so scared of a scandal, of it all coming out about him, that he couldn't think straight. And anyway,' he added reluctantly, 'she wouldn't have done that.'

'You mean Lee Jackson.'

'Yes. Her. I knew she wouldn't do something like that.' He said it reluctantly, loath to give her credit for anything. 'She wasn't the type. She wasn't after money. And she did seem to care about Catherine.'

'So you didn't tell Clifford Hammond that, in your opinion, he had nothing to fear from the letters. That Lee Jackson wouldn't have sold them or used them to blackmail him with.'

'That's what I said, isn't it?' Walter said sulkily. 'No, I didn't say a word to him. I saved my breath. He wouldn't have listened anyway. He was off in a panic. You see,' he said, leaning forward clumsily. Whisky fumes came towards me on his breath, and behind them a minty smell, like mouthwash. 'You see, Catherine had never done anything like this before. She was always completely in control. And he was used to it. She sort of decided how they would live. He relies on her completely.'

Walter snorted.

'He acts the big businessman on the surface, but he's not like that really. Not at all. So when she started losing control, you see, he panicked. He thought he'd lose everything.'

'And what about Laura Archer?'

Walter was genuinely surprised.

'Mrs Archer? She works for him at the bank.'

'I know,' I said impatiently, 'but how does she come into this?'

He looked puzzled. 'I don' know,' he said. 'I din' know she did.'

The whisky was telling on him now. His eyes were beginning to close and his voice was slurred.

'Walter!' I said in my sharpest tone. 'Walter!'

His eyes opened, blearily.

'Catherine didn't know,' he said suddenly. 'That I told him about the letters. She didn't know. You mustn't tell her. Please. You mustn't.'

To my horror, he started to cry. He cried as if he had been bottling everything up for years and once he had started he could not stop. Cradling his glass in his lap, he let the tears roll down his face in twin rivulets. He blinked constantly, making sobbing sounds with his mouth, while the tears plashed miserably into his lap.

'Pleashe,' he kept saying, his voice now slurred with whisky. 'Pleashe.'

'All right,' I said. 'I won't tell her.'

It didn't stop his crying. He had found a handkerchief in his pocket and he was dabbing at his face with it, but the tears kept coming. All he was doing was to clear a path for the next wave.

I averted my eyes and stared at the coffee-table, noticing that the whisky bottle, which had been nearly full when we'd started talking, was now half-empty. There was a dull thud. I looked up. The empty glass had fallen from Walter's nerveless grip and was lying on the floor in front of the sofa.

I wouldn't get any more information out of Walter Quincy tonight. Like the glass, his head had fallen forward, only not quite so far. It was resting on his chest and it looked like it was going to stay there for the near future. He was breathing stertorously through his mouth; his nose was all clogged up with tears. I could hear them bubbling away.

After a few minutes, Walter's breathing settled into a slow, steady rhythm. I scribbled a note to him, saying that I would be back at the same time, nine o'clock, tomorrow night. Tomorrow I would buy a fresh bottle of whisky and ration it out to him with care.

I took the opportunity to look round the flat a little. The most revealing item was a scrapbook in which Walter had painstakingly pasted hundreds of press clippings featuring Catherine Hammond, most accompanied by photographs. Every time her husband made an appearance, his face was blacked out with pen, neatly but viciously, a systematic obliteration.

There was a taste of bile in my mouth. I let myself out and went quickly down the stairs. Outside the night air was cold and clear and I stood outside for a few minutes, inhaling it gratefully. There was a sprinkling of stars in the sky and a small white crescent moon. The street was very still, curtains drawn against the night, making dull gold squares of the lighted windows. A cat yowled in a neighbouring garden. A car went past, engine ticking comfortably.

I got into the van and went home.

17

Nat was on the doorstep when I got back. He said he liked my hat. In return for the compliment I offered him half of the hummus salad pitta sandwich that I had picked up at the kebab shop, but he declined and passed out on the sofa almost immediately, head on my lap. I polished off the sandwich, my mouth stinging from the chilli sauce, and washed it down with some Bulgarian Cabernet Sauvignon. How sophisticated. I had turned on the TV and watched in sequence a cop show and the news; too poor to have a remote control and too lazy to get up and change channels.

Nat was snoring. I looked down at him. He was half-cradling a pillow, his arms wrapped round it, his lashes soft curves above his slashes of cheekbone. Like that, he looked almost vulnerable. Still, the snoring was getting on my nerves. I gave him a shove.

The reaction was immediate and shocking. He was awake in a second, pulling himself back against the sofa in a defensive crouch, hands curling into fists.

'Jesus, Nat,' I said in surprise, 'what's wrong with you?'

'Forgot where I was,' he muttered, looking embarrassed. He sat up and stretched his arms out, making a ritual gesture of uncurling his fingers. Then he yawned widely, like a cat; I could see the red ribbed roof of his mouth. The leather of his jacket creaked. He smiled at me.

'Had a nice dinner?'

'Mmmn. Extra chillies.'

'What's on telly?'

We both looked at the screen. A prim male voice announced that the subject of the panel discussion tonight would be whether the homosexual age of consent should be lowered to sixteen. In another lightning mood swing Nat jumped up instantly and punched the Off button, eyes narrowed in anger.

'I was interested in that!' I protested crossly.

'Well I bloody wasn't.'

'Bad day at the office?' I said sarcastically. When questioned on what he did for a living, Nat had given me to understand that it would be better if I didn't ask. I had received the impression that it was definitely on the shady side.

'Leave it,' he said shortly.

'But—'

'I don't want to watch the bloody TV all evening like a moron, OK? It rots your brains, you just sit there while it goes yak yak yakking on—'

'Look,' I cut in, now as angry as he was, 'this happens to be my house, not yours, and if I want to watch the TV all night I damn well will.'

I stood up and switched on the TV again defiantly. Nat was glaring at me, his eyes bright green and narrowed to slits. I glared back at him, hands on hips. Suddenly he swung away from me and punched the wall. The plaster cracked and he let out a lurid curse. There was a moment's pregnant pause and then I started to giggle. The tension deflated like an old balloon. Nat was smiling too, though he still looked upset. He was nursing his fist in his other hand.

I turned off the TV and sat down on the sofa again. He flopped down next to me. I reached out to touch his hand and the fingers of the uninjured one wrapped themselves around mine.

'What the hell just got into you?' I said.

He looked away sheepishly.

'I can't explain,' he said. 'Don't ask me. I'm really sorry about the wall.'

I dismissed the wall with a wave of my hand. I had noticed before how his eyes seemed to change colour depending on his mood. Now they were a wide, clear grey, open and pleading.

'It's not all the same, is it?' he said, as if to himself.

'What isn't?'

'Let's drop it,' he said quickly. 'I'm sick of talking about it. I brought some puff.' He pulled a tobacco pouch out of his pocket. 'I'll roll up if you like.'

'OK.' I stared at him, feeling that something important was still unresolved. 'But—'

He pulled his hand free and started crumbling the grass beneath his fingers. 'Just leave it, OK?' he said without looking up. I shrugged my shoulders and went to get a beer.

* * *

Something was wrong with the gallery. I felt it as soon as I came into work the next day. You could have cut the atmosphere with a knife. Shelley came quickly out of the back office, bracelets jingling less than usual, her heels beating a fast, uneven rhythm on the floor. She looked relieved to see me.

'Sam!' she exclaimed. 'Did Harriet ring you? Have you heard?'

'Heard what?'

'About what happened yesterday! The theft!'

I looked around me.

'The print stand's gone,' I noticed.

'Yes. Well, no, not the stand itself, I've just moved that into the back office. But all the prints in it were stolen. We're still trying to work out what was in it.'

'Shit,' I said slowly. 'What a thing to happen.'

Shelley led the way into the back office. Harriet was sitting at Judith's desk, her eyes red and swollen. She was certainly having a bad time at the moment. Open in front of her were stock books and boxes of file cards. She was making some kind of list. The print stand, a huge mahogany frame with two sides opening in the shape of a V, stood beside her, empty.

'Hello, Sam,' she said faintly. 'Has Shelley been telling you about it?'

'Just the outline,' Shelley said. 'You're the one who was here, you can tell her.'

She went to make some coffee. Harriet started slowly, her voice still faint. The story seemed automatic by now; she must have already told it several times. It had, she said, been a particularly quiet day, so quiet that Shelley had gone home early, leaving Harriet to lock up at six-thirty, the normal closing time. No-one else had come in. Then, at five-thirty, Johnny had rung. Wanting privacy, Harriet had gone into the back office to talk on one of the phones there.

They were quarrelling when the buzzer sounded, indicating that someone had come into the gallery. It took her a little while – not more than thirty seconds, she said earnestly – to tell Johnny to hold on. As she went out of the office into the gallery, the buzzer went a second time; the door was already closing. She assumed that whoever had come in had taken a look round and left straight away, which sometimes happened.

Then she noticed that the print stand was empty. She ran out into the street. Reluctant to leave the gallery unattended, she craned her neck down the street, but it was already dark outside. All she could remember of the person she had seen disappearing out the door was his back, which had been wearing a belted raincoat. It must have been a man because of the height and width of the shoulders. He had dark hair. That was it.

She and Shelley had then spent a large part of the evening in Vine Street police station. Shelley had been on the phone to the insurance company first thing that morning, and so far there appeared to be no problems with their claim.

'How did the police react?' I asked.

'Not badly at all. They told Harriet she was a fool, but that wasn't exactly news to me or her. It all seemed routine.'

'They don't think we'll get any of the prints back,' Harriet added in a subdued tone.

'Well, we probably don't want to,' Shelley said briskly. 'Unless they find them straight away, of course. But if we've taken the money, then we end up paying back the insurance company the full sale price and we're no better off. They'll probably end up on a stall at Portobello Market.'

'So have you worked out what was taken?' I said. The contents of the print stand tended to change frequently: when prints were sold others would be brought straight out of the storeroom to take their place. I couldn't have said what was in the print stand at any given moment. Shelley gestured sweepingly to the stock books and file card boxes spread out on the table.

'We've been at it for an hour already. Of course, I told the insurance people that we could give them a list of pieces without any problem. If I had said that we're not a hundred per cent sure what was there, they'd have used it as an excuse to hold up payment. So we're trying to remember what was in the stand, and double-check against the file cards and the sales ledger.'

'There were probably about twenty or twenty-five prints in there,' Harriet added. 'I can remember quite a few. And I rang up Judith, and she confirmed most of mine.'

I managed to remember about five prints I had seen in the stand, but they were down on both Harriet's and Judith's lists already. Harriet and Shelley spent most of the day trying to track down the other ones while I sat at the front desk handing out information sheets on the artists and photocopies of favourable reviews of the exhibition.

To prevent myself fossilising with boredom, I thought up questions to ask Walter that evening. He hadn't seemed aware that Laura Archer had approached me and I wanted to pick his brains about her. Also, I assumed that Judith Frank must have told the Hammonds about me, but how much did they know, and why had they set Walter to following me – or was that just Catherine? Speculation raced round in my brain and to be cut off constantly by people asking me questions about the paintings was frustrating in the extreme.

At six-thirty I said goodbye to Shelley and Harriet, who

were still in the back office. Shelley was clearly furious and I didn't give much for Harriet's future employment prospects with Shelley Frank Fine Art. I couldn't help feeling sorry for her. The only positive aspect to the story was the quarrel with Johnny. Maybe they were breaking up. That could only be an improvement in Harriet's life.

I was starving. I stopped at a Soho trattoria for a plate of ravioli with butter and sage and a couple of glasses of red wine and then headed off for Fulham to see Walter. The appointment was for nine but I planned to arrive at eight-thirty to catch him off-guard.

I keep telling myself it's no use speculating. But I still remember that restaurant with its padded orange booths and how I had to wait twenty minutes for the bill, and wonder what would have happened if I had simply gone over to the cash register and paid there, leaving that much earlier. Sometimes stupid things like that can mean the difference between life and death.

Traffic was terrible and when I reached Randolph Terrace the street was packed tight with parked cars. As I crawled past number fourteen, looking for a space, I looked up and saw Walter appear at the window. He was pressed against the glass, hands hanging by his sides, his face distorted with fear. I thought that he was watching out for me, and braked, meaning to roll down the window and wave to him. But there was nothing I could have done then, nothing at all to save him.

It took barely two seconds, maybe less, but it felt like the slowest of slow motion. It looked like the easiest thing in the world, as if he had just leant against the window till he went right through it and out the other side. His head went first, smashing through the window as if it had been made of stunt glass, thin as paper, and his body followed it with a terrible, merciless momentum. I heard the sound first, the cracking, shattering sound of breaking glass, but it seemed strangely disconnected from reality. Then his entire body hurtled forward into the air, straight out of the third-floor window, fragments of glass pouring out around him like breaking ice, flashing as they caught the light of the streetlamps.

He tumbled down the front of the house like a stuffed dummy in an unconvincing film stunt. For a moment I doubted that it was him at all. The body looked like a practical joke: arms and legs awkwardly akimbo in the air, body as heavy as lead, unmoving, not a sign of struggle against the inevitable. The noise he made when he hit the ground was nothing compared with the crashing of the glass. It was a single dull, anticlimactic thump. A few pieces of glass had been slower than he was. They fell over his body, scattering like confetti, tinkling lightly against each other.

I had been too late after all.

I sat in the car, paralysed with disbelief, my foot still clamped rigidly over the brake pedal. I looked up at the smashed window. No movement. Nothing there. No-one came hurriedly out of the front door and down the stairs, hat pulled down to hide a guilty face.

People were starting to collect in the street. The occupants of the basement had come out of their door on the side of the house and were looking down in horror at his body. One of them was screaming, short, panting screams as if she could hardly breathe with panic. I heard running footsteps behind me and turned to look, but it was a man I didn't know. He didn't give the van a glance, but tore across the street and came to a skidding halt beside the body.

'He's dead,' the woman was screaming. 'Dead – dead – dead—'

Their voices carried clearly in the still air.

'He might not be,' the man said helplessly. 'He might still be alive.'

The other woman had recovered from her shock now, enough to move, and was kneeling by the body, touching it. I couldn't see what she was doing.

'No,' she said, her voice unnaturally calm as if to compensate for the panic of her friend. 'He's dead. His neck's broken. Karen, come inside. I'm going to call the police.'

I couldn't afford to bring myself to the attention of the police, not after what had happened to Lee. I let my foot off the brake and slid away into the night. I hoped like hell that no-one had taken down the number on my licence plate.

* * *

I pulled up alongside the house and waited. Lights were shining on every floor. It was an impressive, elegant building, standing back from the street, surrounded by a paved patio, with a large two-car garage on its left. The garage door was down, so I had no way of telling who was home. In any case, I didn't think the person I was waiting for would be using a car.

Ten minutes passed. Then a taxi came down the street and drew up in front of my car. I ducked. Catherine Hammond got out, paid the driver and went into the house, walking very fast. She was wearing her navy coat with the fur collar, pulled up so it obscured the lower half of her face. I gave her five minutes and then rang the doorbell.

It was answered by a Filipina maid in a black dress with a spotless white apron tied over it. She held the door half-open and said, 'Yes? Who is it, please?'

'I'd like to speak to Mrs Hammond,' I said, coming in past her so that she would have had to shut the door in my face to keep me out. She didn't. Instead she frowned at me and closed it behind me.

'I don't know if she here,' she said. 'I go to see.'

'I know she's in,' I said. 'Tell her it's Sam Jones and she'd better see me at once.'

The maid gave me a disapproving stare and went upstairs. I waited. The hall was wide and had black and white tiles on the floor in a diagonal pattern. There was a polished table next to me; on it stood an elaborate arrangement of flowers in a porcelain vase, flanked by twin gilt candlesticks whose candles were pristinely new and white, even their wicks. They were probably changed as soon as they had been lit once. A huge mirror hung over the table, its frame elaborately carved and gilded.

From the centre of the hall floor rose a staircase with an elaborately carved balustrade, its treads covered in a long strip of black carpet. The edges of the treads were painted white. Three other doors led off the hallway; two were closed. The third, half-open, gave onto another staircase, this one going downstairs to the basement. Nestling in the base of the staircase was an antique wood stand, containing another porcelain vase filled with another flower arrangement. How unimaginative.

I looked at myself in the gilt mirror. I was framed between the two candlesticks and I had to swivel a little to see myself beyond the expensive flower petals. I didn't go with the décor. I wasn't polished enough. And my eyes were wild.

A door opened and closed upstairs. Catherine Hammond came down the central staircase. Her hand was on the balustrade, but she wasn't holding onto it, just using it as something convenient to trail her fingers along. She came to a halt a few steps from the bottom and stared at me, one hand resting on a newel post. She looked as beautiful and calm as ever. If you didn't notice the expression in her eyes.

'May I ask what this is about?' she said icily.

'Don't you know, Mrs Hammond?'

'I most certainly do not. Is it something to do with the gallery you work for? If so, I'm surprised it can't wait till tomorrow.'

She was in a navy silk dressing-gown over pyjamas that seemed to be made of the same material. On her long slender feet were velvet slippers. She must have changed quickly. The effect almost convinced me; I was half-ready to believe that she had been at home all evening, and I had seen her come in myself a couple of minutes ago.

'It's about Walter Quincy,' I said. 'Your secretary-cum-confidant. Now permanently retired.'

Her eyes widened. Her colouring was extraordinary, those pale grey eyes startlingly clear against her skin.

'How do you know?' she blurted out. Then she looked horrified.

'I was there, Mrs Hammond,' I said. 'I saw him die less than twenty minutes ago. That's how I know. What about you?'

18

Catherine Hammond stared at me as if she were Lady Macbeth and Banquo's ghost was standing behind my shoulder. I didn't turn round to check.

'You *saw* him die,' she repeated softly. 'I don't understand.'

She ran her hands automatically through her hair in that same nervous gesture I had seen before.

'You were there too,' I said. 'Since you knew that Walter was dead.'

'I—'

She darted a glance around her. The maid seemed to have disappeared, but she said, 'Shall we go into the drawing-room?'

Without waiting for my response she descended the remaining few stairs, opened one of the doors on her right and went through it without looking at me. Her slippers were silent on the tiled floor of the hall. I followed her and found myself in the living-room. Stretching right across the house, with deep bow windows at either end, it was furnished like the hall, with a conspicuous, oppressive opulence: carpets white as milk and thick as cream, mahogany side tables glossy with polish, plenty of brocade sofas and armchairs scattered artfully about, standing on curly little gilt legs. Velvet curtains hung in heavy pleats over each window. The paintings on the walls were the only element of the décor that seemed incongruous. They were all uncompromisingly modern.

Catherine Hammond sat down in the middle of one of the brocade sofas. Its rich material was caught down in a regular pattern with tiny covered buttons. She was staring straight ahead, her legs pulled up to one side, the wide legs of her pyjama trousers in navy silk folds around her feet. She took up poses as a matter of course; now she reminded me of a Jean Muir advertisement in *Vogue*. But she lacked the right model-blank stare. She was thinking too hard.

I sat down on the opposite sofa. It was hard and uncomfortable and the dents made by the little buttons fell away unexpectedly beneath me. Sitting on a series of small crevasses made me feel insecure. It didn't seem to be bothering my hostess. There were some small taffeta pillows behind me, but they too were hard as rocks.

'I know you were out tonight,' I said. 'I've been parked outside for the last twenty minutes. I saw the taxi you arrived in; I took its number. You must have changed pretty quickly. I'd bet your clothes are scattered all over the floor of your bedroom.'

Her mouth opened, but nothing came out. She ran her hands through her hair again.

Finally she said slowly, 'All right. I was there. He rang me. He said he needed to see me at once. He told me you were coming round to see him and had been asking questions about Lee. He was frightened of you. You had threatened him and he was afraid I would think he had betrayed me.'

'Surely it was too late for that,' I said. 'Walter and I already had a long talk last night.'

Her eyes narrowed. She wasn't warming to me with acquaintance.

'I don't see what business it is of yours!' she said haughtily. 'How dare you cross-question my assistant about my private life!'

'And it's too late for that line. You should have tried it when I first walked in the door.'

'You little—'

'No heightist comments please, Mrs Hammond. Shall I tell you what business of mine this is? Lee Jackson meant a great deal to me. And it seems to me that I care a whole lot more about what happened to her than you do.'

'That's not true!' she cried angrily, half-rising from the sofa.

'Then tell me what happened tonight at Walter Quincy's flat. If it's not relevant to Lee's death, I'll leave it alone.'

She stared at me, sinking back on the sofa. I knew she was making some sort of calculation.

After a minute or so she said, 'Walter called me, as I said. He was desperate; he said I had to come at once. I called a taxi but it took a while to come. I told the driver to stop at the end of the street. I wanted a breath of air before I went in. I thought Walter was going to make an ugly scene and I was dreading it.'

'Why should he make a scene?'

Her eyes met mine.

'He was obsessed with me,' she said, as if it were the most obvious thing in the world. 'He was terribly jealous and possessive of me. It was very difficult.'

'Then why did you go to see him at all, if you were dreading a scene? Why didn't you just tell him to wait till tomorrow at work?'

I knew in advance what she was going to say.

'I thought – I didn't know what he might do. He was a depressive, you know. It had been diagnosed. And I was right to worry.'

She looked down.

'I got there too late. Maybe he thought that I wasn't coming at all, that I was furious with him for talking to you. And so he killed himself.'

There was a brocade footstool in front of me, with stumpy gilt legs like a golden dachshund's. I propped my boots up on it and leaned forward.

'So you weren't in the flat with him?'

'No, I was walking towards his house. I heard the crash of the window and then he came flying out—'

Her voice broke. I would have sworn that she was genuinely distressed.

'I turned at once and started walking back the way I'd come. I picked up a taxi almost immediately and came straight here.'

I looked at her. She pushed her hair back behind her ears. Strangely enough, I believed her story. But I knew as surely as I was sitting there that she was also lying through her teeth.

There was a scraping noise from outside; a key turning in the lock of the front door. I jumped. I was pleased to see that Catherine Hammond did too.

'Catherine? Where are you?' came Clifford Hammond's voice brusquely from the hall.

'In here,' she called. 'But—'

He appeared in the doorway, already frowning. When he saw me, sitting across from his wife, distinctly out of place in his smart living-room in my jeans and leather jacket, patent-leather boots up on a footstool, his frown deepened further, carving deep grooves across his forehead and on either side of his mouth. His brows pulled together in twin creases.

'What is *she* doing here?' he said to his wife.

He was still wearing his overcoat. It was black vicuna and looked as heavy as a millstone around his neck. His grey hair was so smooth that he must have just checked his appearance in the hall mirror. Vanity, vanity. He stood there inside the door, feet slightly apart so that his body formed a black triangle, staring at me.

'She came to tell me something,' Catherine Hammond said, her voice trembling for the first time that evening. I thought it might be the realisation of what had happened, finally coming home to her as she sat in her silk lounging pyjamas on the brocade sofa of her lavish reception room. 'It's Walter,' she said. 'He's dead.'

Clifford Hammond did not exclaim, 'Walter, dead? How? Why?' He simply stood there, unmoving, his eyes fixed on me as if he thought that, by staring hard enough, he could make me evaporate into thin air.

'And why did Miss Jones come to inform you of this fact?' he asked. 'No doubt she had a reason.'

The sarcasm in his voice was probably supposed to make me wither up and die. I tried to look flourishing instead.

'I saw him die,' I said. 'And, by a coincidence, so did your wife. Nice to have something in common.'

'What's this?'

He turned at once to Catherine. 'What happened? What were you doing there?'

'Walter threw himself out of his window,' she said carefully. 'He had rung me to come to see him. I hadn't gone in yet. I was outside in the street.'

'And where was Miss Jones?'

Both of them looked at me. Clifford like a prosecuting counsel; Catherine with bemusement.

'I was outside in the street as well,' I said. 'And I can't say that I saw Mrs Hammond.'

'Perhaps that's because you weren't there at all,' Clifford Hammond pounced on this as if I were in the dock. 'Or because you were closer than that. Perhaps you were in the flat with him.'

But there wasn't a jury for him to impress.

'You'll have to get your stories straight,' I said. 'Your wife just suggested that Walter killed himself because he was obsessed with her. Now you're trying to frame me with his murder. You should try talking to one another. Communication is so important in a relationship.'

I hadn't known how near the bone it would go. Clifford Hammond went white as a sheet. The lines in his face were suddenly dark as mud against his pallor. Catherine Hammond seemed frozen to the sofa. I watched them, hoping that one of them would say something revealing. But it wasn't my lucky day. Well, I knew that already.

Finally, Clifford Hammond recovered his voice. It was not as smooth as usual.

'Get out of my house,' he said. 'Now.'

'What, so soon?' I said. 'There are so many things we haven't covered. Walter and I had a long talk last night. I wanted to ask you about some things he told me—'

'Out!' shouted Clifford Hammond, losing it completely.

I shrugged. 'Well, far be it from me to outstay my welcome,' I said, standing up and zipping up my leather jacket. 'I assume you weren't planning to threaten me with the police if I refused to go? I can't imagine that you'd want to explain me to them.'

Clifford Hammond opened his mouth, his lips shaped

in an O. His face was bright red.

'No, don't say "Out" again, I'm going,' I said. I looked over at Catherine Hammond, who was still an ice statue. She would need a bucket of hot water thrown over her to unfreeze her from the sofa.

'Goodbye, Mrs Hammond. I'm sure we'll meet again,' I said. 'Perhaps we could have another pleasant chat about our mutual acquaintances. Now deceased.'

Her eyes flew up to mine, the only thing moving in her whole body. They were extraordinary: full of a furious anger, a terrible resentment, which, like most of this whole messy murderous business, I didn't understand. Against her pale olive skin her eyes looked not grey but two white laser beams of hate. At that moment she would have killed me if she could.

Clifford Hammond stood aside to let me pass, ostentatiously avoiding contact with me. I half-expected him to pull back the skirts of his overcoat like a Victorian lady drawing back in outraged virtue from a loose woman. I didn't much like this Enemy of the People implication, but I swaggered out, doing my best to live up to it, leaving the door swinging open behind me. As I went down the steps, it slammed shut so hard I heard the hinges protest. The Hammonds were about to have a very interesting conversation.

* * *

Nat was waiting for me, pacing up and down the street impatiently. By the time I had parked he was pulling open the driver's door.

'Where have you been?' he said. 'I've been waiting for hours!'

I opened the front door and switched the main studio

203

lights on, an unforgiving pair of fluorescent strips which showed up every dark corner and hammock of cobweb on the ceiling. The room flooded with white light. It stripped down everything beneath it, like lips drawn back over bared teeth.

I turned to look at Nat. It had been raining on and off that evening, not heavily, but he had been caught in it. His hair was slicked back from his face, the shoulders of his raincoat damp. Without the usual short tangle of hair, his face was positively ugly. His bones were too prominent, too sharp, for a covering as fragile as skin; his cheekbones looked as if they would cut him when he smiled. In this deathshead, his eyes were gleaming green and bright. I put up my hand to touch his face. It too was wet, but the skin beneath was burning hot.

'You're soaked,' I said. 'You must have been outside for ages.'

'Hours,' he said, shrugging. 'I told you. It doesn't matter now.'

He took hold of my hand. His fingers were so long and weirdly knobbed with bone that they seemed hardly human; those of an alien hand. Like his face, they were burning hot.

'I think you have a fever,' I said. 'You're hot as an oven.'

He slid my hand under the layers of jacket and shirt, through the buttons, against his ribcage. It almost scorched my fingers. I didn't care. I kept remembering Walter pitching headlong out of his window without even putting his hands forward to save himself. And the sound that he had made when he hit the ground.

'What is it?' he said intently, his fingers tightening over mine.

'Nothing,' I said. 'I don't want to talk about it.'

'But—'

'No. Leave it alone.'

I pressed my body down the length of his, inside his coat. He felt tightly packed with energy, ready to explode, like the grenade with the pin out which I had once said was the only thing that could stop him.

'I want to feel alive,' I said. 'Make me feel alive.'

He knew exactly what I meant; his mood was the same as mine. Cold raindrops on his face and hands, his skin slippery with hot sweat, tasting of salt and excitement. We fought all night like a pair of animals, in an eerie silence, the only sounds those made by our bodies as they met and clung and struggled desperately with one another, finding release only to demand it again at once, never satisfied, restless and greedy and violent by turns. I found myself wanting to hurt him, to punish him, and every emotion I felt seemed to be mirrored in his eyes as if I were looking at myself in him. Even when I was crying out for sleep I could not stop; the craving of my body overrode everything else and drove me on until it had so exhausted itself that it collapsed, only to awake a short time later, the need to batter myself into extinction against his body renewed and urgent as ever.

When I slept I dreamt of Walter, hundreds of Walters falling from the same window again and again as if the ceaselessly tumbling bodies were sheep I should be counting. Sometimes he turned into Humpty Dumpty, a giant egg body with tiny little arms and legs, his shell cracking into thousands of pieces at the bottom of the wall. But mostly he was Walter, and the sound he made when he hit the ground was not that of an eggshell shattering but a human body, one thump, like a sandbag, and then silence.

I would start awake in terror and then memory would flood back, telling me that it was not a dream but reality. I would see Catherine Hammond on her brocade sofa, in her silk dressing-gown and pyjamas with their dull rich sheen. Nothing had changed. I still knew she had been lying.

19

Then, at last, it was the next day, and the dreams of Walter falling over and over again from his window, like a needle stuck in a groove, faded away into darkness. I opened my eyes to the clarity of morning light. Nat was curled around my back, but he was so fast asleep that I slipped out from under his arm and got dressed without even causing him to stir.

I felt stiff and sore and when I looked at myself naked in the mirror I could see why. Bruises like smudgy fingerprints circled my wrists. I could still feel Nat's hands vice-tight around them. More were scattered over my thighs, and in the soft skin under my arm was the imprint of teeth.

I wasn't complaining of unfair treatment; I hadn't left him unmarked either. That wasn't what worried me. It was the sense that we sparked off, or encouraged, something in each other that would have been best left sleeping. And you can't close the box again once you've lifted the lid and looked inside.

I put on my black satin jeans and pulled over them a big black polo-neck sweater. I pinned my hair up in clumps on top of my head and made my face up carefully: pale powder, liquid black eyeliner, red lipstick. Then I filled up all the holes in my ears with little silver hoops and loaded

207

my fingers with silver rings. I looked in the mirror. It was the effect I had wanted. I didn't look like I'd take any shit from anyone.

It was odd to push open the heavy glass door and walk into Shelley Frank Fine Art the next day as if nothing had happened. Knowing now that Clifford Hammond had a financial interest in the gallery, I was half-expecting him to have rung Judith and asked her to sack me summarily. I could sue for unfair dismissal. But everything seemed normal. Judith wasn't even due in today.

Shelley had a pot of coffee, a plate of biscuits and a list of routine tasks as long as her arm for me. Ring the shippers, send off the finally compiled list of stolen prints to the insurance company, run off more biography sheets on the artists in the exhibition, as we were running out . . .

She paused halfway through the torrent and fixed me with a glance.

'Oh Sam, by the way, I've been meaning to ask you – it seems such a long time ago now that you came in here the first time –'

Only a couple of weeks, I thought. But then, Shelley went so fast that to her a couple of weeks were someone else's couple of months.

' – but are you still thinking about what you told me then, all that stuff about Lee and the secret lover and so on? Because I told Judith after I talked to you – I was quite fired up about it myself – and she poured so much cold water on it that I felt completely deflated. Mixed metaphors.'

I was eating a Mocha Macaroon Fancy, and I deliberately waited to finish it and lick the crumbs off my fingers until I answered, wanting to see if she looked preoccupied, waiting for my response. But there was nothing in her face but curiosity.

I shook my head.

'I was a bit fired up myself after Lee's death,' I said. 'Looking back, I expect I wanted to blame someone, or make it seem more complicated than it was. It seemed such a waste for Lee to die that way. But that's how it must have happened. I realised that as soon as I got some perspective on it. And as for her lover, well, that's not really any of my business.'

Shelley looked relieved. 'Oh good,' she said. 'I'll tell Judith. We stirred each other up, didn't we? Conspiracy theories and so on. But things don't really happen like that to people you know. Especially to someone like Lee.'

Judith, I thought, would know better, if Clifford Hammond had been in touch with her; but she wouldn't disillusion Shelley. Judith knew her friend too well to trust her with information like this. If Shelley had been in the know I would never have been hired in the first place. And once it had been done, Judith must have decided it would be more suspicious to cancel it than to let me stay. Even introducing me to the Hammonds herself, what a nice piece of bluff that had been. And it had almost worked. If Walter Quincy hadn't been such an incompetent shadow, or if Laura Archer hadn't got in touch with me . . .

I would go to see Laura Archer this evening. She was my only link left with the Hammonds. Somehow I didn't think they would be confiding in me any further.

* * *

Richard at the shippers had misplaced some of the documents I had sent him last week and the resulting confusion took a while to sort out. There was nothing more boring than the shipping details – no wonder Shelley was so keen to pass them on to me. An hour later I got round to photocopying the list of stolen prints Shelley had given me. I put the original in an envelope and got out the insurance file to check the company's address. I could file the copy of the list at the same time. How efficient.

Two young men were wandering round the gallery. I could tell they were art students by the supercilious air both of them affected; it said that they were easily capable of producing infinitely better stuff than this commercial rubbish any day of the week. One of them had long greasy hair, and he kept scratching his scalp. White flakes of dandruff were already scattered over the shoulders of his greatcoat.

I addressed and stamped the envelope, chucking it in the post tray, and put the copy of the print list in the file. Then I took it out again. Something on it had just caught my attention. Two of the entries were for prints imaginatively called *Untitled VIII* and *Untitled X* by Philip Guthrie. Where had I seen his name before? I didn't remember seeing his prints before, but then I had been so busy hanging the exhibition I had hardly looked at the contents of the print stand.

No, it wasn't that. I strained at the memory and brought it into focus, blurred, but still recognisable. Catherine Hammond, at the opening, had asked me if we had any Guthrie prints in stock. Now of course I knew that she had been trying to distract me from going outside to check on the arrival of their driver and walking straight into Walter Quincy. Walter must have told her that I had given him the slip and that it was possible I had caught a glimpse of his face. She would have panicked at the thought that I might see him and connect him with her. And it had worked; she had sent me in the other direction instead, into the back office, while she ran out herself to tell Walter they were on their way out. And that was why Walter had been late that evening; he had been outside all along but unable to come in for fear of bumping into me.

But when I had looked up Philip Guthrie, the file cards had said that all of his prints had been sold. Now two of them were appearing on the list of stolen prints. How could that have happened? I went into the back office to get the box of artist file cards and brought it out to the front desk.

Rifling through it, I found that the cards I had seen at the opening had disappeared. Their replacements were identical to the originals in every respect but one: they no longer bore the note in Harriet's handwriting that they had already been sold – well before the robbery had taken place.

20

I paused outside Harriet's front door for a moment, swept by a sense of guilt. As soon as I had heard about the robbery I had assumed that Nat had been responsible – Nat, who last night had been wearing a raincoat like the one Harriet described, whose business activities were shrouded in mystery and who I had met wandering round the gallery when he had never shown any interest in modern art since; what had he been doing there if not casing the place? Now he was off the hook I was embarrassed by the conclusion I had drawn. He'd never know, but I'd still buy him a six-pack by way of atonement.

The label next to the bell said 'J. Mitchell'. Damn: I hadn't realised she lived with Johnny. Well, perhaps he was still at work. I pressed the bell anyway. After a few moments the front door swung open and Harriet stood in the doorway.

'Oh, hello, Sam!' she said, surprised to see me.

She didn't look too well. There were dark circles under her eyes and the skin of her face was tired; it had a sallow, unhealthy tint. She wasn't wearing any make-up and her hair, pulled back to the nape of her neck with one of those elastic-centred scrunches of material, lacked lustre. She had on her customary jeans and a big sloppy sweater over the top which probably belonged to Johnny. Comfort dressing.

'Can I come in?' I said.

'Of course.'

She led me into the living-room. It was a bachelor den with excrement-brown leather sofas and a dark green carpet. On the far wall was mounted a large oar painted with lavender and green stripes. Beneath it hung several framed photographs of a rowing eight in action, oars blurred with motion. Johnny sat at four. He was covered with sweat and looked very much like a tortured pig.

'Do you want a drink or something?' Harriet said rather nervously.

'No thanks. Is Johnny due back soon?'

She shook her head.

'Good, then we can talk in peace. Do you know what I've come about?' I sat down on one of the sofas. The leather was slippery and it was hard to get a purchase.

'No!' Harriet said unconvincingly. 'Are you here for something? I thought you just dropped in for a chat.'

'I'm afraid not. It's about the prints that were stolen from the gallery.' I was watching her closely. 'I went back and checked the file cards. You've made new ones for a couple of the Philip Guthries. Originally you'd marked them as sold. That's what made me realise what had happened.'

'I – I don't know what you're talking about,' she said helplessly. She was one of the worst liars I'd ever met, so incompetent it was almost endearing.

'Come on, Harriet. Just last week those prints were marked in your handwriting as having been sold. Then suddenly, whoops, the entire contents of the print stand were stolen while you were in the back office – sorry about that, everyone – and now the Guthrie prints have cards saying they're still in stock, and they appear on the list of stolen prints. I haven't talked to Shelley or Judith yet, but if I did, I'm sure they'd say that it was you who put the Guthries down on the list for the insurance company.'

I paused, to see if Harriet wanted to say anything. She didn't.

'It's a nice little racket,' I continued. 'A print goes missing here and there; you mark it down as having been sold so no-one goes searching for it in the short term, and you hope that by the time of the next stocktaking, when you change the card to say that the print is still in the gallery, no-one will remember that it was supposed to have been sold. There's so much through-trade from day to day that that's perfectly possible. And by the time you come to stocktake, it's easy to account for a few missing prints; they might have fallen out of their mounts and been caught down the back of another one, or maybe even been nicked. Everyone accepts a little wastage. Or, if you're doing the stocktaking yourself, it's even easier. No-one even notices the prints are missing.'

The dark circles under Harriet's eyes seemed to have deepened.

'I wondered why you'd bothered to stage the theft at all,' I continued, 'but then I remembered that Shelley told me at the opening that she wanted to do an extra stocktaking in just a couple of weeks. Usually that doesn't happen till August, does it? You should have been perfectly safe. You might not even have been working in the gallery next August, and no-one would haul you back if you weren't still working there to ask about a couple of prints that went missing ages ago. But this was much too soon. You couldn't take the risk of bluffing it out when anyone asked you about the Guthries – your face would have given you away at once. So you decided to stage a robbery. What did you say?'

Harriet had whispered something I hadn't caught. She said again, 'It wasn't me.'

'Come on, Harriet,' I said sharply. 'If it wasn't you, who else was it? It's your writing on the cards and you were in the gallery when the prints were supposed to have been stolen—'

'I mean it wasn't me who started it,' she said, looking miserable. 'I wouldn't have done it, I wouldn't have even thought of it on my own . . .'

She burst out crying. I went into the kitchen, did a quick forage and returned with a roll of kitchen paper, which I plunked down in front of her. Sympathetic, caring, that's me. I provide my interrogatees with something to cry into.

'So who did think of it?' I said. I believed her automatically. I should have known that Harriet would never have done something like this on her own. Not because she had morals – because she lacked initiative.

'I met him at a party.' She snuffled up some tears, and tore off a large wedge of paper to mop up the traces. 'We got talking. Johnny wasn't there. So, you know, we had a lot to drink, and he had some grass on him. We got pretty out of it. And I was telling him about Johnny, what I told you, how difficult it is when he expects me to come out to all these expensive places and pay for myself.'

She stared up at me woefully.

'I left college with a huge overdraft, you see. I couldn't earn money in the last year because I was so busy getting ready for finals. My bank manager had frozen my account, they'd stopped my Access card, and Johnny was insisting

on going out to all these places, restaurants, clubs . . .
Anyway, he asked me how much I earned, and said that it
was a disgrace to pay me so little, that they were
exploiting me. I agreed at the time. Well, I was a bit
pissed. He made it all sound so convincing, like Shelley
and Judith really were ripping me off.'

She must have seen my face, because she hastened to
add, 'Of course, I know that's not true. Loads of people
want jobs in art galleries, and I was lucky to have one. But
it's easy to make yourself think that you're owed
something, isn't it? Especially when nothing seems to be
going right anywhere else in your life.'

This last miserable sentence set her off crying again.

All in a rush, she said, 'I didn't really think it would be
so easy, you know? It was so . . . easy. I waited till I was
left to lock up one evening and then I just put one of the
Guthrie prints in a big bag and walked out with it. I wrote
on the card that it had been sold and no-one even noticed.
It wasn't in the print stand, it was in a folder in the print
cabinet. I was terrified for a month, and then I just forgot
all about it. Shelley had done the stocktaking at the
beginning of August and I didn't think there'd be another
one till the middle of next year, like you said. I gave it to
him and he sold it to a dealer who he said wouldn't ask
questions. I got £250.'

'And after a while you took another one.'

Harriet looked as if I had hit her.

'My overdraft was more than three grand,' she said
plaintively, 'let alone the Access bill. All the £250 did was
calm down my bank manager for a while. But it didn't last.
So when he rang me up again, I was grateful. It was like
he was helping me. And it was much easier the second
time. There's another one you don't know about, too. One

by Petra Debray. I took three altogether. By the end it was almost like a routine.'

She blew her nose.

'Then it all happened like you said. Shelley said we were going to do an early stocktaking and I panicked. I rang him up and he told me to keep cool, that she couldn't prove anything, but I knew I couldn't convince her. I knew that if she asked me if I'd seen the prints anywhere I'd blurt it all out. He was the one who thought of the robbery. And it worked, didn't it? Shelley thought I was so upset because I'd let her down, not because I was involved. You're the only one who guessed. But you must believe me, Sam, I said to him that it was all over, after that. I got a terrible scare. Even if you hadn't found out, I wouldn't have done it again. I'm not really cut out for that kind of thing.'

I bet he didn't try to change her mind. Harriet was a risky accomplice; he was lucky that she hadn't already cracked and spilled everything to the police.

'Has he rung you up yet with an arrangement to meet you, to give you your share?' I asked.

She shook her head mutely. The information didn't surprise me.

'So why don't you tell me his name?' I said. 'Though I've got a pretty good idea already.'

I had cancelled the idea of the six-pack by now, for obvious reasons.

Harriet stared at me worshipfully. 'You know everything!' she said. 'Of course, I forgot for a moment you knew him!'

'Biblically.'

She looked confused. 'That's how I met him in the first place, at that house where Lee died. There was another party a while ago that I went to, and I met him there. His girlfriend was away and I ended up staying the night.'

She blushed.

'I quite liked him, actually,' she said. 'I was a bit disappointed when she came back unexpectedly the next morning and Paul had to bundle me out so she didn't see me – Sam? Are you OK?'

I was staring at her in disbelief.

'You're telling me it was Paul Perry who got you into stealing the prints?' I said.

Her expression was blank. 'Of course,' she said. 'Who else did you think it was?'

I decided not to answer.

'Are you going to tell Shelley and Judith?' Harriet said nervously. She didn't mention the possibility of my telling the police, I noticed. Nor had she mentioned that she would be resigning forthwith.

'You're not planning to stay on at the gallery, are you, Harriet?' I said disbelievingly. She looked sheepish. Clearly she had been.

'Absolutely not. Go in there tomorrow morning and resign,' I said firmly. 'If you don't, I'll tell them everything.'

'It's just—'

'What?'

'Well, if I resign I don't get unemployment benefit for six weeks. It's the new rule.'

'Oh, for God's sake, Harriet!' The top of my skull nearly exploded with pent-up annoyance. 'Don't you realise what you've got yourself in the middle of?' I demanded, jumping up and striding up and down the room. 'Just try for a moment, if you can bend what passes for your brain that far, to imagine what it'd look like to the police.'

'The police?' Harriet repeated, as if she'd never heard the word before.

'Of course the bloody police, you stupid twat!' I came to a halt in front of Harriet and stared down at her menacingly. 'You've committed theft on not one occasion – which you could plead as a momentary impulse – but three. Three. If it went to court you'd be put away. This is not some little game that went wrong. If the insurance company hadn't believed your story, Shelley and Judith would be short of stock worth fifty grand. And if you hadn't panicked in the first place, and decided to stage the robbery, they would have written off the prints you'd already stolen as missing and never seen back any money for them at all, because they couldn't claim for wastage. I don't suppose you gave that a second thought.'

'I didn't mean—'

'No, don't bother with excuses. You know, the thing that really gets to me is that it was Shelley and Judith you stole from. I mean, if they had been terrible bosses who sexually harassed you or made you work appalling hours, I could understand it better. But from them, there's no excuse. They trust you and treat you well. You have no justification at all, do you?'

Harriet's head was hanging in shame; she didn't even try to answer me. I hoped I had thrown enough of a scare into her to make her think twice before trying anything like this again.

'OK, I've said my piece.' I was softening slightly. 'Now, I'll tell you what's going to happen. You go in tomorrow morning and hand in your resignation.'

I wouldn't tell her that Shelley had been on the verge of firing her anyway.

'Don't get into contact with Paul any more,' I continued. 'If he rings you, hang up. That's the condition on which I'm helping you. If I learn that the two of you have been in communication, I'll go straight to Shelley and Judith. And they'll go straight to the police.'

I wasn't as sure of this as I sounded. Shelley and Judith would probably cover up the whole thing; I doubted their insurance would cover theft by one of their own employees. But I wasn't going to tell Harriet that. I saw her body freeze in tension as I mentioned the police, and I was satisfied.

'All right?' I said. 'Is that a deal?'

Harriet's head lifted. She had been crying again and her face was damp with tears.

'Yes, I promise. He's in Manchester, anyway,' she said. 'He left the day after we . . .' Her voice tailed off.

'OK.'

'I don't understand why you're helping me, Sam,' she said forlornly. 'Why don't you just tell them now?'

'I don't know,' I admitted. 'But I've done some pretty stupid things in my time. It doesn't mean I'm a hardened criminal.'

I felt horribly embarrassed all of a sudden. I was shifting my feet around on the carpet like a tough little boy caught by his friends in the act of doing a good deed. I shrugged.

'Let's just say that I don't like the idea of grassing on someone, and leave it at that, shall we?'

I left before she could thank me. Grateful people make my toes curl.

21

It was raining heavily when I left Harriet's flat. Maybe it was the rain that brought into my mind an image of a weather-clock I was given for my birthday, many, many years ago. It was a little Swiss chalet with two archways for doors and a barometer between them. When rain was predicted a man slid through one of the archways, wearing a bowler hat and an umbrella; for the sunshine, the man retreated and a smiling bare-headed woman in a dirndl skirt took his place. The figures were fixed to a single piece of wood. As it revolved, one figure went out while the other was carried inside. It was impossible for both to emerge at the same time.

Driving home, I thought that Claire and Paul were like that couple; when one goes in, the other comes out. I had suspected Claire at first and now that she seemed to be ruled out, Paul had taken her place in the limelight. I had been so sure Nat had stolen the prints that I hadn't thought of anyone else. But Paul had been there that very afternoon, hanging around, waiting to see if Shelley would leave and give him and Harriet the opportunity they needed to stage the robbery. He had to be there – if he'd let Harriet do it on her own she would have messed it up somehow. And when he had seen me he had reacted brilliantly, pretending it was me he wanted to see all along. I should have realised it wasn't true at once; hadn't he known already that it was my day off? And then mentioned that we had bumped into each other, when his story was that he had come on purpose to see me?

There was a more serious side to this. If Lee had found out about the stolen prints, would Paul have killed her to keep her quiet? That I didn't believe. It was too much of a risk for too minor an offence. Paul was not the type to lose his cool.

But perhaps he had taken Lee down to the end of the garden to try to persuade her not to tell Shelley and Judith about the stolen prints. Perhaps she had refused, and in anger he had made a threatening gesture; Lee, stepping back to avoid it, might have stumbled over a brick, fallen and hit her head on another.

That was how I wanted to picture the events leading up to her death. I wanted to believe that it had been a fatal accident. Not for Paul's sake, but for Lee's. I did not want to imagine someone luring her down to the part of the garden where the remains of the barbecue were lying, discarded, on the ground, retrieving a brick from its position on the bald grass and waiting for their moment to hit her over the head with it, hard and fast. I did not want to think of the same person leaning over her dead or dying body, checking to make sure that they had struck hard enough. Waiting beside her, keeping silent, heart racing; waiting until her pulse stopped beating and her blood stopped flowing. I shivered.

I was home. I parked in the usual place, across the road from my studio in a disused driveway. The rain was still coming down, but more gently now. The sky was draining itself out. Tomorrow, if London was lucky, there would be clear skies over the city.

I switched off the engine and got out, pulling my mackintosh snugly around me. The PVC material squeaked in familiar protest as I drew the belt tightly around the waist of the coat; but it seemed to me that, even with the falling rain, the noise of plastic on plastic was unusually loud in the quiet street. I looked around me quickly, but could see nothing suspicious. That didn't prove a thing. The street was poorly lit and there were some shadows on the far pavement which could have been cast by anything at all. My right hand slid into my jeans pocket and closed over the hilt of my little flick knife. I'm no Boy Scout, but I like to be prepared.

I crossed the street slowly, looking around me, my other hand holding the door keys so I could get inside the studio fast. There was a humming sound to my right; one of the factories next door working a late shift. That meant there would be people around. I felt safer.

With a sudden blinding flash a pair of headlights switched full on, dazzling me as if I had just stepped into a searchlight. Too late I realised that the sound I had heard wasn't industrial machinery, but an engine ticking over. The car surged out from its parking space and hurtled towards me where I stood in the middle of the road, presenting a perfect target.

For a split second I knew exactly how a paralysed rabbit feels. Transfixed by the headlights, I was trapped between them as if they would sear me if I crossed them, not knowing which way to jump. My death had come to meet me and all I could do was stand still.

Then, like a great force gathering in the pit of my stomach, my will surged upwards and took hold of me. I didn't want to die. I wouldn't die. The car was almost upon me. I could feel its hot breath panting towards me as if it were a giant animal with huge burning eyes. I threw myself to the side of the road in a sudden desperate leap, bracing my whole body against the blow that I was about to receive.

I don't know if I would have made it or not. Sometimes I think that I would have done. I ended up well to the side of the road, after all, half under my own van. Other times I remember how close the bumper of that car seemed, how I was engulfed in the beam of its headlights, and I don't believe that I would have survived on my own.

I wasn't expecting to be hit so soon. Almost at once something smashed into me, all down the length of my body, and threw me off-balance. I was flying through the air, further than I had thrown myself, and I knew that this was it: I was dead. The air whirled around me and my ears were full of the sound of squealing tyres. Simultaneously, the headlights flashed past and I crashed to earth, gasping for breath as if I had just run a marathon. I was still conscious and for a moment I thought that I had died but wasn't aware of it yet, that my brain had disassociated itself from my body and was floating just above it.

That made sense. Parts of my body didn't seem to be mine. I was lying half on the tarmac and half on something else, and the arm beneath me wouldn't move no matter how I tried to bend the fingers. Oh God, I had lost an arm. Not my right arm, please God.

Then the arm moved by itself, as if it had taken on a life of its own. I stared at it in horror and disbelief. It suddenly occurred to me that the car might come back; that its driver might want to check if I was already dead or whether it was necessary to reverse back over me. Perhaps I could throw the disembodied arm on whoever it was. That would freak them out. I started to sit up and caught my breath in pain.

'Sam! Sam, are you all right? Sam!'

'Aaaah!' I screamed in shock. The body I was half-lying on jumped. I turned my head and found myself looking directly into Nat's face.

It all happened so fast, clear and sharp as the momentary outline of a lightning flash against grey clouds. In a second Nat had dragged himself from under me and we were both craning our heads round the side of the van, trying to catch a glimpse of the car that had tried to run me down. All we could see was a glimmer of red tail light vanishing round the corner.

Nat sat on the hard tarmac and swore, systematically and thoroughly. He did this for longer than the time it had taken for the whole attempt on my life. I was no slouch at cursing myself, but I was impressed by his facility. He cursed as if he could kill the driver of the car just by the power of his words, as if he had their neck between his hands and were slowly strangling them to death. Relief takes people in different ways. I found I was pounding my fist against the tarmac and couldn't stop even when the skin over my knuckles started to break. Rain trickled down my face and washed it clean, pattering onto my raincoat.

Nat was on his feet, holding out his hand to help me get up. It hurt a lot. Nat's eyes were wild. I assumed that we must both still be in shock. He put his arm around my shoulders for support and I clung to his waist. Nothing seemed broken, or at least nothing major. I could walk and so could he, just about. We staggered across the road like a pair of survivors of a nuclear explosion. Looking down, I saw a huge hole in the knee of my jeans.

LAUREN HENDERSON

You'll have to patch that, said my brain, in a detached, sarcastic little voice; ripped jeans haven't been fashionable for years.

* * *

We sat in the hottest bath our torn muscles and grazed skin could bear. I had poured the entire contents of my bottle of Molton Brown Deep Relaxing Bath Oil into the water and for further relaxation we had a bottle of frozen vodka propped on the edge of the bathtub, fast unfreezing in the steam. I was sitting with my back to Nat's chest, our bodies slotted together like spoons, his legs stretched out on either side of mine. Neither of us had said much.

It wasn't just the knee of my jeans which had ripped. I had a large and spectacular graze on the skin beneath, which was gently oozing blood. My gloves looked as if I had attacked them with a cheese grater and my hands weren't in much better shape. There were various bruises and grazes on elbows and knees, and, according to Nat, my back was a Turner sunset.

Neither of us had lost consciousness at all. We didn't have any ringing in the ears and our pupils weren't unusually dilated. We weren't concussed. That meant we didn't have to go to hospital. We hadn't even bothered to discuss ringing the police. I didn't want to, and fortunately Nat wasn't the kind of person to deliberately involve the police in anything.

For once, Nat's bony body seemed warm and comfortable. Perhaps it was the water lapping around us. I leaned back against his ribs, nuzzling the back of my head into his collarbone. His arms closed around my waist, loosely at first and then they tightened, holding me so snugly that I could hardly breathe. I winced in pain.

'Nat?' I swivelled my head to look up at him. It hurt badly. 'Nat, you're hurting me.'

His face was a mask of anger, his eyes burning green like pools of acid that could eat up the skin around them. His hair was damp and clung to his skull like a cap. He looked as if he were a thousand miles away, stamping with both feet on the head of the driver of the car.

But he heard me. His grip on my waist loosened at once and he bent his head to kiss the point of my shoulder.

'I'm sorry,' he said, letting out a deep breath. 'I was just thinking . . .'

He let the sentence trail off. We both knew what he meant. He picked up the bar of soap and began, slowly, to wash my back.

I remembered a friend of mine who had been hit by a car. Up into the air she had gone, the car catching her hip and sending her spinning, red hair flying loose, red silk skirt flapping, like a doll tossed away by a bored child. And she had landed like a doll, too, legs outspread in front of her, hands behind her, sitting in the middle of the road. For a moment her face was the smooth ivory mask of a china doll, as if any moment her head would loll sideways and her body would crumple. Then the face opened, her mouth stretched wide by an angry scream. She wasn't a doll any longer. She was like a little girl, furious with the world about what had just happened. I had known at that moment that she would be all right.

There was hardly a mark on her. Even her skirt had remained undamaged. I wished I could say the same about myself.

It was the first night that we slept together without making love. We curled up together, carefully at first, easing ourselves into positions in which our bruised bodies felt the minimum of discomfort. Settled at last, in the dark, our involuntary gasps of pain turned imperceptibly into the soft noises of sleep.

'Nat?' I said as we were drifting off. 'Did you just save my life?'

He let out a breath against my ear, warm and scented of his roll-up cigarettes.

Then he said, 'I don't know. You were already jumping when I cannoned into you. You might have made it on your own. No thanks to that drunken moron behind the wheel, though.'

'There's a Chinese saying: if you save someone else's life, then you become responsible for them.'

'Yes,' he said. 'I've heard that too.'

Then we fell asleep.

22

For a moment when I awoke the next day I thought I had been to the gym the day before, doing a particularly punishing set of exercises. Then I remembered what had happened.

It took me two hours and four cups of coffee to get dressed. I did some stretches, trying to ease out my muscles as much as I could. Then I covered every part that hurt with Tiger Balm. I got Nat to do my back. It would have hurt too much to do it myself. I put on my leather jeans, on the principle that they were so constricting themselves that they would stop me making any sudden painful movements. Then a hooded sweater and a padded jerkin over the top. Ready for action. As long as it was only sixty beats per minute.

Nat said I should have stayed in bed. He had it worse than me; his collarbone was a mass of bruises and welts and he was lucky it wasn't broken.

I kept my eye on the rear-view mirror as I drove to Putney. I hadn't been able to see the make of the car last night so everyone behind me was automatically suspect. I doubled back a couple of times but no-one seemed to be on my tail. Maybe they didn't expect me to be up and about so soon.

I hadn't known whether Laura Archer would be at work or not. It was Saturday but for all I knew she could still be at the bank, writing letters to people who had gone overdrawn and charging them £10 each for the service. Or whatever it was that she did at the Wallenstein Trust. The porch had been swept recently and featured a wire milk-bottle container with the arrow pointing to '2', a boot-scraper and a doormat. Very comprehensive.

The door was answered by a man who resembled a model in the Next catalogue. He looked at me as if I were a Jehovah's Witness, but said politely enough that his wife was in and showed me into the living-room. I gave him my name. It meant nothing to him. Laura Archer probably ran her marriage on a strictly need-to-know basis.

The room was furnished comfortably but anonymously, reminding me of a show house in a suburban development for well-paid commuters. I sat down in an armchair. Mr Archer disappeared and in a short while brisk footsteps came down the hallway and Mrs Archer entered the living-room. She shut the door behind her and stood with her back to it.

'I told you not to contact me at home,' she said without preamble. Her tone of voice was as crisp as if she were reprimanding an inefficient cleaning lady.

'I would have contacted you at the office,' I said, 'if I'd known which one you'd be at.'

There was a pause. Then she came over from the door, picked up some cigarettes from a side table and lit one. She didn't sit down.

After taking a long slow drag she said, 'All right, I won't beat around the bush. You've found out I work at Wallenstein's.'

'For Clifford Hammond,' I added.

'I should never have done it,' she said as if to herself. 'I should have known it was a bad idea.'

'Why did you agree to do it, then?' I said.

This took her completely by surprise; she was lost for words. It gave me the key to the mystery.

'Oh, I see. Clifford Hammond didn't ask you to talk to me, did he?' I said slowly. 'You did it behind his back. The fact that you could borrow an empty office at McCott Shaw was convenient for you not just because it concealed from me the fact that you were actually working for him. It kept him from knowing that you had made contact with me.'

I looked at her. It was obvious from her face that I had guessed right.

'It suited you in lots of ways, didn't it?' I said. 'If you got hold of them, you would really win his trust. It wouldn't technically be blackmail, but you could have asked him for anything you wanted and he would have given it to you. Like a high-powered job at the bank. I hear that's what you were angling for.'

I couldn't help admiring her. She took it on the chin.

'My offer still holds,' she said coolly. 'I would be prepared to meet your price.'

'What makes you think I have a price at all?'

'But why else did you go to the gallery Clifford co-owns?' she said. 'And tell that story about wanting to find Mrs Jackson's lover? When Mrs Frank told Clifford he assumed at once that you had the letters and were trying to sound out whether he would buy them back.'

'So why didn't he get in touch with me himself?'

She took another pull on the cigarette. 'He wanted to let things ride for a while, to see what happened,' she said. 'I saw an opportunity to help him out.'

'Hmmn. What did Catherine Hammond have to say about this?'

Another blank stare.

'Oh yes, I was forgetting the limited communication lines between Mr and Mrs Hammond. They're worse than Charles and Di, wouldn't you say? So of course Clifford didn't tell Catherine about me. She must have found out somehow, though. She sent Walter Quincy to follow me.'

'He was poison,' Laura Archer said unexpectedly. 'Always snooping through everything when your back was turned. Clifford wanted her to sack him but she wouldn't. Walter was totally loyal to her. She didn't want to give that up.'

A thought had just struck me.

'How do you know,' I said, 'that I haven't approached Catherine Hammond with the letters? For all you know I could have the two of you bidding against each other to push up the price.'

'What *is* your price?' she said, coming straight to the point.

'Like I said to you before, Mrs Archer, it isn't money. It's information. If you tell me who killed Lee Jackson and Walter Quincy, who searched Lee's flat the morning after she died—'

'You're saying Walter didn't kill himself?' She looked horrified. 'But he was clinically depressed. He was on medication for it. The police are treating it as suicide.'

'I was there, Mrs Archer. I saw him fall. He went straight down the side of the building like a sack of potatoes – he didn't flail the air or even put his hands out to save himself. I think he was dead when he went through the window. Someone broke his neck and shoved him out to make it look like an accident. Just like Lee Jackson's death. That looked like an accident too, didn't it?'

Laura Archer had gone as white as her shirt. The hand that held the cigarette was trembling.

'I'm going to ask you to leave,' she said in a voice that had lost its usual calm.

'What if I say I'll go straight to Clifford Hammond and tell him what you've been doing behind his back?'

It didn't work. She made a small gesture with her hand as if to dismiss the objection. Ash from the cigarette scattered on the carpet. She didn't even notice.

'Just remember, Mrs Archer,' I said, 'you could be in danger if you're too involved in this. Look what's happened to two people already.'

She shook her head. It was definite. She wasn't going to talk to me any more. There was nothing for me to do but leave.

* * *

It was mid-afternoon. Thanks to the new improved licensing laws the pubs were open and I cruised around the side-streets till I found a quiet-looking one. My back was hurting badly and I wanted some medicine.

It was a pretty little pub on a back street with benches outside and pot plants hanging from the eaves. There was a sign up outside which asked customers to leave quietly and not disturb the neighbours. I took it that was a coded request not to relieve oneself over their garden walls. The street had a village atmosphere, with a couple of small shops opposite the pub and a postbox in front of them.

I bought a double vodka and tonic and took it outside. It wasn't exactly the season for alfresco drinking, but inside was smoky and close and I was too sore from my strains and bruises to care much about the weather. I eased myself down onto one of the benches, wincing with the effort, and drank half down in one gulp. I felt better.

A few cars drove by. Along the other side of the street was a woman walking her dog. She wore a padded khaki Barbour jacket and a silk scarf was knotted round her neck. The dog was a small poodle, clipped to resemble a pumped-up body-builder in an alpaca suit. It trotted neatly along in front of her, its bottom clenched tightly. They crossed the road and came slowly towards the pub.

The woman was fishing for something in her pocket.

'Stop, Daisy,' she said, pulling the poodle to a halt in front of the postbox. 'Wait for Mummy.'

Daisy expressed her feelings by squatting down on her back legs, each of which was adorned with a white clump of hair like a pompom, and relieving herself against the pillar box. Mummy found her letter, pushed it through the slot and pulled Daisy away in mid-flow. Daisy hopped along for a few steps, before she got her balance, probably dribbling down her leg.

Something about the scene was familiar to me. I stared at the postbox, wondering what it could be. Then I realised it was the postbox itself with its domed top, the slot beneath, its stumpy Greek pillar-shape . . .

Completely forgetting the pain I was in, I ran to the van and started it up with hands trembling as much as Laura Archer's had done. I was lucky not to be arrested as I tore across London, tyres screeching round corners, jumping lights where I could. Stephen gave me the keys to the studio without bothering to come himself. I tore down the path to the studio as if I were racing against the clock.

Once I knew what I was looking for, it seemed too simple. I walked up to the Leo sculpture. With hindsight, I could see that the face of the lioness, although deliberately disguised by the stylised technique, was that of Catherine Hammond. I knew too that if I looked at the archer I would see a resemblance to Lee.

I put my hand into the slot on the Leo pillar. It was narrow, and I had to manoeuvre my fingers and then my palm through the gap slowly, but I have small hands. Inside, with the tips of my fingers, suspended below the hole itself so that I had not been able to see it before, I felt a structure like a plastic mesh hanging basket. I worked my hand further through the slot, wincing as the sharp metal edges began to cut into my forearm. Then my probing fingers touched not metal, but paper, and I knew that I had found Catherine Hammond's letters.

These two pillars were not, as I had assumed before, the first ones in a Zodiac-influenced series, but complete in themselves. Lee had designed them on a scale that was similar, but not exactly parallel to that of a real postbox. The domed tops were the closest point of reference. And, of course, the postal slots.

23

I put the letters into the pocket of my jerkin. Then I changed my mind, took them out again and stuffed them inside my sweater. I was wearing a body by way of underwear and I worked the letters down inside it till they lay over my stomach. I wouldn't be able to bend over or sit down quickly but then I couldn't do either of those things anyway without screaming in pain.

I returned the keys to Stephen Baldring, telling him that I had found the missing sketches. Out of curiosity, I asked him if Lee had ever discussed with him her work in progress.

'Oh yes, of course,' he said affably. 'She often used to come up here for a drink when she had finished for the day. Recently she was very enthusiastic. I hadn't seen her like that before. She was very pleased with her current project.'

'Those two pillars.'

'That's right, the pillar boxes. Though that wasn't their proper title. She called them something more whimsical.'

I stared at Stephen with a kind of masochistic fascination. If it turned out that he had known all along, that all I had had to do was to ask him . . .

'Do you remember what she called them?' I prompted.

'Oh yes. Well, more or less. It was something along the lines of *Postboxes for Love Letters*. You see what I meant by whimsical.'

I would have hit myself. Only someone had already done that for me.

* * *

I was hungry and I needed to think, so I drove over to the Highgate Tea Rooms and ordered mushrooms and cheese on toast and a pot of tea. I didn't seem to have been doing very well in the fresh vegetable stakes recently. I made a mental note to buy some fruit. Then I made another one, to eat it before it went off. Most of the time I managed Step One but not Step Two.

I was trying to put together three facts: Lee's death, Walter's death and the car attack on me. They were very hard to reconcile. It was plausible to assume that they had all been carried out by the same person. Each followed a similar pattern – a murder, or attempted murder, which was intended to look like an accident – and each had been carried out with a cool head and a high chance of success. Last night, if it hadn't been for Nat, I might well have been killed myself. But if I was looking at a single suspect, the requirements seemed impossibly high. It would be someone who could have come to the party without standing out like a sore thumb; someone connected to the Hammonds, who was strong enough to throw Walter out of a window. All the people in the Hammonds' nexus – themselves, Judith Frank, Laura Archer, Walter – would have been much too obvious at the party. I toyed for a moment with the idea of Clifford Hammond disguised in a long straggly wig and a grungy T-shirt and dismissed it reluctantly.

No-one seemed to fit. Maybe I should try it from another angle; maybe Lee's death really had been an accident, or at least not connected with her affair with

Catherine Hammond. An argument with Paul, say, or even Claire, whose alibi might not be as strong as I had originally thought. After all, Claire might have a stronger tolerance for Valium than Ajay – who was rather naive about drug use – realised. She might have been able to get out of bed after a couple of hours, groggy, but still on the warpath. Which would be after Ajay had seen Lee alive.

That would work. Lee's death would have set off the whole chain of circumstances leading to the Hammonds. But then how would whoever searched her flat have known that she was already dead? The search must have been for the letters. Perhaps the burglar hadn't known Lee was dead but thought she would still be out at the party. Catherine Hammond would have known Lee's movements. Maybe it was she herself, trying to get back her letters. That hardly made sense. Catherine Hammond hadn't approached me about the letters, when everyone had assumed I had them. She didn't seem to care where they were. Someone else, then? But how would anyone else have known Lee was out that night?

I was going round in circles and achieving nothing but a headache. At random I pulled down a book from the shelves next to my head. The Highgate Tea Rooms were on the first floor of a private house and it was like sitting at tables in the living/dining-room of a very eccentric restaurateur; bookshelves and bric-à-brac abounded. I was holding an Agatha Christie in my hand. *At Bertram's Hotel*, a minor part of her oeuvre but nonetheless welcome. I buried my nose in it. I wasn't leaving here until I had finished. Maybe I could pick up pointers from Miss Marple's technique.

* * *

Laura Archer was not at home all that afternoon and evening. Either that, or she wasn't answering the phone. Every time I called I got the answering machine. I was beginning to be concerned. I tried the Wallenstein Trust and McCott Shaw. No joy from either one.

I rang the Hammonds' house. The maid said that they weren't available. I asked if that meant they didn't want to talk to me and she said she didn't understand. Ironic that now I had finally got my paws on the letters, no-one seemed to be around to congratulate me.

I rang off and stared for a while at my kitchen wall. In front of me was a long, narrow picture, painted by a friend at art school. It was a line of fruit: pink apples, blue bananas, green strawberries, purple avocados. They hung from a single black curling vine and looked lusciously ripe but rather bizarre. After a while I shoved my hand down the inside of my body and pulled the letters out. I took down the picture, unclipped the frame and pushed the letters down behind it. As a hiding-place it was mediocre, but it would do for the moment.

The next morning I tried Laura Archer again. By this time I didn't expect any answer at all. I was taken by surprise when she herself answered the phone.

'Mrs Archer?' I said, disproportionately relieved. I only realised now that I had been half-expecting to hear that she had met with an accident. 'It's Sam Jones. I rang you all yesterday— '

She cut through me in a polite voice. 'I'm so sorry,' she said. 'I think you must be mistaking me for my daughter. We do sound rather alike.'

'You're Laura's *mother*?' I said, bemused. What was she doing there? Did she live there too?

'That's right,' she said blithely. 'I'm afraid that Laura isn't here.'

'Do you know where she is?'

'Well, of course!' Laura's mother gave vent to what could only be described as a tinkle of laughter. 'That's why I'm here!'

So she was all right. If not, her mother would scarcely be doing a silver-bell peal impression down the phone. 'Laura's rather dazed by the news, of course,' she was continuing. 'But she's over the moon. So's David. They're both delighted.'

'I'm sorry,' I said frankly. 'I have no idea what you're talking about.'

'Of course, I am silly. There's no reason you should know, it all happened in such a hurry. You must be a friend of Laura's.'

'That's right,' I said unblushingly.

'Well, dear, it's very exciting for her. She rang me up last night, to tell me that she had been offered this very important job in the New York branch of the bank she works for. And apparently it was crucial that she go off to take up this job at once. She's going to be a Vice-President, or something very important-sounding. So she asked me to come in and help her pack, and look after the house till she can organise to have it let or sold. Really, it all happened in the most tearing hurry. I expect that's how these big banks work, though. Next plane to New York, and don't look back!'

The silver bells tinkled again.

'Isn't that rather a nuisance for David?' I said at random.

'Oh, well, he's been freelance for a while anyway. And they both had their hearts set on working in New York.

243

Laura's been hoping this would happen for ages now. Anyway, they're going to be put up in a hotel till the bank finds them an apartment. That's what they call a flat in America, an apartment.'

'I expect you don't know the name of the hotel?' I said, pessimistically. I was right. She didn't. Laura was going to ring her when they arrived.

'I am sorry,' she said again. 'I'm sure she'll be ringing you from New York when she settles in. I hope it was nothing too important?'

'Oh no,' I said. 'Nothing of any importance at all.'

* * *

I had to hand it to Laura Archer. Ideally, of course, what I would have liked to hand her was a grenade with the pin out; but, in lieu of that, she had my reluctant admiration. She had finessed the whole thing as neatly as a run-and-fell seam. She had been scared yesterday. I had seen that. But she had still managed to turn the situation to her advantage. She must have gone straight to Clifford Hammond. Instead of the letters, she had another lever; what she knew. She must have confessed to him that she had been in contact with me, said that I had threatened to publicise everything and that she needed to leave the country so that I could no longer put pressure on her. Clifford would have had no choice but to agree. And thus she had stepped into the job she had been wanting for a long time.

So what did Laura Archer know that made her so dangerous to Clifford Hammond? She had to know something about what had happened to Lee and Walter. If not she would just have dismissed my attempt to frighten her yesterday; after all, one was supposed to have been an

244

accident, the other suicide. Only someone who knew that there was more to it than that would have been scared for her own safety.

But for me it was a brick wall. My only option now was what Clifford Hammond, and maybe Catherine too, had thought I wanted to do all along: to blackmail them. But not for money, as they had thought. For information.

I had my hand on the phone, ready to try the Hammonds again, when it rang, startling me out of all proportion. After I had calmed down slightly, I raised the receiver.

'Sam?' a little voice said nervously. 'Sam, it's Judy. From the co-op?'

'Oh, hi, Judy.' I racked my brains to think why she would be calling me.

'Sam, are you doing anything at the moment? Could you come round?'

'Why?'

She said something in such a low voice I could hardly hear her.

'What?' I said impatiently. I really don't like hippies.

'I can't tell you on the phone!' she whispered loudly.

'Ah.' I understood. There were only two phones in the co-op, one in the hall, the other on an extension lead in the lounge. Neither were exactly private places.

'It's sort of what we were talking about before—'

'You mean Claire? Lee?'

'Sort of—'

'Hold on. I'll be there at once.'

24

'Open it. Go on.'

Judy had plonked a parcel in my lap and was sitting watching me, nervously fiddling with the end of her plait. She was wearing a nasty sweater and a big felt skirt appliquéd with further coloured pieces of the same material, like Fuzzy Felt shapes. I wondered if she'd made it herself. Probably. Instead of being hemmed it had been cut inexpertly with pinking shears.

I started to unwrap the parcel. It was long and flat, like several sheets of cardboard wrapped up in brown paper.

'Is it really this shape, or are we playing Pass the Parcel?' I said flippantly. Judy frowned. She hadn't even offered me a cup of tea. It must be serious.

I pulled off the paper. Inside was a big sheet of cardboard, bent in half to make a rough folder. I opened it up. Then I was bereft of words. Inside the folder were what looked to me at first glance very like the prints that had been stolen from Shelley Frank Fine Art.

They were all in mounts, held in with stamp paper. Someone, presumably Paul, had placed a sheet of protective tissue paper over each print and then closed the mount over it to hold it in place. I checked a couple of them, remembering the list in the gallery. No question, these were the ones.

I closed the folder and looked up at Judy, shifting position slightly. The floorboards weren't any more comfortable this time round.

'Do you know what these are?' I said incredulously.

'They're from the gallery where you work, aren't they?'

'But what are you doing with them? Hasn't Paul gone by now?' I hadn't got a grip on this at all. Harriet had told me that Paul had already left for Manchester; surely he would have taken the prints with him.

Judy's pointed nose was already pink, but then so were her eyes. She looked like a mouse who has been doing a lot of crying.

'That's why I did it,' she said, looking down at her hands. 'I couldn't bear it that he was leaving with her, after everything that had happened . . . they were quarrelling all the time, too, things weren't any better between them . . . why didn't he stay? He could have stayed! And after everything he said to me—'

'How far had things gone between you?'

She blushed. Now her whole face was pink. At least it evened things up a bit.

'That far. I see.'

'He asked me if he could put these in my room for a while. He didn't tell me what they were, I mean, they were all wrapped up. He just said they were important. When Claire gets cross she throws things around, and he didn't want to leave them in their room.'

'So if he didn't tell you what they were, how did you know?'

'I listened in on a phone conversation,' she said, looking embarrassed. 'I didn't really mean to eavesdrop but this girl Harriet rang up for him. I took the call, and I thought—'

'You were jealous.'

She nodded. 'So I picked up the other phone when he was talking. It wasn't what I thought it was. She was really upset – she was saying that the gallery was about to do a check of the prints and they'd notice some were gone. Paul told her to pull herself together but she just got worse, so finally he said—'

I cut Judy short. Her whiny little voice was getting on my nerves.

'The fake burglary. I know about it.'

'Oh.' She was disappointed. 'Anyway, I guessed what they were when he gave them to me to hide, but I didn't tell him I knew. And then he said he was leaving with Claire. I was so miserable, I still can't believe it . . .' Judy looked worn out, as if she had no more tears left to cry.

'But why didn't he take them with him?'

She ducked her head again. 'He thinks he has,' she said softly. 'I made another parcel which looked just like this and gave it to him instead. Only it's just got cardboard inside.'

My hand went up to my mouth to hide a giggle. I was impressed.

'I want you to take them,' she said. 'You can take them back to the gallery.'

'No,' I said patiently, 'I can post them back anonymously. I'd look pretty silly walking in with them under my arm, wouldn't I?'

'Why? Oh yes, I see.'

Despite the neat way she had turned the tables on Paul, Judy would always be a few joss-sticks short of a packet.

'Judy,' I said thoughtfully, 'while you were listening in, did Paul or Harriet say anything about Lee finding out about the stolen prints? Or later on, did Paul say anything about it?'

249

Judy shook her head. Then she realised why I had asked. Her eyes widened.

'You don't think—'

'I don't know what I think any more.'

Judy still looked like a mouse. But now it was a frightened one.

* * *

While I was here, I decided to drop in on Tom. I thought I'd tell him he was forgiven for being a touchy bastard. He was in his room, hunched over his desk like an actor playing Richard III, pen disappearing between his huge banana fingers.

'Hello, Sammy,' he said gloomily.

'Haiku keeping?'

Tom didn't even flinch. Normally when I mocked the sacred Muse of Poetry he would hold up his crossed index fingers at me and thunder 'Antichrist!' in his deepest bass voice. It must have been going pretty badly.

'I'm going to pack it all in and become a primary teacher,' he said. 'I'm really going to do it this time. I've got to face it – I'll never be as good as Tony Harrison.'

I tried to think of something to cheer him up.

'You could marry a glamorous opera singer,' I suggested, 'like Tony. Get some inspiration that way.'

'What the fuck are you talking about?'

'He's married to Teresa Stratas, didn't you know? You could hitch up with Montserrat Caballé.'

'Who's that singer on the ENO posters?' Tom was brightening up. 'The normal-sized one with the nice bottom?'

'Lesley Jarrett?'

'Yes. I'll marry her. The others would cost too much to feed.'

'She's not a blonde, though.'

'She'd just have to dye her hair,' Tom said firmly. 'I would insist.'

'I'm sure if you turned on the full spotlight of your manly charm—'

'I could introduce you to that guy on the other ENO poster, the muscly one,' Tom said generously. 'He's a stagehand or something. We could double-date – me and Lesley, you and Mr Muscle.'

Tom has a very good idea of my sexual tastes.

'Talking about dating—' I began. He cut me off abruptly.

'Julia and I have agreed just to be friends.'

There was a little pause.

'Want to hear a blonde joke?' I offered. 'What's a blonde's chat-up line at a party?'

'Don't know.'

' "Hello, I'm drunk!" '

I got a grudging smile.

* * *

By coincidence I bumped into Julia Seddon in the courtyard as I was leaving. She smiled at me without too much warmth.

'Have you come to see Tom?' I said.

She nodded.

'I'm a bit worried about him,' she said rather dramatically.

'Really? I just left him and he seemed OK. A bit down, but—'

'No, he's taken it very hard. I haven't treated him well.'

'Then you should stay away from him,' I suggested firmly. 'Don't rub salt in the wound.'

'But I feel responsible. I led him on without realising how he felt about me.' Julia Seddon obviously relished presenting herself as a femme fatale. 'He was so angry at the party when he found out I didn't feel the same way about him – I mean, he's just not my physical type. He blamed Lee, which wasn't really fair. I wouldn't have gone for him anyway. But it's true we'd been spending a lot of time together and I can see how he got the wrong idea.'

She looked at me with her big blue eyes. I had to admit she was terribly pretty.

'And he feels things so deeply, doesn't he? I worry he'll do something to hurt himself.'

'Don't worry.' I wanted to cut her down to size. 'Tom's not the type. He's much more likely to get apocalyptically drunk, pick a fight with someone and then not remember a thing about it the next day.'

She looked faintly revolted.

'I suppose you're right,' she said reluctantly. 'He was very drunk at the party. But I don't think he picked a fight with anyone . . .'

Her voice tailed off, as if she had just thought of something. Suddenly she wheeled round and went inside. I stared after her curiously, half-inclined to follow her and ask what that had been about. Then I remembered I had some stolen prints to dispose of. No rest for the wicked.

25

I hid the prints in the back of my van, under an unpromising welter of bits of metal, dirty old dust-sheets and tools. Tomorrow I'd go to some big anonymous post office far away from where I lived and post the wretched things back. Tonight, what with all the illicit items in my possession, I felt like a receiver of stolen goods. I wondered whether to tell Nat about the prints. He would probably think it was funny that I had suspected him of stealing them; he had as twisted a sense of humour as I did.

He turned up a few hours later with his usual pack of beers.

'Jesus,' he said as I let him in, 'don't you ever read your post? Look at all that rubbish.'

'Oh yeah.' I looked dispiritedly at the pile of brown envelopes that had collected on the mat. 'It's just that I know they're all bills.'

'Even so.' Nat threw himself on the sofa, plonking the beers at his side. 'You're going to have to do it sooner or later.'

'Yeah, OK.' I picked up the pile. It tried to slither away. I took it over to the kitchen table and started to open the envelopes. Nat had found one of my magazines and was engrossed; probably a bikini fashion spread or a feature article on multiple orgasms. Sometimes I think those things are really written for men.

Electricity, gas, telephone, tax, the usual collection. One larger brown envelope, addressed by hand to me at the wrong street name and redirected at least twice by the pencilled scrawls over the address. Probably the social services. I ripped it open. Inside was a letter written on a piece of paper ripped from a lined notebook, and a photograph. I read the letter first. It had obviously been scribbled in haste, maybe on a bus or a train; the pen dipped crazily at intervals.

'I don't think I'll be seeing you tonight. I've seen him waiting for me already and I know he won't let me meet you. Ask him who his brother is. Please don't let him hurt Catherine.'

The photograph had been taken about fifteen years ago. It showed Clifford Hammond with his arm round a boy. Clifford was smiling paternally down at him. The boy was not smiling. His whole body looked tense and his arms were clamped rigidly by his sides. He was about ten years old but there was no mistaking who he was. Even if the original wasn't lying across my sofa at this very moment.

* * *

On the sofa I heard Nat shift position. The small sound of creaking springs was suddenly infinitely menacing. All the world was turning upside down.

'Loads of bills?' he said.

'And a letter.'

'Anything interesting?'

He could have had no idea that Walter had managed to write to me. Perhaps he had been following Walter at the time. The letter was full of barely controlled panic.

His eyes were clear grey and he looked totally relaxed, even peaceful, his limbs stretched out in his familar open, surrendering sprawl. I stared into them, watching their expression change with my words.

'It's from a mutual acquaintance,' I said. 'Walter Quincy. Remember him?'

As I said before: I can't turn my back on anything, even as a matter of strategy. I have to push and push at things till I run the risk that what I'm looking for may end up broken in my hands.

'He used to work for your brother's wife,' I said. 'Clifford Hammond, well-known banker-about-town. I can't say I think much of Nathan Hammond as a name. Too many "n"s in it.'

There was an unexpected sound in the room. It was Nat, slow-clapping me, three times. He was sitting up now.

'Could we cut to the point?' he said.

'That is the point. You must be working for Clifford. Catherine had Walter. And those two have always been at cross-purposes, haven't they, Clifford and Catherine?'

Nat smiled. It was one of those smiles of his that showed the teeth but had no merriment behind it, just the bare bone.

'You're pretty clever, aren't you? At least, that's what my brother thinks. He's got quite a paranoia about you.'

He said the word 'brother' with a mocking emphasis, as if he were jeering at Clifford Hammond, or at least at his own relation to him.

'And what do you think?'

'I think you're pretty clever too,' Nat said. 'You don't know it all. But then, who does? I bet there are things you know that I don't.'

He stretched his legs out in front of him and stared at the scuffed toe-caps of his shoes.

'Like where those letters of his wife's are, for instance,' he added.

I stared at him incredulously.

'Are you saying that it's all still about the letters?' I said. 'After everything that's happened?'

Nat shrugged again.

'But that's what it was always about,' he said simply. 'Getting the letters back. Scaring her off.'

'You mean Lee.'

'Of course.'

'Why did you agree to do that?'

He looked straight at me. It hurt now to look into his eyes.

'Needed the money, didn't I,' he said half-flippantly. 'I thought that Clifford owed me something. No, put that another way. Clifford owed me, big time. I was just collecting what I was due. He said he had this job that needed doing, and then he'd pay me. So I said OK.'

He looked strangely embarrassed. The room was so quiet that in the silences I could hear every incidental sound, the intake of breath, feet scuffing on the floor as our bodies changed positions, my own heartbeat. Not his. He was too far away.

'I didn't mean it to happen,' he said suddenly. 'It was – I don't know what I meant.'

'I assume you're still talking about Lee.' My throat was dry.

He nodded.

'It wasn't supposed to happen, either. Not that Cliff cared, after the event.'

'He didn't mean you to kill her?'

'God, no. Just put the frighteners on her. Tell her to stay away from Catherine.'

'And did you?'

Nat shifted uncomfortably on the sofa.

'Sort of. Yes.'

'How did you know where she would be?' I said curiously.

'That little creep who worked for Catherine,' Nat said. 'He'd have done anything to get at Lee Jackson. He was completely obsessed with Catherine, you know. It was because of that Walter guy that Cliff knew about the letters in the first place. He was a little shit, that one. He was mad jealous of Catherine – drivelled on about how loyal he was to her and then he'd tell you anything if he thought it might break up this thing she had going with the Jackson woman. Cliff asked him if he knew where she would be that night and he told him at once. He'd heard from Catherine.'

I noticed the way Nat called Clifford Hammond 'Cliff'. I bet that Clifford didn't like that one bit. And I bet that Nat was perfectly aware of it and kept calling him Cliff anyway.

'I found her at the party,' Nat was saying. 'It wasn't difficult. I said could we have a private word about Catherine. She came straight away. We went down into the garden. I'd picked it out beforehand because it was so dark down there, nice and private. But it all went wrong.'

'How?'

'It was her fault,' he said. 'She should just have listened to me. I wasn't going to come the heavy, it didn't seem necessary at that stage. But she realised who I was. I don't know how. She just looked up at me and said, "You're Clifford's brother, aren't you?" It took me by surprise and I said "yes" without thinking.'

He was staring off into the distance now.

'Catherine must have told her,' he said, his voice filled with pain and anger. 'I didn't know even she knew. Maybe she guessed. Cliff wouldn't have told her himself, the bastard.'

I was thinking about the photograph Walter had sent me, and of what he had told me about Clifford Hammond's sexual tastes. I had an idea now of how he wanted his boys to look.

'She started going on about it. I couldn't bear it. She said how come I was doing this kind of work for Clifford, after everything that had happened. Shit. *Shit*.'

'Nat—'

'I pushed her,' he said straight at me. His eyes were burning green. 'I pushed her and she fell. It happened so fast. I couldn't – I thought of walking away, when she was talking, just walking away, but I couldn't do it, I couldn't *bear* the thought that there she was, right in front of me, someone I'd never met before, and she knew, she knew what had happened – but I didn't mean to kill her. I really didn't. She seemed OK. And she was pissing Clifford off, too, so she was the last person who should have died. What a fucking irony. She was a friend of yours, wasn't she?'

I nodded.

'She hit her head on a brick when she fell,' Nat said. 'I checked her pulse. She was dead. Bang, just like that. I waited there for a while. I couldn't believe it. Then I went to ring Clifford from a phone down the road and he said to go and search her flat. I went back and got the keys from her pocket.'

'Lee's neighbour heard you.'

'Did she? I'm not surprised. My hands were still trembling, I must have made a hell of a racket.'

Something clicked in my brain.

'How stupid of me,' I said slowly. 'I should have realised all along you were at that party. You told me that when Baby was talking to you at the gallery opening she said you were the only person tall enough to appreciate her earrings. But that night she was wearing little hoops that no-one would ever notice. It was on the night of the party that she was wearing those massive chandeliers. Baby must have made that remark to you then. I bet you were nervous when you saw her at the opening. She came up to you to say hello, didn't she? So you scarpered as soon as you could – you didn't want to be anywhere near me once you knew that she was around and might say something that would indicate that you'd been at the party. When I asked you what you two had been talking about, you just repeated what she had originally said to you. But someone else actually told me that he thought Baby knew you, and went up to say hello to you. I didn't think it was significant.'

'She's got a mouth as big as a bucket,' he said dismissively.

'Then she's lucky you didn't kill her to shut her up, isn't she?' I snapped back at him. 'Like you did with Walter.'

I stood up and went over to the sink, palming behind me the wrench that had been lying there for weeks. It fit nicely into my hand. I turned round to look at him.

'Walter.' Nat spat out the name. 'God, that I was glad to do, I can tell you.' He grinned nastily. 'I can make excuses for myself when I make a mistake,' he said. 'But not with Walter Quincy. That wasn't a mistake. I was happy to do it. Hit him over the head and chucked him out the window.'

'Did Clifford tell you to do it?'

'He didn't *tell* me,' Nat said. 'No-one tells me to do anything. He said he'd pay me. And, like I said, I needed the money.'

He stood up.

'Walter used to look at me with those little black eyes,' he said. 'Very knowing, as if he knew everything about you. He did know a lot. Too much. He went way too far, that one. It wasn't just his look. He'd say things too. Things he shouldn't even have known about. He was fucking crazy about Catherine, of course, he couldn't think straight, but that was no excuse.'

'Did Clifford tell you to kill me?' I said, pleased to hear how unruffled my voice still sounded. I was leaning against the kitchen table, hands propped behind me for support. The wrench was filmed with sweat by now. 'I've been wondering why he won't answer my calls, why he let Laura Archer go off to the States without making another effort to buy the letters. It must be because of you. He thinks you're going to do it for him.'

'Yeah. He told me to get the letters back and to find out what you knew.'

'You don't seem to have done a particularly good job with either one.'

'Yeah. Well.' Nat looked at me. 'I got sidetracked. I thought Cliff could go to hell for a change.'

'Isn't he getting impatient?'

'So? What do I care?'

Nat was walking towards me, slowly. The sound of his feet sent echoes right up to the ceiling, resonating round the room. I stayed right where I was. He reached me. My arms were at my sides. I didn't try to move them.

'Sam,' he said gently. 'Sam.'

And then he reached out and put his arms around me.

'I wish it hadn't been like this,' he said into my hair. 'I didn't get involved with you because of Clifford. It wasn't to do with that. It just happened between us. I couldn't have stopped it, and I didn't want to anyway. Please believe that. I'll take care of him. I'll make sure he doesn't try anything stupid again.'

This was the worst of all to bear. I closed my eyes, then opened them again. My sight was clear and so was my head.

'Just one small point,' I said. 'You killed my friend. You killed Lee.'

He pulled back a little so he could look down into my face.

'I told you, it was an accident!' he said with indignation.

'You killed her,' I repeated. 'Even if it was manslaughter. And you killed Walter deliberately.'

'Walter,' he said with contempt. 'I'd do that again in a minute.'

'Exactly—'

'What are you saying?'

'You didn't kill Walter because Clifford told you to,' I said slowly. 'And you didn't hit Lee because Clifford said so, either. You killed them because they knew something about you that you didn't want known.'

I looked up at him.

'So are you going to kill me too?' I said, my voice hard. 'I know what Clifford did to you when you were young, just like they did. Are you going to kill me for it?'

I watched the soft expression fade out of his face. Not all at once, but gradually, like an eclipse. For a moment his face was wiped clean as a slate. Then his fingers tightened on my shoulders and his eyes were blazing with anger.

261

'Don't say that,' he said, his voice almost childish in its naked rage. 'I – I—'

He turned away, pounding one fist into the other palm, his shoulders fixed. 'I can't,' he said, 'I can't—'

He was angry but not beyond the bounds of reason. It wasn't enough. I couldn't let him walk out of here after what he had done; and there wasn't a shred of proof I could bring against him. So it would have to be personal, my revenge for Lee. And it was for Lee I wanted revenge. Not my own pride: I didn't believe that Nat was having an affair with me to get information for his brother. That part of it was genuine enough.

But I was damned if I was going to let my feelings for him get in the way of what I had to do.

'You bastard,' I said furiously. 'I'm going to turn you in to the police right now and your brother with you. What are you going to do about me? I'm going to tell them everything you've just told me and show them this—'

I fumbled around on the table with my left hand and grabbed the picture that Walter had sent me, shoving it at him. It meant nothing to me but it obviously did to him. His face blanched with pain.

'You *bitch*—'

He raised his hand to hit me, his face inches from mine. I ducked away and in the same movement I brought up the wrench from behind my back in a long powerful swing, smashing it up into his face.

The blow sent him reeling back, his hands to his face, but he didn't go down. The front door was locked and it would take far too long to unbolt it. I ran for the ladder up to the sleeping platform. Before he recovered I was busy at the top.

He straightened up, taking his hands from his face.

There was a deep bloody welt across his cheek. The cheekbone must be broken. I had heard something crack under the wrench.

His face was feral, the skin drawn tight as a drum over the sharp bones. His lips pulled back from his teeth, baring them in a lupine snarl. What big teeth you have, Mr Wolf. He looked as if he would sink them into my throat and tear it out without a second thought. His eyes glittered bright and feverish.

He came up the ladder slowly. He was nearly at the top when he stopped, his hands on the highest rung. I was on my hands and knees and our faces were level. I tensed every muscle, expecting him to make a sudden spring up at me. Our eyes met. Our breathing had synchronised; it sounded as if there was only one person in the room. We stared at each other across the top rung of the ladder, across a huge chasm of silence, only a foot apart.

His voice was rusty. It rattled up through his windpipe as if he hadn't used it for years.

'Why couldn't you just leave it alone?'

I heard mine through a sea of my own blood, roaring in my ears.

'You know I couldn't.'

I grinned at him, feeling my face stretch into a rictus. Strangely, he smiled back at me. For a moment I thought he would give it up. Or I hoped he would.

Then he came up over the top of the ladder, his hands reaching out for me, and I jerked out the pins which moored the ladder to the platform, the pins which I had just loosened, and kicked the ladder away into space with all the strength in my body.

One of his hands caught onto the edge of the platform as he went back. His long fingers curled around it, clinging till the knuckles showed pure white with the effort. The ladder was heavy, and the great shove I had given it had sent it too far back for him to right it again. For the longest moment he was anchored only by the lone hand on the platform. Its grip was weakening, gravity ripping his fingers away. The ladder looked as if it were leaning against an invisible wall.

He threw his head back to look up into my face. 'Sam?' he said, like a question. I couldn't answer it.

'I wouldn't really have hurt you,' he said, gasping with the effort of holding on. 'I saved your life, didn't I?'

'Nat—' My heart was pounding. I reached down with both hands to grab his wrist, my fingers closing round it. No flesh on it, just bones, hard to grasp—

It was too late. The ladder realised that the wall it was leaning on didn't exist. Nat's wrist slipped through my fingers, though they too were white-knuckled with the effort of clinging on. A grinding noise dragged along the stone floor. The ladder crashed down, echoes resounding high into the air, and then there was nothing but empty space and my own empty hands in front of me.

The ladder had broken, and he was sprawled under it. His long thin limbs were all askew, like a huge spider dropped by a giant hand. I waited, long enough for him to move; but there was no sound, none at all.

I didn't have to go down. I could still climb out of the skylight, leave him lying there: do the safe thing. For once.

Down the side of the wall next to the platform was a series of rough bricks, hollowed out at intervals. I swung myself over the edge and went down them too fast. I had shoved the wrench down the back of my jeans. As I jumped to the ground, I pulled it out and held it in my hand as I went over to where he lay. But even before I reached him, I could see that I didn't need to protect myself. Not only his limbs were askew, but his head was turned at a crooked angle. Too crooked. His neck was broken.

The wrench dropped out of my hand and clanged on the concrete floor. I sat down next to him. One of his arms was flung out, close to me. I put out my hand and clasped my fingers around his wrist.

I stayed there for a long time, till it got dark. Then I got up and dialled Clifford Hammond's number.

26

I was sitting in the bar of the Connaught Hotel, drinking a vodka martini. Not my usual neck of the woods. I was waiting for Catherine Hammond and the choice of rendezvous had been hers, not mine. If it had been designed to intimidate me, it hadn't succeeded. I had dressed for the occasion: leather jacket, leather boots, little black Lycra dress and fishnet tights. I had wanted to wear my rubber dress but I had run out of talcum powder. It was probably as well. The barman hadn't wanted to serve me anyway.

My cocktail was nearly finished by now. Catherine Hammond was late. Still, I wasn't going to leave yet. I was too curious. She had been leaving messages on my answering machine every day for a week till finally I had cracked and rung her back.

I couldn't have seen her at once. I had needed some time on my own.

So far I hadn't had much solitude. The police had been keeping me busy. Thanks to Clifford Hammond, though, I was in the clear. He had pulled more strings than a marionette company that night, suggesting that the line to take was that I was a victim of domestic violence who had been defending myself from God knew what. After all, look at the injuries I already bore. I showed them my bruises, both sets of them. They garnered me plenty of sympathy, especially after the part of Clifford Hammond's statement that covered his brother's violent tendencies.

They put me in a special suite at the police station with flowers and sofas and pastel prints on the walls, and sent a woman officer to take my statement. She told me that Nat had two previous convictions for breaking and entering. That didn't hurt my story either. It was an ironic reversal of circumstances – it's usually the men who get off for domestic violence and the women who go down.

'Lucky you tried to knock me down with your car the other night, eh, Clifford?' I said to him in the back of the car that was taking us to the police station, pitching my voice so that only he could hear me. 'Otherwise I wouldn't have these fetching bruises. Nat told me it was you at the wheel.'

Stretching a point; all Nat had said was that he'd make sure Clifford didn't try anything stupid again. But I'd guessed right. Even in the dim light I could see him blanch.

'You were getting impatient, weren't you?' I said. 'You thought Nat wasn't doing enough for you. Funny, because you'd done enough to him in your time, hadn't you?'

'You're in shock,' he said loudly. 'There'll be a doctor to see her at the station, won't there, Inspector?'

The policeman in the front seat swivelled round. 'Absolutely, sir.'

'That's right. I could do with some sedatives,' I said sarcastically. 'Why don't you be on the safe side and tell him to cut my tongue out while I'm under?'

But I shut up. I couldn't prove a thing. And I had my

own safety to think about. Clifford Hammond would throw me to the wolves if I started talking.

* * *

We had made a deal, he and I, over the dead body of his brother. I mean that literally. I had let him into the studio and gone straight back to sit on the floor beside Nat. Clifford Hammond had had to squat opposite him to talk to me. A part of me relished forcing this on him.

I had got myself under more control by then. I wasn't still holding onto Nat's hand.

The deal was simple: protection for me from the police. In return I would guarantee to give back the letters. He had wanted them himself but I had refused: I would give them to Catherine Hammond or to no-one. And I would keep photocopies. I wanted to cover my back and I had reasons for not trusting him an inch.

Walter Quincy had been right. Clifford Hammond was completely irrational on the subject of the letters. He didn't seem to realise that they would be of little interest to any journalist, and in themselves proved nothing – least of all whether Lee had been murdered or not. But I wasn't such a fool as to point this out to him. As Walter had said, Clifford seemed to associate the letters in some way with his own crimes. In his mind, exposure of his wife's secret meant that his own would inevitably come to light.

We went back and forth over the same ground for a while, a wearisome process, till he finally gave in. He wanted the letters back so badly he didn't have much choice. It was strange to sit there in the dark with someone I knew wanted very badly to kill me, talking in quiet voices as if we were negotiating a settlement of no particular importance. I didn't let myself get angry. I was too frightened of what I might do to him.

Nat was cold by the time the police arrived.

* * *

The police officer left me in the interview suite while she went to get the doctor. By this time my tongue was practically hanging out for Mogadon. Take me away from here, make me forget. But much to my disappointment, when the door opened next it wasn't the doctor, but DI Fincham, of all people.

'I was very sorry to hear what happened,' he said. 'How are you feeling? Do you mind if I come in?'

'Be my guest.' I gestured at the other sofa. 'Welcome to the Rape and Domestic Violence Suite. I hope you like carnations.'

He sat down. It was the middle of the night but he looked as neat as ever.

'Do you get your suits from Burton?' I said flippantly. I was probably in shock.

He didn't answer this.

'Miss Jones—' he started.

'It's Ms.' I didn't have much to lose at this point. Then I softened up. I could see he was trying to be nice. 'But you can call me Sam.'

He looked hard at me. 'I wondered if you wanted to tell me anything,' he said. 'About what happened. I can't help feeling that it would be a coincidence if there weren't some connection between this and Mrs Jackson's death.'

I didn't say anything.

'There's no-one listening in, if that's what you're concerned about,' he said, nodding towards the mirror on the opposite wall. 'It's the middle of the night. And I'm not taping this either.'

'Thanks.' Suddenly I was very tired. 'But I can't. I mean, there wouldn't be any point.'

'So I'm wrong in assuming that Mr Hammond – *Clifford* Hammond, I mean – is more involved in this than meets the eye?'

I said nothing. After a while he sighed, and scribbled something on a piece of paper. He put it on the table in front of me.

'That's my direct line,' he said, standing up. 'Call me if you change your mind. I'll treat it in confidence.' He went over to the door. 'I'll send in the doctor now.'

I looked at the piece of paper. DI Fincham put his head back through the door.

'Oh, and it's Marks and Spencer's,' he said. 'My suits.'

I crumpled the paper up into a ball and threw it across the room. Then I felt guilty. I retrieved it and put it in my pocket. The doctor came in. I rolled up my sleeve and held out my arm.

'I've got a very high tolerance,' I said. 'Can you give me double the normal dose?'

* * *

A few days later I sent the prints back to the gallery, taking care not to leave any fingerprints on them or the wrapping. An arrest for art theft was the last thing I needed at the moment.

There would be an inquest into Nat's death, but everyone assured me I had nothing to worry about. Clifford Hammond was going to testify on my behalf. All the loose ends had been knotted up and severed in the space of a few days. All except one. And I was waiting for her now.

My glass was empty. I gestured with it at the waiter. In

a moment he was by my side, clearing away the dregs of my old drink. Whisking away the little paper coaster underneath it, he laid down a fresh one, white and padded, embossed with the name of the hotel. On it he set another vodka martini. I crossed my legs and for a second his eyes dropped to my boots in reflexive disapproval, before he straightened up and asked if I would like anything else. I smiled at him sweetly and said no, thank you, I was fine. He turned his back on me and walked away eloquently.

Next to the drink he had placed a glass bowl of crisps and one of olives. I didn't touch them; I wasn't hungry. I hadn't been hungry for a week.

Catherine Hammond appeared in the doorway of the bar. The waiter bounded over to her, took her coat, pulled out her chair and fetched her a Laphraoig with an eagerness he had withheld from me. She was wearing a black double-breasted coat dress with silver buttons and a wide belt of the same material and looked wonderful, as ever. I wondered if the black were in Nat's honour. I didn't like to ask.

'You must have been surprised to hear from me,' she said.

I shrugged.

'I had other things to think about,' I said. 'Making sure I wasn't going to be arrested. That kind of thing. Your husband kindly took a personal interest in my case. You may have heard.'

'Yes.' She took a big slug of her whisky. She must have been more nervous than she seemed. 'I hardly knew him,' she said. 'Nathan, I mean. Oh, I knew who he was, of course –' her eyes met mine for a moment – 'but I had hardly ever met him. He only came round a few times, asking for money. I didn't know that he killed Lee till afterwards.'

'How did you find out? Clifford wouldn't have told you.'

'Oh no.' She smiled wryly. 'Walter told me.'

'Walter told you plenty, didn't he? It must have been Walter, nosing round what Clifford was doing, who let you know who I was in the first place.'

She nodded. 'Walter was a born spy,' she said. 'Always eavesdropping. That's the main reason I would write to Lee, you know, instead of phoning. I didn't want Walter listening to my phone calls to her.'

'And when she died you wanted the letters back, so you sent Walter to follow me—'

'No. I didn't care about the letters. Once I heard Lee was dead I didn't care much about anything.'

'Then why did you put Walter onto me?'

She stared into her tumbler. 'I wanted to find out about you. Clifford thought you were a blackmailer, but I didn't know what to think. It was hard to believe that you would be so concerned over the death of someone who was only a friend—'

And now she was staring at me as if trying to read something in my face.

'I have to ask you this,' she said abruptly. She pushed her hair back behind her ears with one trembling hand. 'After all, it's the reason I wanted to meet you . . .'

'Yes, I was wondering when we'd get to that.'

I had finished my drink by now, and so had she. The waiter appeared at her shoulder but she gestured him away imperiously and he retreated at once. All the colour had ebbed from her face, leaving it paper-white. The hand holding the cigarette was trembling too. Her whole body was drawn up tight as a knot.

'Were you – was the reason you were so concerned to find out how Lee had died—' She stopped, took a deep breath, and came out with it. 'Were you and Lee lovers?'

I looked at her. For a second I thought of lying to her. It would break her completely; at that moment she was brittle as fine china. What a fine revenge that would be.

'No, we weren't,' I said.

I was sick of lies and my taste for revenge had soured. Besides, Lee would not have wanted it. Catherine leant towards me, reaching out to press my hand, her face ablaze with happiness. I flinched away from her as if her fingers were tipped with acid, and she drew back without having touched me.

'Would you have left your husband for her?' I asked.

'I don't know,' she said after a long pause. 'I don't know if I would have been brave enough.'

She looked at me as if she were seeing me for the first time. Maybe she was. The cloud of jealousy had lifted.

'Do you know,' she said wonderingly, 'you're the only one I can talk to about Lee? The only one? How bizarre, when I've been so tortured by the idea of you and her together.'

It made sense now: that was the explanation for the look of hate she had shot me in her living-room.

'And what do you want to say about her?' I said drily.

Her eyes fell. 'I don't know,' she said after a while. 'Just – I really meant that you're the only person now who knows about us and who knew Lee, how – wonderful she was. Who would understand why I took such a risk.'

'Lee took a risk too,' I pointed out. 'That you wouldn't leave your husband. That she would get her heart broken.'

A faint flush rose to her cheekbones. For a moment I thought it was embarrassment and then I noticed the brightness of her eyes, her little smile, and I realised it was pleasure at the idea that Lee cared that much for her, that she might have been destroyed if Catherine had chosen to stay with her husband.

I was swept by a wave of dislike for Catherine Hammond. Apart from her affair with Lee – or perhaps even including that – none of her actions seemed to have been motivated by anything higher than pure selfishness.

I said nastily, 'So *are* you going to stay with your husband?'

She shrugged. 'I expect so,' she said indifferently.

Well, that was that. I reached into my bag and pulled out a fat brown envelope, passing it across the table to her. She stared at me curiously and opened the flap. It took her a moment to recognise the contents.

'Where were they?' she said.

'In the new sculpture she was making. She called it *Postboxes for Love Letters*. Something like that.'

She stared at me with wide anguished eyes. 'Really?' she said painfully. 'Lee wouldn't show me her new work. Do you mean she kept my letters in it?'

'She made it especially for them, as far as I could see. She probably wanted to show it to you when it was finished.'

'Yes.'

Her mouth twisted. She looked at the envelope for a long moment, turning it over in her hands. For a moment I thought she was about to cry and I braced myself against it. Then she put the envelope in her bag and shut the clasp. It was a small final click. She looked over at the barman and gestured at our empty glasses. The refills were brought in seconds.

'It was pointless being concerned about them,' she

said. 'Lee would have kept them safe. And even when she died, it didn't matter. Clifford was obsessed with finding them. He has an obsession about proof.'

'Tell me,' I said curiously, 'when I came round that night after Walter died – did you know then what had happened?'

She nodded. 'Walter did ring me, but it wasn't quite as I said. He told me Nathan had been following him. He said you were coming to see him that evening and he thought Nathan knew that he'd already been talking to you. He was petrified. Clifford was out so I couldn't ask him what Nathan was up to – I knew it would be on his orders. I went round at once but it was too late.'

She drank down half of her whisky. 'The rest is as I told you. I was down the street when I saw him falling. When I realised you knew that I'd been there I got the shock of my life. I didn't know what to say.'

'Why didn't you just tell me what had happened? After all, it was Nat who killed the woman you loved, even if it was a kind of accident. Why didn't you go to the police?'

'The police?' Her eyes widened. It had obviously never occurred to her. 'But everything would have come out—'

'Literally,' I said drily. Selfishness again. It was as if her beauty cocooned her from having to think about anyone else but herself.

I had nothing more to say. By mutual agreement, we finished our drinks and stood up. Catherine Hammond dropped some money on the table to cover the cost of our drinks. The waiter brought her coat and helped her into it. I put on my jacket myself – I was used to it. She fastened her coat and drew on her gloves. Then she hesitated for a moment, looking me up and down.

'You must be very strong,' she said. 'I mean physically.' She shivered.

'I found him quite frightening. Nathan, I mean. There was something very wrong with him, you know. It was Clifford's fault. You must know that by now. Clifford warped him in some terrible deep way.'

I didn't want to hear this.

'And this is the man you wouldn't have been brave enough to leave for Lee. The man you're going to stay with, after all that's happened.' My voice was rising. 'So don't talk about Nat to me. Yes, he killed Lee and Walter. But he saved my life when your husband tried to run me down. You didn't know that, did you? Or maybe you did. And Nat wouldn't have hurt me. I made it happen because I wanted revenge for Lee. He wouldn't have come after me otherwise.'

She was silent. We walked outside. The doorman, splendid in his uniform, hailed a taxi for her from the rank opposite the hotel. She did not look back at me as it drove away. I followed it with my eyes till it turned into Grosvenor Square and I could see it no longer.

It was chilly outside after the central heating of the hotel, but the cold was welcome. I set off down the street, not caring where I was going, just needing to be in motion. I was very tired, not physically, but mentally. And there was a strange sense of anticlimax, that something which had occupied me so intensely for so long could finish like this, over a drink in a hotel bar with a woman I would probably never see again. I wondered if she would keep the letters; Clifford would surely want them destroyed.

After a while I was warm from the exercise and the three martinis, and no longer noticed the frost in the air. I was trying not to think about Nat, and not doing too well. Perhaps I should be trying to remember him, instead. The first step to forgetfulness is to remember someone properly – the way they really were, not the way you wanted them to be – stripping away the gloss and the romance you painted over their face.

I began to replay in my head the first night, or morning, that Nat had come to the studio. He had called Baby 'Madame Fifi with the false tits'. It had endeared him to me straight away. Then he had started to wander around the studio while I was pouring our drinks, and he had come to a halt in front of my sculpture, saying that it looked like a meteor that had fallen to earth . . .

I stopped dead in the middle of the pavement, struck by a sudden idea. Maybe, unconsciously, Nat had put his finger on what the Thing needed. What if the reason it looked so malevolent at the moment was that it wasn't meant to be on the ground at all? That it needed to be up in the air, with plenty of space around it, room to breathe?

How would that work? Well, there was no harm in trying. God knew I needed a distraction. I could go to a hardware shop right now, buy a length of chain, rope up the Thing and haul it up over one of the metal beams in my ceiling. It looked a lot heavier than it was. It shouldn't put any strain on the ceiling supports; in fact, I had been meaning to put a swing over one of the beams for a year now . . .

I pictured it hanging in the air, no longer seeming monumentally heavy, but a silver sphere, grand and beautiful, like a meteor suspended for ever in space, and my heart started to pound in excitement.

I couldn't wait to try out the idea. I turned on my heel and headed back to where I had left the van, walking fast now, eager to get my hands on a length of chain. Where would the nearest hardware shop be to the Connaught? I could always try asking the doorman . . .

Exclusive CDs to enhance your reading pleasure

There is nothing better than a relaxing read and nothing quite like your favourite music to compliment your mood.

Each of the CD compilations are performed by the world's top artists. The choice is yours, all you need to do is send £1.98*per CD to cover postage and handling and indicate which CDs you would like. Please allow up to 28 days for delivery.

HOW TO GET YOUR CDS:
Simply complete the coupon below with the quantity of each CD you wish to purchase and send with your cheque to Hodder Headline CD offer, P.O. Box 2000, Romford, RM3 8GP.

Hodder Headline CD offer
Please send me:
Qty........HH01 Essential Opera @ £1.98 p&h each
Qty........HH02 Classical Masterpieces @ £1.98 p&h each
Qty........HH03 Rockin' n' Reading' Hits of the 60's @ £1.98 p&h each
Qty........HH04 Unmistakably Jazz @ £1.98 p&h each
Qty........HH05 Movie Sensations @ £1.98 p&h each
Qty........HH06 Gregorian Chants @ £1.98 p&h each
*Please note these prices apply to the UK addresses only. Please see below for other areas.

Enclose a cheque/postal order payable to FM LTD. Please write your name and address on the back of your cheque/postal order.

Name & Address...
....
....Postcode ☐☐☐☐☐☐☐☐

POSTAGE AND HANDLING PAYMENT METHOD
UK & Ireland – Cheques or Postal Orders ONLY £1.98 per CD
Europe including Eire – Eurocheque in £Sterling ONLY or Visa/Mastercard Credit Cards £3.25 per CD
Rest of the World including USA and Canada – Eurocheque in £Sterling ONLY or Visa/Mastercard Credit Cards £4.25 per CD

Please debit £................ from my ☐ Visa ☐ Access

Card No ☐☐☐☐ ☐☐☐☐ ☐☐☐☐ ☐☐☐☐

Expiry Date ☐☐ Signature...

ENQUIRY HOTLINE: 01708 336888
If you do not wish to receive further mailings for products within the Hodder Headline Group or carefully selected companies please tick here. ☐ Offer subject to availability. Please allow up to 28 days for delivery.

Offer closes 31st December 1996   *you may photocopy this form*